"Vivid, convincing characters . [...]
empathy so adroitly, Hoffman dra[...]
selves to the kind of pain—the pain of commitment—that haunts
her story. [With] an uncommon insight . . . Hoffman [explores]
an observation that is commonplace yet infinitely complex: people suffer, they rage, they come to terms with the randomness of
life."   —*People*

"Not-so-delicate questions are raised in a wonderfully delicate
way in Alice Hoffman's latest novel . . . Explorations of the tangled strands of parenthood and friendship, self-protection and
generosity, dream and disillusionment are made achingly vivid
by Hoffman's ability to ground them in the finely etched details
of her characters' daily lives."   —*Newsday*

"There is a cumulative power to *Illumination Night* that is won-
drous . . . It's enough to make one search out other books
by Alice Hoffman."   —*Chicago Tribune*

"Reading an authentic prose stylist of high order is an uncommon privilege."   —*The Boston Globe*

"Alice Hoffman hits bull's-eyes on the incomprehensions between
the young and the old, on the magic and pain of ordinary life. She
is erotic and romantic . . . funny . . . clever and humane."
                                                 —*The London Times*

continued . . .

Local Girls

"She is one of the best writers we have today—insightful, funny, intelligent, with a distinctive voice . . . [*Local Girls*] does a lot to show that Hoffman is an established artist at her peak."

—*The Cleveland Plain Dealer*

"Wonderfully sly and unforgettable scenes . . . Hoffman gets it just right."

—*The Boston Globe*

"Moving and deadpan funny . . . Epiphanies about passion, pain, and resiliency induce smiles and shivers in equal measure."

—*Entertainment Weekly*

"Disarming wit . . . she balances the down-to-earth and the ethereal, and indicates that the human spirit can survive despite the cruel workings of fate."

—*Publishers Weekly* (starred review)

"The reader reluctantly parts with these local girls."

—*Raleigh News & Observer*

Second Nature

"Magical and daring . . . very possibly her best."

—*The New York Times Book Review*

"Suspenseful . . . a dark, romantic meditation on what it means to be human."

—*The New Yorker*

"Hoffman tells a great story. Expect to finish this one in a single, guilty sitting."

—*Mirabella*

"*Second Nature* may be best read at full speed, hurtling down the mountain, as if falling in love."

—*San Francisco Examiner & Chronicle*

continued . . .

ILLUMINATION NIGHT

Alice Hoffman

B

BERKLEY BOOKS, NEW YORK

THE BERKLEY PUBLISHING GROUP
Published by the Penguin Group
Penguin Group (USA) Inc.
375 Hudson Street, New York, New York 10014, USA
Penguin Group (Canada), 90 Eglinton Avenue East, Suite 700, Toronto, Ontario M4P 2Y3, Canada
(a division of Pearson Penguin Canada Inc.)
Penguin Books Ltd., 80 Strand, London WC2R 0RL, England
Penguin Group Ireland, 25 St. Stephen's Green, Dublin 2, Ireland (a division of Penguin Books Ltd.)
Penguin Group (Australia), 250 Camberwell Road, Camberwell, Victoria 3124, Australia
(a division of Pearson Australia Group Pty. Ltd.)
Penguin Books India Pvt. Ltd., 11 Community Centre, Panchsheel Park, New Delhi—110 017, India
Penguin Group (NZ), 67 Apollo Drive, Mairangi Bay, Auckland 1310, New Zealand
(a division of Pearson New Zealand Ltd.)
Penguin Books (South Africa) (Pty.) Ltd., 24 Sturdee Avenue, Rosebank, Johannesburg 2196,
South Africa

Penguin Books Ltd., Registered Offices: 80 Strand, London WC2R 0RL, England

This is a work of fiction. Names, characters, places, and incidents either are the product of the author's imagination or are used fictitiously, and any resemblance to actual persons, living or dead, business establishments, events, or locales is entirely coincidental. The publisher does not have any control over and does not assume any responsibility for author or third-party websites or their content.

PRINTING HISTORY
G. P. Putnam's Sons hardcover edition / August 1987
Berkley trade paperback edition / February 2002
Berkley trade paperback ISBN: 978-0-425-18326-7

The Library of Congress has cataloged the G. P. Putnam's Sons hardcover edition as follows:

Hoffman, Alice.
Illumination night.
I. Title.
PS3558.03447I57 1987   813'.54   86-30472
ISBN 0-399-13282-1

PRINTED IN THE UNITED STATES OF AMERICA

13

Please visit the author's website at
www.alicehoffman.com

ILLUMINATION NIGHT

Alice Hoffman

To Sara Hoffman
1900–1985

To Lillie Lulkin
1903–1987

Chapter One

ILLUMINATION NIGHT

SIMON looks out his window and sees something white moving in the window of the house next door. It is the first Saturday in July and so hot that dragonflies light on his window ledge, too weak to fly. Simon lifts himself up by leaning his arms on the ledge; his toes are pressed against the baseboard molding. He can hear the ocean, which lies beyond a tangled field of beach plums and scrub pines. He can hear the white material in the window next door flapping against the bright blue sky, and his dog, an old German shepherd named Nelson, digging himself a hole in the dirt.

Simon, who will be four in November, has his own room, painted blue, up under the eaves. From here he can hear his father, Andre, working on his motorcycle out in the shed. The radio is turned on in the shed, and music spirals upward. Downstairs, in the kitchen, Simon's mother, Vonny, lights the right rear burner of the stove. It's an old black stove, and beneath the heavy metal the floorboards sway. The stove was installed in the twenties, as were the plumbing and the electricity that flickers whenever there's a thunderstorm. The house itself—two small bedrooms upstairs, a kitchen, parlor, living room, bath, and sun porch downstairs—is a brown shingled cottage that sags in odd places. The ceilings are too low and the pipes moan. Outside, along a low stockade fence, old, dusky roses grow. The first time they saw the house, the year before Simon was born, Vonny could not believe Andre was actually considering it. There were bats in the upstairs bedrooms then, and a family of skunks lived under the porch. Andre had just sold his company—he designed and manufactured three-wheeled motorcycles—and they bought the house the way they got married, suddenly, startling themselves with their own recklessness. The weekend they bought the property was the first time either of them had been to Martha's Vineyard. After the realtor showed them the house, they went out to lunch, then came back to explore on their own. Andre went immediately to the cellar, to inspect the foundation, and when Vonny went to look for him, her foot went right through the rotted wood of one of the steps. She lurched forward, then suddenly, as though the wood had released her, regained her balance. She sat down on the second step and began to cry. The flashlight Andre held made circles of light as he knelt to examine the rotten stair. He wore a white shirt and blue jeans and an old black jacket. He swung one leg over the splintered wood and watched her cry. Two hours later they bought the house.

It has been five years and Andre has never regretted it. On the other hand, in the dead of winter Vonny thinks a lot about Beacon Street. She hates the stove here; a draft always blows out the pilot light as she cooks, even on hot, still days. Today, she is fighting with the stove as she boils potatoes for potato salad. Simon can hear her reach into the cabinet for the big lobster pot as he takes off his pajama pants and gets shorts and a T-shirt out of his dresser. He pulls his p.j. top up and gets stuck inside. When he opens his eyes everything looks blue. He finally gets his p.j.s over his head, then sits down to dress himself. He is extremely proud of some of the things he is able to do. He loves the way his mother's eyes widen when he manages something that was impossible even a week earlier. If the world ended at the front door, Simon would not care, although he might like to extend it a bit to include the shed and the stony path where he rides his bike—his father has bolted two wooden blocks to each pedal—as far as he's allowed. Beyond that spot there is a cliff and, after a drop of twenty feet, a salt-water pond. The water there is so murky it is impossible to swim, but the beach is littered with false angel wings and bone-white crab claws and, in the height of summer, pink marsh mallows grow wild in the thickets.

Next door, Elizabeth Renny, who will be seventy-four this winter, holds up a white scarf. Through it, the wide expanse of lawn looks gauzy and far away. Beside her there are thin curtains that cling to her skin. This cottage is newer than the one next door, built at the turn of the century. She has lived here, in Chilmark, for more than fifty years. Last night, two starlings got caught in her chimney and Elizabeth Renny could hear them beating their wings all night. She could not sleep, and then this morning there was silence. Awake in her bed, Elizabeth suddenly felt light-headed and she has felt more and more giddy as the morning wears on. She wonders if the starlings managed to rise up in the chimney without moving their wings. When she looks outside, the sleeplessness and heat have a strange effect on her. She has been worried about the coming winter since May. She is all alone; her daughter lives in a suburb of Hartford, Connecticut. For the past year, there has been a film over her right eye. Lately a black spot has formed in the center of her vision. At night, she is frightened by silly things: the sound of crickets, branches brushing against the window, the pressure of a cat's paw against her mattress. Now, she couldn't care less. Through the scarf, everything looks white and she can feel her body lessen its pull on her. Usually, her bones feel as if they're already drawing her into the earth. It smells sweet up here. Clover and rose of Sharon. In the pine tree a mockingbird leaves its perch and soars above the highest branches. Elizabeth Renny hears the calls of the birds she leaves bread for every morning: starling, cardinal, mockingbird, nuthatch. When she leans forward she sees that what she thought was a cloud is a cluster of white herons, effortlessly sweeping across the sky. Outside, there is music from the portable radio in the neighbor's shed, but she doesn't hear it. Simon is the only one who sees the white thing move into the air. Against the sky it's like a cloud. For a moment it drifts toward the trees, then drops quickly. Up in his room, Simon can hear the sound of pinecones hitting the ground, or bones breaking. A clattering sound, which makes him think of his own kitchen. A spoon hitting against a metal pot.

THEY had fought over the shed and each thinks the other has won. Vonny had wanted it for her potter's wheel, Andre for his motorcycles, and in the end there was an uneasy compromise. Andre set up Vonny's kiln against the wall near a small window barred with wire mesh. On days when she fires pottery he pulls the bike he's working on—currently a 1934 Norton—into the yard and spends the rest of the day in a black mood. When Vonny finally withdraws her plates and mugs, the shed is still so hot Andre has to wait hours before going back inside. On these days he works until midnight, although he has no timetable. He has come here to do what he wants— restore old motorcycles that he sells to collectors. Growing up in New Hampshire, he was taught not to talk too much, and not to listen much either. Now Vonny, who knew exactly what he was like when she married him, wants more from him. It would be as though he expected her to cross a bridge, when he knew from the start she would go a hundred miles out of her way to avoid one. He had been used to New Hampshire girls who went to bed with him for a price: a declaration of love, the possibility of a future, dinner at a steak house with several glasses of wine. When he moved to Boston, a sudden decision based on two feet of snow and the sound of his father coughing in the middle of the night, he spent a great deal of time going out with women who all seemed to have complicated plans they continued to think about while he was kissing them. Most of them left him because they were uncomfortable with his silence. Vonny did not—then, at any rate—expect him to talk. When they made love the first time, in his apartment, Vonny wore nothing but black knee socks patterned with blue roses. It had taken him completely by surprise that a woman who declared she was terrified of bridges would suggest they go to bed only a few hours after they'd met. When she closed her eyes and arched her back, Andre felt his skin grow hot and his chest constrict. He fell in love with the way she closed her eyes long before he fell in love with her.

This wanting to talk began with her pregnancy. She would wake him at three in the morning and want to discuss his childhood. She would grill him about his father—a county employee who drove a snow plow—and insist he consider the effects of his mother's death—the car she was in had gone out of control on a stretch of ice when Andre was eleven. The way Vonny wanted him to talk was different from the other women he had known. There was an urgency to it that made him pull even further away. Sometimes, during her pregnancy, Andre dreamed he had to swim to shore in an ocean that grew deeper with every stroke he took, and when he woke the next morning his arms felt the strain.

He would never tell Vonny, but he enjoys being alone more than ever. He is alone, working on the Norton, when he hears the crash. Two of Vonny's unglazed plates roll off the top of the kiln. Through the small window he can see a white thing with arms and legs. He sees it as it bounces upward from the ground, then collapses. The plates, which hadn't broken when they fell, are shattered as Andre runs over them. He keeps right on running, through the hedge of lilacs that separates their yards. He can feel his body expanding and he feels the same sort of pounding in his head as he used to—and had forgotten about until this moment—the year his mother died, when he ran home from school every day, panicked until he reached his own front door.

When he kneels down, she looks like a bird caught in a net. His hands shake as he begins to pull the scarf that is wrapped around her off her face. Then, because he has the strong sense of interfering in something much too private, he stops and feels over the chiffon for her pulse. Her wrist bone is amazingly sharp; though he can't tell if her pulse is weak or strong, it seems regular. He stands, not knowing whether he should leave the old woman alone. Then he runs to her house, in the back door, to the telephone on the kitchen counter. Two cats are on the table, lapping milk from a cereal bowl. Neatly creased and folded paper bags are wedged between the refrigerator and the counter. He dials 911 and in a voice that doesn't sound at all like his own tells them that Mrs. Renny has had an accident.

AT the end of the month, when an ambulance delivers Elizabeth Renny back home, it has already been decided. Her daughter's girl, Jody, will come to stay for the rest of the summer. Mrs. Renny's daughter, Laura, who is a school psychologist in Hartford, has two other children, young sons, and a husband and can't be expected to look after her mother, even if she has a broken collarbone and a broken leg, which, at her age, may or may not heal. When Jody was told about the decision she stayed out all night and refused to tell her parents where she had been. She alluded to a seedy nightclub in Pawtucket, Rhode Island, but in fact she had spent the night at her best friend Becky's house, smoking cigarettes and crying and watching late-night TV. Her parents, who have problems of their own, now have the good fortune of simultaneously doing a good deed and getting rid of her. They settle Mrs. Renny in, move her bedroom from upstairs to the downstairs parlor, do enough food shopping to last two weeks, and leave on the ferry, distant enough at last to comment on how quickly time passes, how their daughter is growing up.

After her parents leave, Jody takes one look at the bedroom that was once Elizabeth Renny's and is now hers, and realizes the depth of her parents' betrayal. She is sixteen. Her hair, though long in the back, is clipped short in front; she wears a smudged line on each eyelid. She has been planning to escape from Hartford all along, but not to a house that smells like cats. They have gotten her a bicycle with a basket so she can ride to the local market, and have opened a checking account which, they have pointedly told her, will never contain more than a hundred dollars. Because there is no escape, Jody unpacks all of the things she has hidden from her mother: three bottles of nail polish, a tiny blue bathing suit, a package of red hair dye, her birth-control pills.

ALL that first evening Jody worries that now that they're alone, she will have to actually talk to her grandmother. But Elizabeth Renny says next to nothing. Jody can tell she's in pain; her grandmother keeps her eyes lowered as though she has done something wrong. Rather than be bored to death, Jody cleans the kitchen, feeds the two disgusting cats, and makes scrambled eggs and English muffins for dinner. She would kill for a frozen pizza. When she brings the tray into the parlor her grandmother says, "Oh, you shouldn't. You don't have to cook for me." Yet she eats every bite, even though Jody knows she's a terrible cook. Afterward, Jody rinses off the dishes, and when she comes back into the parlor with her grandmother's medicine, she finds the old lady has fallen asleep. Jody wakes her and, as she holds out grandmother's pills, their hands accidentally touch. Jody withdraws hers so quickly that several pills fall onto the carpet and she has to search for them in the cat hair and dust.

She knows her mother would love to see her groveling like a slave. At home, she wouldn't even carry her own plate to the dishwasher. The whole thing is mortifying and she prays that her grandmother can go to the bathroom without her help. At seven o'clock she lets the cats out. At seven thirty she phones her friend Becky collect, and when Becky accepts the charges Jody bursts into tears.

"My parents will kill me when they get the phone bill," Becky says, but Jody can tell she's delighted, her kindness knows no bounds now that Jody has literally been cast into the sea.

"I'll probably lose my mind in less than twenty-four hours," Jody says.

Talking to Becky brings back some of her old spark, and when the cats start clawing at the screen, Jody kicks open the door with her bare foot. There are thin blue clouds in the sky and the high call of a mockingbird. Becky carefully recounts the reactions of all their friends when they heard that Jody had been sent away. Already, there are interesting rumors: a pregnancy, a drug problem, a divorce in the family. It is not even eight o'clock when Jody gets off the phone. At first this place seems absolutely silent, then there are strange noises: the hum of the refrigerator, gravel hitting against hubcaps when a car speeds by, the creak of the stairs when she goes up to her bedroom after locking the back door (something she would never think of doing at home) and making certain her grandmother is still asleep and—this she doesn't admit to herself—alive.

She spreads out her comb and brush and nail polish on top of the painted white bureau, but it doesn't help. She gets into her nightgown, but once in bed she hears squirrels running in the walls. Their weight against the plaster makes it seem as though they will break right through the walls and into her bed at any moment. She gets out of bed, pulls on a pair of shorts and a white sleeveless undershirt, then goes to the open window and lights a cigarette to calm her nerves. She has brought a clear glass ashtray up from the kitchen and now she balances it on the window ledge. Her eyeliner has rubbed off on the pillowcase and without it her gray eyes look much bigger. Impossible as it seems, the sky has only begun to grow dark. The leaves of the lilacs make a whispering sound and it's still too hot. Jody smokes her cigarette, and just when she's feeling a little better she hears footsteps outside. She's not exactly a country girl; she imagines bloodthirsty wolves in the bushes. But it's only a German shepherd come to lie halfway between her grandmother's yard and the neighbors'. When Andre leaves the shed, Jody leans both elbows on the windowsill. He wears blue jeans and, because it's still so hot, no shirt. She can't make out his features, but he has long dark hair, which he shakes out of his eyes as he leans down to lock the padlock on the shed. Then he whistles sharply, for the dog. The memory of something white makes him look up, directly into her window. Jody quickly moves back and not until he turns away, the dog trotting to catch up to him then following him through the door, does she lean forward, vainly hoping that if she sits there long enough she will see him once more.

In seventy-three years Elizabeth Renny has made only two decisions of consequence: when she married Jack Renny and left New York for Chilmark, and when she imagined that she could fly. Now, she thinks that if embarrassment could really kill you, she'd be dead. She had not been unconscious, though she pretended to be when Andre rushed to her. She had closed her eyes, frightened that he might lift the scarf from her face.

She had been intoxicated by July. After years of not seeing much—the confines of her house, her cats, peculiar patterns of moonlight when she tried and failed to sleep on hot summer nights—she had suddenly seen everything. For the first time in months the black spot in her eye seemed unimportant; her fear of blindness evaporated. Now, she has ruined her granddaughter's summer and, frankly, her own. She has always believed she hates living alone, but as she listens to Tina Turner, in stereo—on portable radios in the shed next door and up in Jody's room—she realizes she prefers cats. The white one is Margot, the big tom, Sinbad. She keeps bells tied around their necks to warn birds away. Her granddaughter tosses hunks of old bread out onto the porch, instead of breaking the crusts into pieces. Jody spends most of her time sitting out in the yard writing letters, and in the afternoon she bicycles into town for groceries. Mrs. Renny makes out a small list each morning—usually lettuce, cat food, some sort of jam, bread, plums. She had worried that Jody would run wild, but Jody always comes straight home from the market. The worst her granddaughter has done is to put a red streak in her hair, which is rapidly fading. When Elizabeth Renny was sixteen she was still a child. She was never out by herself at night until her own daughter was eight years old, and then only because her husband was away and there was the threat of a hurricane. She drove them to the town hall, where mattresses had been laid down and coffee and crullers were set out on a bridge table. She would like to be inside her granddaughter's body for an hour, just to see how it feels. How would Tina Turner sound through her granddaughter's ears? What would the sun feel like on her skin? How fast would her legs move when she bicycled down the road?

She can tell her granddaughter is afraid of her. She catches her staring when they eat dinner. Elizabeth can move around the house now, dragging her leg behind her, using two canes. When the doctor came to visit, she could tell he was amazed not to find her in bed, wasting away. She has always been strong. When she was younger she picked beach plums and spent an entire week making jelly. For a whole week her skin was flushed and pink. The oddest thing of all is, should her bones mend she is not at all certain she won't go upstairs, open the window, and try it again.

SIMON wakes Vonny. She puts on a robe and takes him downstairs, leaving Andre to sleep. Simon rolls snakes out of Play-Doh while Vonny makes French toast, using the last egg. Later she will go to the farmstand where the eggs are always freshest. It is a little before seven and bands of light angle through the trees. Teenagers are supposed to sleep late, but when Vonny looks out the window Mrs. Renny's granddaughter is already out on the back porch, drinking a can of soda. When Vonny squints it could well be herself out there, fifteen years earlier, balancing the can of soda on her knee so she can light a cigarette, not noticing that the starlings are calling in the birch tree.

When Andre comes down, he goes to the stove and pours himself a cup of coffee. He stands by the window and watches Mrs. Renny's granddaughter idly stroke the back of the white cat. Her fingernails are painted blood red. "What the hell does she do out there all day?" he says.

"She plots her future," Vonny says. "Don't you remember?"

"No," Andre says.

He rinses out his coffee cup, then begins to pack a lunch for himself and Simon to take to the beach.

"Two kinds of cookies," Simon insists, and Andre adds a paper bag of chocolate-chip and lemon cookies to the thermal lunch bag. Vonny tips her chair against the radiator to watch Andre; in the murky kitchen light his skin looks unnaturally pale. Simon comes to sit on her lap. She puts her arms around him and notices that his dangling legs do not reach the chair rungs. Once, she was the sort of person who never wore seat belts, who didn't think twice about mixing Valium and gin. Now she worries all the time. Perhaps she should have known she would turn out like this; there was always her fear of bridges. She watches Simon too carefully. Lately, she worries not only about chicken pox and ear infections, but about Simon's height. People often judge Simon to be younger than he is. They're surprised when he talks in full sentences, when he fearlessly jumps into the surf. Secretly, Vonny measures him twice a month against the kitchen counter, setting cookies up high for him to reach.

All that morning, Vonny works at her wheel on the sun porch off the living room. Her vases and mugs are sold at shops in Edgartown and Vineyard Haven, and some of the larger, more expensive pieces are crated and shipped to Cambridge. Unless there is a special order, she prefers to use varying proportions of copper oxide in her glazes so that her pottery runs from a pale mossy color to a green so dark it seems black. Often, she scratches away at the glaze to reveal the red-hued local clay she favors. Some of her customers say that the figures and patterns this sgraffito technique reveals are what distinguishes Vonny's pottery, but this is not her concern. What she likes best is that moment just before the clay takes shape. It is the time when if startled, by her child's voice or a sudden rainstorm, Vonny is always amazed to look up from the clay and see the world around her.

In the afternoon, after Andre and Simon have returned from the beach, Vonny scrapes her wheel clean, then bathes Simon and puts him down for his nap. On these hot days he doesn't cry and insist he's not tired, and sometimes he sleeps for more than two hours. Vonny takes a shower, then puts on white shorts and a T-shirt with the logo of Andre's defunct company—a small red motorcycle inside a hot-pink heart. When she goes down to the kitchen, Andre is on the phone, trying to reach the client in New Jersey who has bought the Norton, sight unseen. Vonny fills a wicker basket with blueberries, grapes, apricots, and oranges. On a piece of yellow note paper she writes: *I'm taking this next door.* She slips the paper in front of Andre, waits for him to nod, then goes out

the door. She should be taking homemade baked goods or
jam rather than fruit, but she's certain that Elizabeth Renny
is twice the cook she is. Since they have lived as neighbors,
Vonny has been inside Mrs. Renny's house only once, when
the pipes in her kitchen froze and Andre went to help. Vonny,
carrying Simon in a Snugli then, brought over a wrench.
Sometimes, when they are both outside, they talk to each
other through the lilacs. Eventually they will have to confer
over the half-dead pine that borders on both their properties.
They have had one disagreement—when Nelson chased the
white cat up a tree. Nelson loves cats, but figures they're fair
game outside. He likes to trap them between his paws and
gently chew on their backs.

Vonny walks up the steps to Mrs. Renny's house, but before she can knock on the screen door Jody says, "My grandmother's asleep."

The girl stands hidden against the silver mesh of the screen.
Vonny has the uneasy feeling that she has been carefully
watched as she crossed the lawn.

"Oh, that's all right," Vonny says. She holds up the basket
of fruit. "I brought this over as a get-well present. I can leave
it with you."

The girl opens the screen door. She is tan and her shoulders
are a little stooped. She has beautiful eyes and a wide, sullen
mouth.

"You can come in," she says.

Vonny does, then puts the basket of fruit on the counter.
"You're Jody?" she says.

Jody nods. She has taken an orange out of the basket and is peeling it.

"How long will you be staying?" Vonny asks. When she first heard that a teenager would be living next door she naturally assumed her search for a regular babysitter was over. Now, watching the girl coolly consider a slice of orange, she's not so sure.

"I guess time will tell," Jody says. This is exactly the sort of thing her mother says when she doesn't want to answer a question. "I'm starting to like it here," Jody says. "The people I know in Hartford are extremely immature."

They can hear Elizabeth Renny stirring in the parlor Something—a cane?——falls to the floor. Vonny looks down the hallway and sees Mrs. Renny struggling with her canes. When she turns back, Jody is studying her, a dreamy look on her face. When Mrs. Renny reaches the doorway, Jody jumps to help her into the kitchen.

"I thought I heard voices," Mrs. Renny says, and then, about the fruit, "You shouldn't have. Now I'll never be able to thank you and your husband enough."

Vonny finds it difficult to smile. Jody stands in the doorway. Though she's looking directly at Vonny carefully, she seems a million miles away. Vonny remembers that when she was sixteen and seemed that cool, she was burning up inside. If pressed, she would have to admit that she had wanted a daughter. Seeing Jody makes her doubly glad for what she's gotten. She could not bear a daughter this aloof and self-contained. When Vonny leaves, grateful to be back out in the hot sun, Elizabeth Renny takes the fruit to the sink and, leaning her canes up against the counter, washes each piece.

"She's a nice girl," Mrs. Renny says, and Jody smiles. As far as she can tell, Vonny is absolutely no competition.

IT is the first week in August, and Simon is so excited he can't sleep during his afternoon nap. Instead, he crawls under the thin quilt with a flashlight. His mother has told him that Illumination Night is like thousands of fireflies. For more than a hundred years, since Oak Bluffs was a Methodist camp with believers' tents set beneath the old, enormous trees, there has been a Grand Illumination once a year. The Victorian cottages that ring Trinity Park are hung with Japanese lanterns, lit by candles, illuminated all at once by a signal from within the Tabernacle in the center of the park.

Simon knows his mother has been getting ready all day. She is making a special supper and before they go to Oak Bluffs they'll have a picnic of tunafish-and-olive sandwiches, carrots, Doritos, and chocolate cupcakes Simon helped to make. His father will let him have several swallows of cold, dark beer. The streets will be crowded and most of the children will have light sticks that glow in the dark.

Today Simon's parents are angry at each other. Whenever this happens his father goes directly to work in the shed and his mother cooks something with brisk, controlled movements. Today it is blueberry muffins, which Simon will have for a snack when he finishes with his alleged nap. When his mother is angry she thinks she speaks calmly, but her voice cracks. While Simon is in bed with his flashlight, they are downstairs arguing about money. The customer in New Jersey who was supposed to buy the Norton has canceled at the last moment, and his father is left with an expensive antique bike that may be difficult to sell. His response was to go off the Island this morning and return from Hyannis with an old Vincent Black Shadow that cost two thousand dollars. They still have money from the sale of Andre's business, but they have bought this house outright and have nothing much to fall back on, no health insurance for instance. Vonny is furious. She never wants to be so broke that she'll have to beg her father for money. Her father has a new family and would prefer to imagine that his old family, the one that didn't work out, never existed. Once Simon asked Vonny who her daddy was, and she began to cry, suddenly, as though she'd been stuck with a pin.

When Vonny comes in to check on Simon at three o'clock, he is asleep under the quilt. The flashlight is still turned on. Vonny sits on the edge of the bed and turns down the quilt. Simon is curled up in a ball and Vonny feels her throat tighten as she watches him. Andre has threatened not to go to the picnic, or to Oak Bluffs either. Vonny lies down beside Simon. She loves him most when he's asleep. When he is awake, Vonny never knows if something will delight him or make him burst into tears. They have an on-again, off-again battle of the wills, which Vonny never wins. A battle that, whenever Simon is asleep, seems both pointless and unavoidable.

When Simon wakes up, his mother's arms are around him. He wriggles away and, though he is still half-asleep, says, "I want you to play the drum." They are often a marching band, just the two of them on a trail that winds through every room in the house. Before he gets off the bed, Simon throws his arms around Vonny's neck and kisses her. Against her own face, his face is damp.

ANDRE has the truck pulled right up to the back of the shed. The Vincent Black Shadow is in the bed of the pickup, and he pulls out the metal ramp so he can walk the bike down. He knows the girl next door is watching him. She is studying his back as he strains to slide the metal plank out. Being watched should make him uncomfortable, but there's something pleasurable about it. He gets into the back of the truck, wondering if he would have walked up the plank rather than jump in if she hadn't been watching.

As he lifts the bike, which scrapes along the blue metal, leaving what looks like a silver scar, Jody takes a deep breath and walks across the lawn. She knows you can fall in love with someone without ever having spoken, because that is exactly what's happened to her. She has sat in the sun so long thinking about him that now there is a band of sunburn on both her cheeks. She thinks to herself, This is how people get into terrible situations. Even ruin their lives. But she keeps on walking. She knows the time is right because all this week the moon has been red, a lover's moon that keeps her awake. She has been planning this carefully; she will tell him straight out that she needs a ride to a real supermarket, like the A&P in Edgartown. Just to be on the safe side, she has punctured one of her bike tires with a rusty nail. She will be telling him the truth.

Her grandmother has been talking more lately, maybe it's the painkillers. Today at breakfast she told Jody about the sailors on the docks who used to say, "Foul deeds are done in fair weather." Another one of those sayings Jody hates. When she reaches the truck she puts a hand on the cool metal and everything clever she was going to say completely eludes her. She covers her eyes with one hand so she will not have to squint looking up at him.

"Hi," she says.

Andre looks over his shoulder, then leans the bike back against the truck.

"Hi," he says. "Jody, right?"

She nods. If she thought she wouldn't squeak when she opened her mouth, she would answer him.

"Want to help?"

He reaches down, takes her hand, and pulls her up. Now that he is actually touching her, she can't feel it. Andre grabs the bike. Jody goes around to its far side and together they lead it down the metal plank. The old bike is much heavier than Jody would have expected. Once the Vincent lurches toward her and she gasps, but Andre steadies it and they roll it through the open shed door. Jody stands there, stupidly she thinks, while Andre kicks out the kickstands. It's really hot

in the shed, and for some reason the heat makes them feel
they have to whisper.

"How're you doing over there?" Andre says.

"All right," Jody tells him. She is in ecstasy.

"Need a ride somewhere?" Andre says. "I have to get some
parts. Need to pick up some groceries?"

She cannot believe her luck. She needn't have bothered
with the rusty nail.

He puts on a blue workshirt and reaches for the keys to
the truck. When they walk out from the shed the sunlight is
dazzling and, for one brief moment, they are both blinded.

VONNY sees the angles of Jody's thin shoulder blades beneath
her cotton shirt as she gets into the passenger seat. A cloud
of exhaust rises from the tailpipe. The worst thing Vonny sees
is that across the lawn, at the kitchen window, Mrs. Renny
is also watching as the pickup makes a left turn and disappears down the road. It is a mirror image that makes Vonny
shudder. She closes the curtains and plays with Legos at the
kitchen table with Simon. At six, Andre has still not returned.
At six thirty, Simon complains that he's hungry. He's been
looking forward to this night all summer. They had planned
to picnic at the beach, then get to Oak Bluffs before the
crowds arrived. Now it is too late for either. Because she
knows they intend to go to Oak Bluffs, Vonny phones some
neighbors, summer people, Hal and Eleanor Freed, who have
a little girl a year older than Simon. In their car, Vonny has

to keep Simon on her lap and the bag of food between her feet. Luckily, she is not asked to be sociable; the Freeds' little girl, Samantha, talks nonstop. Simon watches her, mesmerized, and Vonny wonders if he is puzzled that another child can have so much to say. The roads are already choked with traffic, but Vonny doesn't see one blue pickup truck.

At the edge of Oak Bluffs, the Freeds, who have always kept their distance and believe that all year-round residents are somehow aberrant, ask Vonny to be at the car by eleven if she wants a ride back. Vonny has a moment of panic. She had never imagined they'd planned to stay so late; she doubts that she'll be able to keep Simon awake. They say goodbye to the Freeds and have their picnic by the bandstand at Ocean Park. After he eats half a sandwich and drinks two paper cups full of lemonade, Vonny surprises Simon when she lets him have not one but two chocolate cupcakes.

By the time they start for the Tabernacle, the road is jammed and the sky has turned deep blue. Vonny holds Simon's hand and drags him a little, so he'll keep up. As they walk through the gate leading to Trinity Park, the air around them darkens. It seems later than it is. In this crowd, Vonny feels as though there's no such thing as gravity. She can't help but wonder if Elizabeth Renny actually stumbled out the window. As hard as she tries, she cannot imagine how that could have been accomplished without first climbing onto the window ledge.

The path they take is narrow, and Vonny can hear Simon's breathing deepen, the way it does when he's excited. The lanterns are not yet lit, but there are so many it's startling. All day Simon has been imagining fireflies strung on thread from house to house. Now when he sees the Japanese lanterns it is as though he has never seen color before. He wants them lit right now, he wants the rose and white to glow, the aqua and yellow to burst into light.

Vonny buys Simon a light stick, then she sits on the grass while he twirls the stick in a circle. Before the band begins to play there is a sing-along, and Vonny is glad she doesn't know the words to the first song. It is "Let Me Call You Sweetheart," sung a cappella. Vonny tells herself it's just a song. It means nothing to her. From within the Tabernacle the voices are distant and deep; they seem to be coming out of the sky.

After they stand for the anthem, Vonny pulls Simon onto her lap. He knows all the words to "Someone's in the Kitchen with Dinah" and "Yankee Doodle Dandy." He lies on his back and watches the stars. It is so dark, Vonny would not know Simon was there if he didn't balance the light stick on his chest.

At last a lantern is brought down to the stage in the Tabernacle. An elderly woman holds a taper to the candle inside and everyone applauds. Vonny lifts Simon up to see as the lanterns surrounding the Tabernacle are lit. Now candles may be placed in all of the other lanterns. Every porch, every rafter of the cottages around Trinity Park is irradiated with color and heat. Everyone promenades through the meeting ground to view the illuminated houses, and Vonny holds Simon's hand so he will not be lost among the legions of strangers.

Simon feels as though he has stumbled into a dream, and because of this he is immediately sleepy. He cannot see the path he walks on, but the distance is filled with light.

As they peer into the houses whose doors are flung open, it's as though Vonny were watching a play. The path beneath her feet seems less real than a stranger's living room. The band in the Tabernacle begins to play a march and Vonny holds Simon's hand tighter. She suddenly feels the way she does when she is about to cross a bridge. Her legs turn to rubber; her mouth is dry. She pulls Simon onto the sidewalk and stands absolutely still. She knows she is breathing too quickly and shallowly, so she bends over and concentrates on a crack in the sidewalk. As soon as Vonny can move, they sit on the sidewalk, up against a low fence that borders a patch of lawn lined with seashells and bleeding hearts and ferns. Vonny helps Simon onto her lap and they watch the Illumination in silence. Less than two feet away is a cottage painted sky blue and white. Lanterns hang from the scrollwork, the archways, the ornamental brackets. Bags of sand hold candles on the path leading to its door. Simon leans his head against her. She can feel the heat of his body through her shirt and her thin sweater, and when he grows heavier she knows he has fallen asleep. If she has to carry him back to the Freeds' car at eleven he will tighten his arms around her neck in his sleep and she will sway in the dark from the strain of carrying him. But now, the fence behind her back feels cold, and when she closes her eyes she can still see circles of yellow light.

*   *   *

HE planned to take the long way home and show her Lambert's Cove, but it took Jody more time than he'd expected at the grocery store, and as soon as they get back he carries the bags into her grandmother's kitchen. In the truck, she didn't take her eyes off him. With Vonny there has never been the carelessness he associates with young lovers, the intensity of not caring what happens next, of looking no farther than the backseat of a borrowed car for a frantic embrace.

In Mrs. Renny's kitchen he feels as if he'd been slapped in the face. What is he doing here? Now all he wants to do is get home, though he wonders what price he'll have to pay for this ride to the store. It's not a crime to give a young girl a ride, to imagine, briefly, that you're kissing her.

"I just wish I could thank you some way," Jody says to him.

His silence is extremely embarrassing; they both know what she means. When Andre doesn't answer, Jody quickly adds, "I could babysit for your little boy sometime."

Mrs. Renny comes into the kitchen and thanks him too.

"I hope it's not all frozen foods," she says to her granddaughter, and Jody wrinkles her nose and keeps loading the refrigerator with diet soda and oranges and eggs.

When Andre looks out the window he notices his house is dark. Usually, at this time of night, the kitchen light is on, the porch light turns a pale gold, an illusion caused by dozens of moths. He remembers their picnic, and with a sinking feeling knows Vonny and Simon haven't waited for him.

"I forgot an appointment," he says suddenly.

Jody turns to study him. It's as lame an excuse as she's heard. Once, when a boy she didn't want to talk to called her, she shouted that a truck had just pulled up on her front lawn, then quickly hung up on him.

"Seriously," Andre says. "It's Illumination Night."

Jody closes the refrigerator door and wipes her palms on her shorts. She doesn't know what Illumination Night is, and she doesn't much care. All she knows is that he's about to leave her.

Though she has not been to the Grand Illumination for years, Elizabeth Renny remembers that the first time she went she wore a pale pink skirt, a blouse with a wide collar, small gold earrings. Although she was already married, she thinks she may have fallen in love with her husband on Illumination Night. Stars had been plucked out of the sky and set into lanterns. She broke the heel of one of her shoes and walked down Trinity Avenue barefoot.

"I wish I could take you there," she says to her granddaughter.

Andre fervently hopes they will decline but, cornered, he invites both Jody and her grandmother along.

"We couldn't impose on you," Elizabeth Renny says.

Jody grabs her pocketbook off the back of a kitchen chair and swings it over her shoulder.

"Oh, well," Elizabeth Renny says. "You two go on. I'm too old."

Jody waits in the truck while Andre goes to check his house and make sure it's empty. Then they drive without talking.

Jody knows he doesn't want her there, but there's always the possibility that he'll change his mind. Bugs hit the windshield and Andre turns on the wipers; soon the glass is streaked with their remains. There is no place to park, but Andre keeps going anyway, and he parks illegally, blocking a driveway. Getting out of the truck, Jody stumbles. After such a promising start, everything has gone wrong. They walk down the road in the dark and she thinks how stupid she is to be wearing shorts. Her legs are freezing. She has to struggle to keep up with Andre.

"Hey, wait up," she says, casually she hopes. If she's left on this road she'll never find her way back. She runs and grabs Andre's arm and imagines that everyone they pass assumes they're a couple. She wants him in some strange, deep way she doesn't understand. When they reach Trinity Park, Jody blinks in the sudden pools of light.

If she had grown up here, Jody thinks, she might have been happy. If every night there were red stars and pink paper lanterns. They walk up and down the streets, looking for Simon and Vonny, Jody hoping not to find them. On a crowded corner, Andre suddenly stops. He stares beyond the Tabernacle, then turns to Jody. He puts his hands on her arms, and for one dizzy instant Jody thinks at last he's going to kiss her. Instead, he bends down so he can be heard above the noise of the crowd.

"There they are," he says.

Vonny is watching the band. Simon looks like a baby sleeping crossways on his mother's lap, his legs pressed against the sidewalk. In the morning, there will be tiny red scratches above his anklebones. Andre lets go of Jody, and as she follows him across the street, Jody knows that on the ride home she will sit in the back of the truck, and by then the stars will be as white and sharp as dragon's teeth.

Chapter Two

OUT ALL NIGHT

IN October a cold snap freezes pumpkins on the vine, and horses left out to pasture return to their barns with ice on their hooves. There are yellow leaves lining the ditches and the roadsides, frozen in place. Jody hates the change in the weather. The cold raises welts on her skin. The stars seem much too bright. Ever since August, Jody has put her desire on hold, which is not to say she has given up hope. Instead of leaving after Labor Day she had registered for the school term, and is now a junior at Martha's Vineyard Regional High School. She is convinced that if her feelings for Andre were as one-sided as they seemed, he would be able to look at her, no problem. Twice this week Andre has passed her on the road. Both times he was driving the pickup alone and she was walking home from the school-bus stop. He didn't look at her as he went by, but she imagines that he looked at her pretty damn hard in his rearview mirror.

She wants to know the smallest details of his life. Does he sleep with his arms around Vonny? Does he shave in the morning or at night? Does he ever think of her, the way she thinks of him when she can't fall asleep? She grows more and more impatient. She weaves a thousand plans. She will hide in the pickup truck, dressed in nothing but a long black sweater. She will call him at midnight, after first making certain that her grandmother is asleep, and beg him to come and trap a bat lodged in the rafters of her bedroom. She will kidnap the little boy, Simon, and hold him hostage for the price of a kiss. Instead of taking notes during class she writes tactical possibilities in careful script until her looseleaf notebook is filled. But when she does finally seek him out she does so before she realizes what she's doing. There is no design, it's just something that happens. That's how she knows it was meant to be. Her grandmother has been asleep for hours and Jody is already in bed when she realizes she's forgotten to let the cats in. They don't come when she calls so she puts a raincoat on over her flannel nightgown and pulls on a pair of leather boots she doesn't bother to tie. Out on the porch Jody hisses the way her grandmother has taught her. When she makes this urgent sound, Jody is calling not to the cats but to Andre. She thinks he may hear her because in his house the kitchen light is switched on. Sinbad comes running for the house. Jody opens the door for him and he slips inside. Then she walks across the yard.

She has to find out who it is in the kitchen. She goes to the window and peers in, past a sink filled with dirty dishes. He is at the table drinking something—coffee, maybe—flipping through a stack of papers. Bills. He wears a green flannel shirt and blue jeans. With one hand he moves his coffee cup back and forth in its saucer. Jody feels some of the excitement robbers must feel. There is enormous power in watching someone act completely natural and unawares. Before she can stop herself, Jody taps on the window. The cold glass against her knuckles feels sharp. When Andre turns to the window Jody holds her breath. If nothing more she will always have this moment when he sees her and nothing else. She knows she will be crushed if he simply looks away, so she breaks their locked gaze and backs off. She stands beside the rose of Sharon that grows by the side of the house. She reaches into her pocket, and when Andre comes outside, without having bothered to put on a sweater, Jody is smoking a cigarette. Andre lets the door slam behind him and follows the orange light of her cigarette. He thinks his heart is beating so fast because he's angry.

"What do you think you're doing here?" he says.

The white cat Jody originally came out to look for is on the porch next door, mewing and scratching at the door.

Jody can no longer measure her own behavior. She has always been well practiced at manipulation. It isn't difficult for her to get what she wants from her parents and friends when she plays her cards right. She's sure the way to get to Andre is to tell him a sad story that will make him feel responsible not only for her but for the way she feels about him. But she's so close to him she can't think straight, and so she tells him the truth.

"I just wanted to see you," Jody says.

Her honesty catches Andre off guard. He realizes just how cold it is. Inside, everyone is sleeping. Even the dog on the kitchen floor seems miles away, distanced by sleep. Lately Andre and Vonny have been careful with each other. Until tonight Andre has made certain to avoid the yard when Jody is out there, waiting, he knows, for him, and Vonny has not complained when Andre brought home a second, then a third, old motorcycle. But careful isn't enough. Something between them is cracking.

"You should be going out with boys your own age," Andre tells Jody.

"Thanks a lot," Jody says in a tone that reminds Andre exactly how young she is.

"Jody, go home," Andre says. They both know he means all the way, Connecticut, not next door.

"I wouldn't even ask you for anything," Jody says.

"Look, I don't want to see you," Andre says cruelly. "I don't know how to make that clear to you."

Jody feels her face grow hot. It would be easy to hate him.

"You're just lonely," Andre says.

It is the worst possible thing he could have said.

"All right," Jody says. "If that's the way you want it. I'll never come back here again."

"Good," Andre says.

"I really mean it," Jody says.

Andre watches as she runs between their yards and disappears in the dark. When he hears the door slam behind her, he walks back to his house. He turns off the downstairs lights, then goes upstairs. In the bathroom, he avoids looking at himself. He washes his face, then goes to Simon's door and opens it. There is a night-light, a wedge of white plastic, plugged into the wall. The rice-paper shades have been pulled down. Simon lies sideways across the bed. He's kicked off the blankets and his feet dangle over the mattress. Andre leans down and shifts his son so that his head is once more on the pillow, then covers him. It amazes Andre that Simon can sleep so deeply, that he can even be carried from room to room without waking. If Andre ever slept as peacefully he no longer remembers. Can it be that every night in his childhood was broken in two by the sound of sleet against the roof, by the hum of the TV his father watched in the living room? Can it be that even in August there were always cold sheets? He wants to be everything to Simon his own father was not, but already Simon runs to Vonny for comfort. When Simon is with Andre it's as though he doesn't think his father can recognize pain. If Simon falls when they're together, he picks himself up and keeps running and Andre never finds out until later, when Simon sits on Vonny's lap and shows her the scrape, that his son has been hurt. Andre doesn't want to believe that his own father's indifference was anything other than what it seemed. And yet, when he thinks of his father getting up long before dawn, maneuvering his Ford down snow-blocked roads he would later plow, Andre wishes that just once, instead of lying in bed until he heard the car start, he had gotten up and made a Thermos full of black coffee.

When Andre gets into bed beside her, Vonny opens her eyes.

"Simon?" she says, thinking Andre has just been roused.

"Asleep," Andre says.

Vonny smiles and moves closer. Andre knows this girl next door is just bad timing. If she had come along a few months ago, he and Vonny would have laughed over it. Now, he will not mention her visit to Vonny. And, because of this, he will not be able to fall asleep until dawn.

When he dreams he dreams about the Flying Horses, the old carousel in Oak Bluffs. He is in a terrible hurry. He knows it is winter because the streets are deserted. The carousel should be shut down, yet he can hear music. Who is he meeting here? Why is he frightened? He thinks perhaps Simon has been locked inside the wooden building that houses the carousel, and he breaks into a run.

The clouds are much too low. He cannot tell if the sky is above him or directly in front of him. As Andre runs he knows he is too late, but in spite of that he runs faster. Luckily, an ax has been left for him. He must chop through the building. He knows that. As he swings the ax, snow begins to fall. Finally the wood splinters, and he sees that the carousel is motionless. How strange, then, that mirrors set in a circle sway back and forth, distorting what he sees, making it impossible to tell what is real and what is a reflection. When he hears a hissing noise, Andre breaks into a sweat. He studies the carved horses—they are wood, their mouths forever open, frozen in place. Along one of the carousel coaches is a painted dragon. It flexes its talons once. When it opens its mouth Andre can see two sharp white fangs. A stream of mosquitoes and hot air pours out of its mouth, and the hiss, which moves mirrors, which alters reflections, winds itself around Andre's throat.

Andre tries to tear away what is choking him. When he leans his head back he sees a painted sign but cannot read if it says *This is the beginning* or *This is the end*.

In the morning, Andre finds that he has lost his voice. He can communicate only by writing notes. He drinks hot tea with honey and gulps cough medicine straight from the bottle. When this has no effect, he drinks three cups of scalding black coffee in a row, and by noon he's able to speak.

JODY can feel spite curling beneath her tongue as she checks out the cafeteria. Usually she brings a book and ignores everyone. Today nothing escapes her attention. She wears tight black jeans and a gray sweater that makes her eyes look like smooth, flat stones. She has chosen her black boots and red bangle bracelets carefully. For nearly two months she has paid no attention to her fellow students, so she has to make up for lost time. The entire student body of the Martha's Vineyard Regional High School is smaller than the senior class back home. No one approaches her anymore, and she can't blame them. During her first week of school Jody let the girls who tried to be friendly know right away—she wasn't interested. Now they don't speak to her unless they have to. Jody has no confidante to fill her in on the social hierarchies, so she has to figure them out herself and it isn't easy. People blend together here, there's no clear-cut caste system as there is at her old school. The most awful-looking boys sit with the prettiest girls. Jody figures that people can't afford to be as nasty to each other when they live on an island. No matter where they go, they're bound to run into each other.

She sees two distinct possibilities at tables up front. One is blond and tall, wearing a flannel shirt and jeans. The other has reddish hair and a pair of wire-rimmed sunglasses in his shirt pocket. They're both, Jody supposes, acceptable, although even the handsomest boys at school are pitiful compared to Andre. She has never been more calculating. She doesn't care what they think of her and she has nothing to lose. Andre has told her to go out with boys her own age, and that's exactly what she plans to do.

She brings her tray up front and watches carefully. The boy with the red hair has his back to her, but the blond boy looks. At his table are two other boys and a girl with short hair who clearly is desperate for his attention. Jody stops a few feet away and meets his gaze. All she has to do is wait and he will walk over to her. When he does she'll have only two questions: does he have his own car and what time can he meet her after school?

SIMON has already decided he does not want a birthday party. He refuses to be any older until he is taller. He does not tell his mother about his decision as she puts a peanut-butter sandwich on the table for him, or when she quickly hugs him. The pressure he feels in his chest comes from keeping his secret, but he cannot be moved or intimidated. Vonny senses something and when she brings him some juice she touches her lips to his forehead. In fact he's hot, not with fever, but with shame.

He knows he is wicked. He must be. He is under a spell. Something pulls at his clothes, stretching them out so that cuffs have to be rolled up, new boots have to be packed with newspaper before they'll fit. Something sits on him, pressing down hard so he cannot grow. His parents think he is stupid. They think he doesn't know that his mother is measuring him against the kitchen counter, or that his father never throws a ball to him, but bounces it instead, the way he would to a baby. Simon sees the way they look at him, and now, even when they are not measuring him, he's measuring himself.

As Simon eats his lunch, Vonny kneels by a cupboard and searches for her cake pans. Simon's stomach hurts. She is already planning his birthday party. If he can put off being four he can use the time to try to grow.

"Maybe I'll be sick next Saturday," he says casually.

"Oh?" Vonny says. She pulls out two round pans and puts them on the counter.

"I might get chicken pox," Simon says.

While his mother's back is to him, Simon pinches himself. A red welt rises on his forearm.

"Look," he calls. "A red spot."

Vonny comes over and examines his arm. Simon watches her carefully. He can always tell when she believes him.

"I guess you might," Vonny says.

Simon begins to feel better.

"It's a good thing the spots are showing up now," Vonny says. "They only last for three days. After that you won't be contagious."

"Maybe it's another kind of pox," Simon says. "A longer-lasting one."

Vonny smiles as she rinses out the cake pans. "I'll let you choose," she says to Simon. "Chocolate or vanilla?"

Every morning the first thing Simon does when he wakes up is take hold of the wooden spindles of the headboard and stretch out on his mattress to see how far his toes reach. He closes his eyes and blocks out the sounds of birds and cars. If it's quiet enough, if he listens hard enough, he may be able to hear his bones growing.

AT Simon's party there is chocolate cake, two kinds of ice cream, blue balloons taped to the windows, and party hats with elastic chin bands and gold fringe. The guests are two other four-year-olds—Kate and Matt—and their parents, two couples Vonny and Andre would never have spoken to had they not all been in a natural childbirth class together. Matt's parents, Jane and Doug, are architects from Boston, and the houses they design have decks jutting out at odd angles and walls made entirely of glass. Most of these houses are occu-

pied only two or three months out of the year and their owners belong to associations that own private beaches. Rather
than tell them he thinks locked beaches are immoral, rather
than ask why anyone in his right mind would build a house
of glass overlooking the Edgartown airport, Andre does not
talk to Jane and Doug at all. And Kate's parents, who both
teach at the regional high school, cannot seem to bring themselves to speak to Andre for reasons of their own. For nearly
three years the mothers have had a weekly playgroup, which
Vonny and Simon have both come to dread. Kate will not
share any of her toys, and Matt is a biter. Whenever Matt
controls his urge to sink his teeth into someone, he's given a
yellow sticker of a smiling face. He now has hundreds of
stickers, perhaps the largest smiling-face collection in the
world. Twenty minutes after Simon's birthday party has begun, Matt bites Simon on the leg. Vonny rushes over to see
if the skin has been broken, and Andre swoops down on Matt
and carries him over to a corner.

"No biting here," Andre says to the startled offender. "Got
it?"

After Simon has been given ice to press to his leg, Vonny
signals Jane into the kitchen and tells her she and Simon won't
be able to make it to play group anymore.

"I don't blame you for dropping out," Jane says. "Actually,
I'm relieved. Can you believe the way Kate hoards her toys?"

"It's not just Kate," Vonny says. "It took me all this time
to realize Simon's not going to be friends with someone just
because I chose them for him."

"I know just what you mean," Jane says. "They have such disgusting little minds of their own."

Vonny is making coffee for the grownups, hot chocolate for the kids.

Jane, who has straight blond hair and an assured, direct gaze, leans her elbows on the counter and watches. "Only give Matt half a cup," she tells Vonny. "Chocolate makes him bite more."

Jane has confided that she has considered divorcing Doug, but she's afraid to lose him as a business partner. They have both had affairs, but for some reason it makes Vonny uncomfortable to know that Doug sleeps with his clients. She knows it is awful to think his is the worse betrayal because he's a man. Every now and then, Vonny plots what she will do if Andre betrays her. She will leave the Vineyard and go back to Boston. She will rent an apartment in a good school district and buy a car and a color TV. When Andre comes for his visit with Simon every second weekend, because that's all the judge will allow him, she will wear gorgeous clothes that will drive him crazy. He will spend hours wondering how she can afford them and who it is exactly she's dressing for. Whenever the thought that Andre might want custody of Simon enters her mind, Vonny quickly stops thinking. And anyway, if she has to she will beg her father for a loan so she can afford the best lawyer in Boston. Or she will go all the way and use a New York lawyer, who may fall in love with her.

That evening, when the guests have gone home and presents are scattered all over the living room floor, Vonny can't stop thinking about her New York lawyer. She's exhausted and Simon is still wound up. He has turned four and is still exactly the same size. He wonders if parents can return their children and get brand-new ones. He whines and pouts and calls Vonny stupid. When told to sit in the corner he kicks at the wall until a small chunk of plaster falls onto the floor. He will not eat supper and when it's time for bed he throws himself on the floor and refuses to let Vonny put on his pajamas. Outside, a cold rain soon turns to sleet.

"All right!" Vonny shouts. "Go to bed without pajamas. Freeze!"

"Don't yell at me!" Simon says. His lips are trembling. His eyes are wet with tears.

"Are you putting these on or not?" Vonny says meanly. Let him cry buckets, she thinks.

Simon stands and tries to make a break for it, but Vonny reaches for his arm, knowing as she does so she is grabbing him too hard. She pulls Simon down on the rug and forces one foot into pajamas. Simon is so surprised and wounded by her cruelty that his breath comes out in little gasps. Vonny can see terror on his face, but she can't seem to stop. She is still screaming.

"You're four years old," she says, "and you're acting like a big baby."

"I'm not a baby!" Simon shouts. His face is wet with tears.

Vonny drops the pajamas and sits back on her heels. She has forgotten that he is. He is afraid of the dark. He has never heard the word *death*. Vonny's made sure of that. Andre has been forcing himself not to interrupt, knowing Vonny will be furious if he does. Now he walks over and picks up Simon. Simon throws his arms around Andre's neck and begins to weep. Crouched on the floor, Vonny herself feels like weeping.

"I'll put him to bed," Andre says.

"Sure," Vonny says, just as if she were a normal person and not a monster.

Later, when Simon has been bathed and dressed for bed, Andre brings him back into the living room to say good night. Simon walks over slowly and hugs Vonny. She cannot bear how tentative he is. When Vonny whispers that she's sorry, Simon nobly acts as though he's forgotten the entire episode. In fact, he kisses her twice. Later still, when Vonny and Andre get into bed, Vonny remembers crying in her room after fighting with her mother. Though she has no idea what their fight was about, she remembers how hot her tears were and how they stopped, as though a spigot had been turned off, as soon as her mother came into her room to kiss and make up.

The sleet comes down harder. Ice coats the bare rose of Sharon and the pickets of the wooden fence out front. By morning there will be traffic warnings and Nelson will have to be walked on a leash so he won't slip. Tonight there is no moon and the only sound is something hard falling from the sky. When Andre and Vonny make love they try to forget that in the room next to theirs a child shifts in his sleep. They do not think about how many times they will disappoint him or each other. As the house settles, birds line the eaves to escape the bad weather, and even those sparrows who never sing at night call a hoarse warning.

ELIZABETH Renny is too old to be someone's caretaker. She has been the voice of reason to the screaming fury of adolescence once and that was more than enough. It surprises Elizabeth Renny to discover that she no longer cares about much of what seemed so terribly important when her own daughter, Laura, was young. Things that should shock her do not. She knows Jody lies to her constantly; is she really expected to believe that this girl with a red streak in her hair and smudged eye makeup comes home late from school every day because she has joined the chorus? She doubts that Jody knows the difference between an alto and a soprano but she can well imagine that the blond boy with the red car is already her granddaughter's lover. Though she has never seen marijuana, she can imagine that too, smoked in pipes in the backseat of the boy's car. Laura's rebellions were nothing compared to Jody's reckless spirit. Every move she makes spells out her desire for danger. In time, Elizabeth Renny can tell, this blond boy will no longer please her granddaughter.

What surprises Elizabeth Renny most of all is that she doesn't want to send Jody away. It has nothing to do with Laura's cheerful announcement that she and her husband, Glenn, are considering a trial separation. Living with Jody is like living with an interesting time bomb, and it takes Elizabeth's mind off the dark spot in her eye.

Jody's newest trick is to come home at ten or eleven, then sneak out again at one and stay out till dawn. The first time it happened, Elizabeth Renny thought a robber had entered the house. She slipped off her wedding ring and hid it beneath her pillow. The cats mewed when the door opened, and when it closed again Elizabeth Renny got out of bed and went to the window. Jody was running across the lawn to the waiting red Toyota. At least the boy had had the decency to cut the headlights so he wouldn't wake the neighbors. Jody grows braver and more careless all the time. Often she has the blond boy park in the bushes near Andre's shed and then takes off all her clothes, daring Andre to see. Staying out all night gives her gray eyes an unearthly cast. She gets only a few hours of sleep in the morning, and always has to rush to get ready for school.

Jody has overslept again. She runs downstairs, still buttoning her shirt, and finds her grandmother has made breakfast for her. On the table are plates of scrambled eggs, two half grapefruits, English tea.

"I don't have time," Jody explains as she pulls on her black boots. "I'm late for school."

"I'd like to talk to you," Elizabeth Renny says.

Jody slings her canvas bookbag over her shoulder. She wears a pink necklace she doesn't particularly admire. A present from James, the blond boy.

"I'll be back by four," Jody says, "unless I have chorus practice."

"Sit down," Elizabeth Renny insists.

Jody sighs and sits down heavily. Her bookbag slides down her arm and falls between her feet. She can hear James's car pull into the driveway, and for some reason the idea that he's out there waiting irritates her.

Elizabeth Renny has prepared for this conversation and she hopes she doesn't seem too prepared. She has dressed carefully, and is perhaps a little too formal in her black wool dress and heels. Just below her collar she wears a garnet pin in the shape of a dog.

"I'd rather you stayed out all night on weekends," Elizabeth Renny says.

Jody looks up at her grandmother.

"Wouldn't it be better to stay out on a Friday rather than a Monday when you have to get up early? Then you could sleep late on Saturday."

Jody clears her throat. She knows she made absolutely no noise going out last night. Maybe it was when she came back this morning. Or those damn cats following her upstairs.

"Doesn't it make sense?" Elizabeth Renny says.

"Oh sure," Jody says. She is studying her grandmother carefully, just to make certain there's no sarcasm intended.

"Well that's settled," Elizabeth Renny says.

"I'm not in love with him or anything like that," Jody says suddenly. "He's all right, but I'm not about to marry him."

"In my day," Elizabeth Renny begins, but Jody cuts her off.

"Girls didn't throw themselves on the first boy who came along," Jody says contemptuously.

"Girls always thought they were in love," Elizabeth Renny says.

Jody looks down at her hands. The red Toyota has been idling in the driveway for some time, and now the horn honks impatiently.

"I guess I'm going to be real late," she says.

Elizabeth Renny wishes her granddaughter would leave. She has brought up the subject of Jody's night rambling because she is, after all, the girl's temporary guardian. And, she realizes now, it would be impossible for Jody to stay on if she failed every single one of her classes.

"Don't worry," Elizabeth Renny says without thinking. "You'll fall in love."

"I'm not worried," Jody says coldly. "I never worry."

She grabs her coat off the hook and walks outside. After she gets into the Toyota, she slams the door. In the past, Jody has thought of her grandmother not as a person but as a piece of furniture that had to be navigated around on her nightly route. She's not about to care what her grandmother thinks. She refuses to be upset. She will make James stop on the way to school so she can get a can of Diet Coke and some cigarettes. He is in her power. He is a slave to the things she will do when they are alone, if she feels like it. For all she knows they may not make it to school at all. Of course she will never feel quite the same, sneaking out at night. But when she limits her all-night dates to Fridays and Saturdays it's not because her grandmother has asked her to but because she's growing tired of James. After a while, she'll do almost anything to avoid him. And that is the only reason she stops on her way home to get the Sunday papers for her grandmother after she's been out all Saturday night. She has a good excuse not to touch him when there's newsprint on her hands.

NELSON lies on the floor of the porch as Vonny works. Vonny can almost feel the pain in his hips, which are stiff and arthritic, as he stretches to find the comfortable position that forever eludes him. Sometimes he comes and puts his large head on Vonny's knee. He stares at her dreamily. His eyes are cloudy and, because of cataracts, a phosphorescent green when the light hits them.

Nelson has taken to following Vonny from room to room. She stumbles over him sometimes. She has to brush dried clay out of his coat each time he insists on accompanying her into the sun porch where he lies near a barrel of wet clay as Vonny works. Perhaps she allows him to follow her and get in her way because Nelson is the canine equivalent of herself, overly sensitive—what Vonny's mother, Suzanne, calls an empath, what others might call easily overwhelmed. Both Vonny and her dog are prone to take on another creature's pain. When Simon has a tantrum and howls, it's Nelson who hides in a corner and whimpers. When anyone stubs a toe, Nelson limps and licks his paw.

Vonny's mother insists that empathy is a gift, but then Suzanne is a woman who, although married to an optometrist and living in a condominium, battles the acidic Florida soil so she can grow ginger in her backyard, a plant she believes will ensure her second husband's fidelity. Vonny, on the other hand, does not believe in astrology, black magic, or even dreams. She thinks of her empathy as a flaw, like a scratch on her soul that lets in vibrations. She stays clear of people with strong vibrations, and she's thankful that her flaw doesn't take a physical form. She sees no blue auras around people's heads, no sparks of light shooting out from their fingertips. She pities her mother's next-door neighbor, who swears she has seen a silver spaceship floating above Delray Beach. She pities herself because this gift of hers allows her to feel Andre's recent torment. Every time he walks past a window, she knows he is thinking about the girl next door.

Of course she has no proof. But Vonny is sure enough of his attraction to imagine murdering him in various ways several times a day. What can she do to save her marriage before Andre does something stupid? She has long telephone conversations with her childhood friend, Jill, who advises her to wear silk and act as though she's got a lover of her own. She can wait it out. She can cook the sort of dinners he prefers, those without green leafy vegetables. She can have it out with him, punch him, disappear into the night. Or she can startle him by doing what he least expects, which is hire Jody to babysit so they can go to a dinner party at Jane and Doug's where she will show him exactly how much he's got to lose. Vonny wears a red satin dress and black high heels with open toes in spite of the weather. Although Andre hates parties and has stated, for the record, that Simon doesn't know Jody well enough to be left with her, Vonny knows she's made the right move as soon as Jody comes over. Jody is wearing jeans and a sweatshirt, and Vonny makes certain to stand close to the girl when Andre comes downstairs. Beside her red satin Jody all but disappears. Andre pays no attention to Jody, and Vonny is somewhat annoyed when Simon seems pleased to see her and doesn't mind when they leave him.

At the party, Vonny lets Andre see that other men are interested in her. She smiles anytime a man talks to her, no matter what he says. She drinks four glasses of wine and lets Doug's squash partner stand a little too close to her. Andre spends most of the evening in a corner, but Vonny can feel him watching her. By midnight she figures she's proved her point. When they get home, Simon has been asleep for hours and Jody is on the couch, reading magazines, an open bag of pretzels propped up beside her. Vonny almost feels sorry for her and adds a two-dollar tip when she pays her. Andre and Jody ignore each other so completely that, for a moment, Vonny wonders if she needn't have bothered to put on her red dress.

"Ten bucks to be bored by Doug's friends," Andre complains when Jody has left. "Next time let's stay home."

While Andre rinses out the coffeepot for the morning, Vonny goes upstairs to check on Simon. Jody has dressed him in summer pajamas and he's huddled, knees to chest, for warmth. Vonny tucks him in with an extra blanket. In the bedroom, she takes off her dress and kicks her high heels into the back of the closet and unclasps her pearls. On her way to the dresser, she bumps into the bed and Andre's pillow falls onto the floor. Vonny is holding her pearls in one hand. In the place where the pillow has been there is a sheet of note-book paper. Vonny sits down. She can hear the door slam downstairs as Andre takes the dog out. She thinks, at first, she has found a love note, but when she unfolds the paper she sees that "I hate you" is written in blue ink. Vonny quickly crumples the paper and, because she can not bring herself to throw out the evidence, sticks it in her top dresser drawer. She doesn't mention the note when Andre comes to bed.

In the morning she makes breakfast, then begins to pack their summer things in boxes that will later be carried up to the attic. She can never get herself to do this task, cleaning away summer once and for all, until the weather report pre-dicts snow. Soon the upstairs hallway is littered with Simon's summer toys: buckets and shovels and his three-wheeled bike. The beds are covered with folded T-shirts and shorts. After lunch, Simon goes down for his nap, and Andre goes off to Vineyard Haven to buy new snow tires that are now on sale. Because there is nothing to stop her, Vonny leaves the folded clothes unboxed and the toys scattered in the hall. She goes downstairs, pulls her hair back with a rubber band, then dials Elizabeth Renny's number and asks to speak to Jody.

AFTER she hangs up, Jody gulps down orange juice. She is actually shivering. She wishes she had gone with James to a deserted cottage in Gay Head he knows about. She could have waited while he climbed in an unlocked window, she could be there with him now. Certainly, she could have tolerated him for an afternoon. And there's another boy who's interested in her, a senior, who seems more dangerous and therefore more promising than James. She could have been waiting for him in the backseat of his car, a black convertible, instead of being here to answer the phone. She was so startled to hear Vonny's voice that she agreed to go over before she could think it all out. Jody knows what's about to happen. She's been lectured to plenty of times. She can squeeze all the expression out of her face so she appears to be listening. She can recognize the long intake of breath that precedes the end of the lecture, the rush of freedom when you know you're about to be released.

Vonny wouldn't dare invite her over if Andre were home. Walking across the lawn, she sees that his truck isn't parked in the driveway. She wraps her sweater around her. It's freezing today, but her face is burning hot. Even her shadow is red. She imagines Vonny reaching out and slapping her and her face grows hotter. At sixteen, having never slept with Andre, she knows she has become the other woman.

When she sees Vonny waiting for her at the door, Jody has the urge to bolt and run. Instead, she decides she won't say anything at all unless she's asked a direct question. Vonny swings the door open, and Jody walks past her, bringing in cold air. Vonny has the chance to study Jody as she walks inside. It somehow gives her an edge. She feels like a principal who has called a student in for detention.

"Have a seat," Vonny says.

Jody sits down and rubs her hands together.

Like a spider, Vonny thinks.

"Do you drink coffee yet?" Vonny says archly.

One for Vonny, and Jody knows it. She also knows her next line. Is that why you asked me here? To drink coffee? But she doesn't want to rush Vonny into anything. Her voice when she answers, sounds girlish, even to herself. "Sure," she says. "With milk and sugar."

Vonny fixes two cups of coffee, one with milk, the other black. Her hands are shaking. She wonders if this is how murderers feel before they grab a knife. She gets the canister of sugar, puts it down on the table, then sits across from Jody. In the past, Nelson would have barked like mad as soon as someone walked through the door. Now, he wanders into the kitchen and as he slinks under the table Jody reaches out and pats his back.

"I'll bet you enjoy causing trouble," Vonny says.

Jody's expression is absolutely impassive. This, she knows, drives them crazy.

"Not that you have a chance with Andre," Vonny says. "I just want you to know I'm on to you."

Jody takes a sip of her coffee. She has added two heaping spoonfuls of sugar and it's still too bitter. It is time, and she knows it. Now Jody uses her line. "Is that why you asked me here? To tell me I don't have a chance?"

"To let you know you'll regret it," Vonny says.

"I don't have to talk to you," Jody says. She starts to get

up, but Vonny reaches across the table and grabs one of her wrists. Her grip is strong.

"Sit," Vonny says, and without thinking Jody obeys. "Let me tell you something," Vonny says. "You wouldn't even know what to do with him if you got him."

There is a very deep threat here, and Jody is momentarily derailed.

"Men and boys are different," Vonny says, no longer certain if she's telling the truth or inventing something to scare Jody off.

"You don't scare me," Jody says flatly, but she is thinking, for the first time, that she might not be able to live up to what she's hoped to start.

Jody's face seems so open that Vonny can't help but notice how clear her skin is. Vonny's own face has tiny lines in unexpected places. She can well imagine how Jody could have fallen for Andre. A girl her age would be mystified by his silence, appreciate it.

There is a thump upstairs, and Vonny hopes it's not Simon, up early from his nap. When he wakes, his moods are unpredictable, and Vonny gives in to him, more, she knows, than she would if he were not so small for his age. She would hate for Jody to see her pleading with Simon to be good, to have a cookie, to stop kicking his feet on the floor. When there is another thump, Vonny stands abruptly.

"I think that's all we have to say to each other," she says.

"Oh, no it's not," Jody says. At this moment there seems no point to life if she can't win Andre. She has tried to make him jealous enough to act. She has flaunted James, but Andre is like a stone. If he cried his tears would be made out of granite. Still, Jody knows that if he were free they would find real love, nights that lasted as long as other people's entire lifetimes. "Just don't think you can tell me how to feel," she says.

There is another sound, a sharp creak, and Vonny tilts her head. Sunlight through the kitchen window falls across her face. To someone like Jody, Vonny's face has a strength Vonny has never seen or even imagined she possessed. She has high cheekbones and dark eyes. Her hair is cut bluntly and angled toward her neck. When she hears the creak a second time, a shadow crosses her face. Even Jody knows the damp smell of fear. When Vonny runs out of the kitchen, Jody follows right behind her. It's hard for Vonny to breathe. The lighting has shifted and it's dark in the living room. Vonny stumbles over the coffee table. She comes to a stop at the foot of the stairs and doesn't even notice when Jody bumps into her, then backs away. She can hear Simon's bike barreling along the upstairs hallway.

"Stop!" she yells.

Vonny starts to climb the stairs. And then she sees him, coming toward the stairs at full speed.

"Stop right now!" Vonny yells. "Right now!"

Her words seem enormous, they echo inside her head as Simon goes down the first step. He throws his head back, laughing, delighted by the speed he's managed and the thrill of the bump of the first step. Jody reaches up and grabs the back of Vonny's shirt, as though she had to steady herself.

The stairs are old and so steep Andre has to bow his head when he walks up them. As soon as Vonny realizes there is nothing she can do, time takes on a curious quality. Everything is happening fast to Vonny—her heartbeat, the shadows moving across her skin—only Simon moves slowly. At this instant she can see his death. She can see his blood on the stairs. She knows the way she will lean toward him, seconds too late, unable to break his fall.

If it does not happen, she will change her life. She will not hide how much she loves Simon anymore for fear of spoiling him. If she has to, she will give Jody her husband. Simon goes down five more steps. His head snaps back and he's laughing harder. It's like a carnival ride. He gets to the turn in the steps, and because he has gathered too much speed it is possible that he will take the rest of the stairs at once.

"Stop!" Vonny shouts, hoping that Simon will jump off the bike, grab on to the banister, stop his own fall. Amazingly, the bike stops. The front wheel dangles over the edge of a stair and spins in place. Vonny runs, grabs the front wheel, and lifts it. Simon is out of breath but still giddy. Vonny pulls him off the bike with one hand, then lets go of the bike so that it crashes down the rest of the stairs. She smacks Simon on the bottom so hard that tears immediately come to his eyes. Vonny has never hit him before and Simon's howls follow as soon as he's realized what's happened.

Vonny's fingers are like tentacles wrapped around the thin bones of Simon's arm, but she's no longer paying attention to him. Goose bumps rise along her arms and legs. She looks down and her eyes meet Jody's. She wonders if she's as pale as Jody is. She picks Simon up and takes him downstairs. He's still crying but his sobs have turned to hiccups. Standing in the hallway, Jody and Vonny stare at the light coming through the landing window. The panes of glass are old and thick; they distort both clouds and sky. When a car horn outside honks, James's perhaps, they're both startled. Vonny kneels and comforts Simon. Jody combs her hair away from her face with her fingertips. She has completely forgotten why she has come here. She has the urge to sit in someone's lap. Instead, she follows Vonny into the kitchen, where Simon is given cookies and apple juice. He swears never again to ride his bike indoors and he is not scolded when he eats five Fig Newtons instead of the three he's usually allowed. It is perhaps the greatest surprise of Andre's life when he comes back from Vineyard Haven and finds Vonny and Jody at the kitchen table, drinking hot tea with honey, neither of them bothering to greet him or even noticing that he has come home.

Chapter Three

TO THOSE IN THE DARK

IT is a starless winter night when Vonny leaves the Chilmark Store and discovers that the engine of the truck won't turn over. Beside her is a half gallon of milk and some rolls for the morning. She had wasted time, dropping off some overdue books at the library, and had to bang on the market door to be allowed in after closing. She had forgotten how dark it can be at six o'clock. She had forgotten how deserted Beetlebung Corner, the center of Chilmark, can be.

She turns the key in the ignition again and again, each time more panicked by the sound of the grinding motor. While she concentrates on the truck, the clerk locks the store and drives off. Vonny looks up and the parking lot is empty. There is not one pay phone between here and home. She should have known something like this would happen. It is too cold to leave home. Before she drove to the library Vonny had to hold a cigarette lighter to the door handle to force the key into the lock. This should have been warning enough. The Vineyard is encased in ice. Boats that left this morning will not be returning tonight.

Vonny can hear the paper bag rip as she grabs the groceries. When she gets out of the truck the crunch of her own boots in the snow makes her heart race. She doesn't bother to lock the truck, since anyone who might manage to steal the damned thing tonight is welcome to it.

You have nothing to fear.

Not even a maniac would be out on a night like this.

Of course it is a mistake to think the word *maniac*. It is quite possible that weather like this is just the thing to give a madman the taste for blood. Were it not for the brightness of the snow, Vonny would not be able to distinguish between field and road. If she could run, she would, but the snow is slick with treacherous patches of ice. It is only a little past six, but it might as well be midnight. The night is deep and silver-edged, like a cloak wrapped around her. The darkness vibrates with a life of its own. Vonny knows that the sort of terror she feels is not rational. It is the terror of a woman who believes she may lose her way in the dark and step right over the icy periphery of the earth.

As a child, Vonny had to sleep with a light turned on. At ten she was still prone to nightmares. Each house in their development was exactly the same, and she often imagined she wouldn't be able to find her way home from school. After her parents' divorce, she came to dread Sundays, for that was when her father, Reynolds, took her for drives in the country. She was so certain he would desert her on some unfamiliar road that she wouldn't let him out of her sight. She followed him into gas stations and package stores. When it was too cold and he insisted she stay in the idling car, she did so with canine obedience. But she watched through the steamy window, frantic until she could see him on his way back to the car.

When Vonny was eleven Reynolds remarried and that put an end to the Sunday drives. Reynolds's new wife, Gale, invited her to spend the night and because Vonny could not think of a proper excuse, she agreed. Vonny's mother and father were not speaking, so Vonny waited out on the curb for her father. As his car pulled up she had a strange, numb feeling along the backs of her legs. Secretly, she had hoped her mother would not allow her to go. On the way into Manhattan the radio was turned on so they didn't have to talk. When they arrived, Vonny realized her father had kept a secret from her. He was rich. In that instant, Vonny discovered the divisibility of "we." Never once did she think "we are rich." This was all his. The living room, with its knotted rugs; the library Reynolds used as his office, with its red walls and blue couches; each room was large enough to get lost in, to have an echo all its own. Flanking the door to the dining room were two porcelain peacocks, so lifelike their throats seemed to pulse.

Vonny was given a pink robe, which Gale said they would keep just for her. At bedtime, Vonny kissed her father and

Gale good night, then went into the guest room. As always, she left the light on. Later that night, Vonny woke to hear voices in the hall. She kept her eyes closed when someone, her father or Gale, opened the door and switched out the light. She forced herself to remain motionless until she heard them walk down the hall to their own room. She began to search for the light switch, slowly at first and then frantically. Instead of the switch, she found the door. She went out into the pitch-black hallway, feeling her way along the wall. More than anything, she was afraid she would stumble and shatter the ceramic peacocks. A sort of paralysis came over her and so she stayed right where she was in the hallway, for hours, until the sky grew light. When she was able to make out the tops of trees through the tall French windows she realized she was facing the living room. She crept back into her room and sat in bed until her father came in at nine and told her it would soon be time for him to drive her home. Vonny dressed, packed her overnight case, then went in, past the peacocks, for breakfast. For weeks after her visit, she couldn't sleep, and when her mother vowed never to let her spend the night in Manhattan again, Vonny was relieved.

Vonny thinks of creatures far more dangerous than peacocks as she walks in the dark. She can feel the carton of milk she carries freezing, growing heavier in her arms. She does not allow herself to think of numbers, because if she did she would be reminded that she has three miles to go. Her breathing is so labored she swears there is ice inside her lungs. She will either die of fright on this walk or not. She will either be attacked by wild dogs or keep right on going. By the time she turns down their long dirt road, lined on both sides by summer houses closed down until Memorial Day, Vonny doesn't know if she can make it. It is the worst part of her walk. She begins to hate Andre, who probably doesn't realize that the store closed over an hour ago. Her own road seems unfamiliar, oddly narrow, oddly pitched. She wonders if it is her road or if, somehow, she has taken a wrong turn.

You would be able to hear a wild dog long before it attacked.

She knows that. That is a fact.

You would hear it slipping on the ice.

There is a sudden flare of color against the flat, white landscape. Vonny thinks she is seeing stars but soon realizes it is Simon dressed in his orange snowsuit. Simon and Andre run to meet her at the edge of the driveway. There is snow in Vonny's hair and on her boots. Simon grabs her around her legs.

"You're back!" Simon yells, and he tugs on Vonny, hard, so that her legs buckle.

The woman who panicked on the road is turning into smoke, evaporating so quickly Vonny can barely remember her. This is Vonny's road after all. This is her house.

"What happened to you?" Andre says. "Christ."

Vonny looks at Andre, unable to tell if he's angry or just concerned.

"The truck died," she tells him. "You'll have to go get it in the morning."

"We thought you were lost," Simon says.

"Oh, no," Vonny assures him.

You will be amazed to find how easy it is to lie, even to those you love best.

"Not at all."

VONNY and Jody talk about everything but the way they feel. Jody babysits at least twice a week, and that gives them a lot to discuss. They talk about what time Simon went to bed while Vonny and Andre were out at the movies, what he snacked on, what books he asked to have read. They talk about recipes for making Play-Doh out of peanut butter and Oobleck out of cornstarch. They make certain never to talk about Andre. His name is not in their vocabulary. His name would make it impossible for them to speak at all. Sometimes, Andre stands on the porch and listens to their muffled voices through the closed window. He can't stand to have Jody in his house. She's getting into everything; she leaves lipstick marks on teacups and her scent on his couch and in his carpets. He knows she has dropped her boyfriend with the red Toyota and now sees several others. He's surprised that she's good with children and jealous of his own son when Simon curls up in her lap.

"Why do you have to hang around with a teenager?" Andre asks Vonny.

"Why does it bother you?" she snaps back. "What's your problem?"

Of course he cannot answer. He has to let it go.

"Teenagers," he says.

Somehow he has been displaced. He can't understand why women like to talk so much, although he likes to hear their voices when he can't make out the words. He imagines it's a song he doesn't know and has no hopes of ever learning. He's not at all involved when they give each other presents for Christmas. Jody brings over a yellow metal bulldozer for Simon and one of her grandmother's sour-cream coffee cakes for Vonny and Andre. All the time Vonny works on her present for Jody she is aware that their friendship, if that's what it is, has nothing to do with trust. It is not unlike befriending a wild animal who would sink its teeth into your forearm without a moment's hesitation. And yet, Vonny feels drawn to her. When she's with Jody it's almost as though she were with herself, as though she were reaching back for the sixteen-year-old girl she once was.

The bowl Vonny makes for Jody is a dark, jeweled green, with a border of sgrafitto leopards circling the rim. When she sees the bowl, Jody wishes she had gotten Vonny something as beautiful. She keeps her earrings and necklaces inside and when she spins the bowl, the leopards run in a circle. Jody has learned quite a lot since coming to the Vineyard. How to defrost a refrigerator, how to fake an orgasm, how not to flinch when she helps her grandmother into the bathtub. Her parents have now officially separated. Her father has an apartment in New Haven. He's invited her to visit, but not to stay. Her mother calls once a week and complains that all the good men are either married or dead. Both of them assume that Jody will be coming home after the school term. They think that Jody misses her friends, the local mall, her two younger brothers. Jody wonders sometimes if Vonny is the only person who understands her. Vonny knows she doesn't want to leave. And, Jody is certain, she knows how much Jody wants Andre. If Jody goes back to Connecticut he will forget all about her. She will die if this happens, yet she tells herself she is trying to forget about him. She takes hot baths to burn out whatever it is that makes her so bad. Her fingers and toes grow pruny. Steam rises from the old white bathtub. When she steps onto the bathmat she is weak from the heat. Where is her heart? Why doesn't she feel anything when her mother phones late one night and, in a desperate moment, asks Jody to come home because she's lonely? Is she the sort of girl who could watch her family perish in a burning building, then go out and buy eyeliner? Why does she go on robbing other girls of their worthless boyfriends when, having done so, she's more repelled when she has to kiss them than when they take off her clothes?

She feels closer to Vonny than anyone else and yet she would betray her in a minute. Her desires are huge. Her tears blood red with fury. Every day she pretends to be normal. She drinks orange juice, she combs her hair, she babysits for two fifty an hour. She wants to explode. She wants to be so fresh that strangers on the street will slap her. If she doesn't go home something awful will happen. Every morning when she passes Elizabeth Renny, who is out on the porch feeding birds, Jody bites her tongue so she will not beg her grand-mother to let her stay. The cats, Margot and Sinbad, always perch beneath a bird feeder. They know their bells would give them away, scattering the birds, so they dare not leap. Instead they lick their lips and lie unmoving, as though completely relaxed, but their ears twitch.

It is the week after New Year's, finals week, and Jody has a history test she will probably fail since she has not opened a book once or even considered studying. She makes a last-minute check of her bookbag before going outside: mascara, cigarettes, notebooks, twelve dollars and fourteen cents. She zips her bookbag closed and swings it over her shoulder. She's wearing an old pair of her grandmother's shoes she found in a closet, shoes she thinks Vonny would appreciate, black open-toed pumps with three-inch heels. So that they'll fit, she's put on thick white socks. Since people at school stare at her, she might as well give them something to stare at.

Elizabeth Renny is at the far end of the porch, shredding crusts of bread.

"See you later," Jody calls to her grandmother.

Elizabeth Renny is trying to follow the flight of a pine war-bler, but it's not a fair test. The warbler always takes his bread up to the top branches of the pine tree and she can never judge if she's imagining the bird or still seeing him.

Jody stands with one hand on her hip. She thinks it must be her fate to be ignored by everyone but boys she doesn't care about. She wants to be stopped. She wants to be sent home, to be caught at something and punished. She thinks about all the possible varieties of trouble she can get into. It's not fair that she can't break bones. If she forced a fight with another girl at school, the most she would get is hair pulled. She wants a boy's kind of trouble. Something with sirens. Something serious.

Elizabeth Renny doesn't notice her granddaughter until she's walking down the driveway on her way to the school bus.

"Have a nice day," she calls.

"Sure," Jody says, knowing already that's not what she's after.

The school bus makes so many stops on the way to Oak Bluffs that Jody is tempted to get off at one. When they pull up in front of the high school, she clipclops down the steps in her high heels and takes out a cigarette while the other kids walk on toward school.

A girl named Garland, who's also a junior, lags behind. She's been studying Jody's shoes.

"Those are pretty neat," she tells Jody.

"They're ancient," Jody says coldly.

"I like old things," Garland says.

"I don't do things because other people will like them," Jody informs her. She blows out smoke in short puffs.

Garland nods, interested. She's often left out of things and she doesn't know it is social suicide to be friendly to Jody. As they walk together through the teachers' parking lot, Jody slows her pace to match Garland's without thinking. But when they reach the door, Jody stops.

"Go on," Jody tells Garland.

"You don't want to be out in this parking lot alone," Garland tells her. "Weird things go on here. Some seniors saw a werewolf over the summer."

"Hah," Jody says. "Don't make me laugh."

"Seriously. There's also a giant who lives on the road to Chilmark."

"Have you ever seen him?" Jody asks.

"Not personally," Garland admits. Jody tosses her cigarette down and crushes it with her toe.

"I'm perfectly safe," Jody says.

The first bell rings for homeroom. A teacher opens her hatchback and begins to collect parts of a science project. The pieces make no sense. The teacher carries a plastic model of the digestive tract past Jody and Garland. Still in the hatchback are three white rats in a mesh cage, some wire tubing, and a basket of lettuce.

"We'd better go in," Garland says.

"I guess it's not a school day for me," Jody says.

"You're going to get in trouble," Garland says.

"Well, that's my business," Jody says. "Isn't it?"

When Garland goes inside, Jody feels a moment of regret. If she had a real friend, not someone like Becky back home, not Vonny whom she can't be honest with, she might be able to explain and understand her feelings about Andre. But she's bad and she knows it. Why should someone be her friend? She walks back to the parking area and sees that the science teacher has left her keys in the car. Without hesitating, she flips the hatchback closed, then gets into the driver's seat. She slams the door and turns the key in the ignition. The motor drowns out the sound of the rats scraping against their cage.

Jody can feel a wave of heat as she presses down hard on the gas. She pulls out of the parking lot and onto Edgartown–Vineyard Haven Road, surprised by the ease with which the wheel turns. She has driven her father's car once, and his car didn't have power steering. A little pressure from her fingertips, and she's up on the curb. Jody regains control and keeps on going. She has no idea where the switches for the lights or windshield wipers are and hopes she will not have to drive in the dark or sleet. Before turning onto County Road she tries the brakes. The car jerks to a stop so violent that Jody's head snaps back. Jody guns the engine and the car flows onto the road like cream. She cranks the window all the way down so she will not die of the heat her body is giving off. She tries her best to stay within the yellow lines.

If she knew how to read the speedometer, she'd be delighted to know she was going eighty-four miles an hour. The other cars she passes are blurs of color. The wind is fierce. For a moment, when the speedometer has passed ninety, Jody is so giddy she nearly passes out. Then, quite suddenly, she realizes she is driving a car. She has taken a car that belongs to a teacher. She doesn't know how to stop it. She has trouble finding the brake. She pulls the car over, fifteen minutes after she has stolen it, swerving over a low embankment, then wrenching the car into park. Her clothes are drenched with sweat. If anything, she feels worse than before. Now she knows she cannot be stopped. She leaves the car and starts walking back toward the high school. Even though she's back at school in time for second period, she'll continue to sweat for days afterward whenever she hears a siren, not knowing it is virtually impossible to solve a petty crime like this without an eyewitness. Three of the eyewitnesses escape when the police arrive and one officer mistakenly lifts the cage's latch. The rats jump out of the cage and disappear into the woods before the officer can convince his partner the cage has ever been anything but empty. The only other witness, a high-school girl named Garland, calls Jody after school to ask if she'd like to get together over the weekend and share a pizza. Jody considers, and then says yes. When she hangs up the phone, she realizes that she's staying.

She will make herself indispensable. She carves out green peppers and fills them with a mixture of hamburger, rice, and tomato sauce.

"Oh, hi!" she says cheerfully when Elizabeth Renny peeks into the kitchen to see what all the banging and sizzling is about. "I thought I'd make something great for dinner."

Elizabeth Renny notices the recipe page from an old issue of *Ladies' Home Journal* on the counter. Jody's hands are slick from the chopped meat, and without her eye makeup she looks about twelve years old. An unusual amount of steam is pouring out of the sides of the lid on the rice pot. Elizabeth Renny knows her granddaughter wants something. The stuffed peppers are soggy and have a burnt taste, but Elizabeth Renny and Jody both politely eat everything on their plates.

After she's cleared the table, Jody sits down. "My parents think I should come back home," she says. She clears her throat, then goes on. "I think I should stay and help you out."

Elizabeth Renny wonders if helping out means leaving homework untouched for weeks, wearing purple nail polish, having a string of boyfriends who rudely honk their horns to announce their arrival. If Jody went home Elizabeth Renny would hear the wind again at night instead of rock music.

"It's real hard to switch schools in the middle of the year," Jody says. "It's disorienting. I won't have any of the right books."

"And you'd miss chorus," Elizabeth Renny says.

"That's right," Jody quickly agrees. "I'd miss it like crazy."

Jody puts up the kettle for Elizabeth Renny's tea and gets herself a Diet Coke from the refrigerator. She's lost weight, Elizabeth Renny is sure, from all her running around and diet drinks.

"It would be a waste to spend all winter here and then miss out on summer," Elizabeth Renny says.

Jody is not certain she understands. It is more than she'd hoped for.

"Through the summer?" she says.

Elizabeth Renny wonders if by then she will be blind. She frequently tests to check if a film has begun to spread over her good eye. Once that happens, she will have to send Jody away. It would not do at all for Jody to be the one to find her. Elizabeth Renny has decided that she will not allow herself to become sightless. She knows what they would do to her. They'd take her to a nursing home somewhere near Hartford, they'd tie her into a wheelchair, lock all the windows, feed her applesauce and milk. If she's lucky, she'll last long enough to see the orioles who nested under the eaves last summer return. She knows that if you set out seed for birds in the spring and summer, some won't migrate because of you. You have to go on feeding them all that following winter or they'll starve. She has not yet decided whether to order a fifty-pound bag of birdseed this spring. The truth is, she has never been able to ignore even the freshest birds, not even the bluejay who, when Mrs. Renny takes her breakfast outside on sunny mornings, swoops down to her plate and carries off pieces of toast.

SHE should not babysit for them anymore and she knows it. But it's hard to turn Vonny down when she asks. Harder still to give up the chance to be in Andre's house. She has found one of his sweaters in the dresser upstairs and has slipped it on. The T-shirt she's wearing is warm enough, but she wants the feel of wool next to her skin. She wants something that belongs to him.

After Simon's had his supper—a grilled-cheese-and-tomato sandwich Jody cooked a little too long—they make popcorn. Simon carries the bowl into the living room and watches as Jody picks blocks off the floor and throws them into a large cardboard box. She slides the box into the toy corner, collects a few books, and goes to sit next to him.

"Not these," Simon says when he sees the books. "Tell me a story."

" 'The Three Little Pigs'?" Jody says.

"No," Simon says. "Something scary. Something good."

"You're going to be sorry," Jody says.

"No, I won't," Simon says. "Please!"

Andre and Vonny went out to dinner and are probably at the movies by now. Jody can't help but wonder if they're holding hands. If she were the one beside him, he wouldn't be able to stop at just holding her hand.

"How about a werewolf?" Jody says.

"What's that?" Simon asks.

"I know," Jody says, "a giant."

Simon nods and reaches his hand into the popcorn.

"If anyone looks at him they get so scared their hair turns white overnight."

"Even kids?" Simon says.

"Oh, yeah," Jody tells him. "He keeps a treasure under his pillow, but if you try to steal it you're in trouble. There's a ring of nails around the treasure, but the giant's head is so hard he doesn't even feel them through the pillow." She tosses some popcorn into her mouth, then makes a face. "We need salt."

Jody goes into the kitchen. Simon stays alone on the couch until he notices that the corners of the room are dark. Then he gets up and follows her. Jody opens the cabinet above the stove and when she turns around Simon is right behind her.

"I told you you'd be scared," she says.

"I'm not," Simon insists. He hears something, huge foot-steps on the porch. They're getting closer.

"Yes, you are," Jody says.

She goes to the door, opens it, and lets Nelson inside.

"What else does the giant do?" Simon asks.

"He snores so hard he blows down trees," Jody says.

"No, he doesn't." Simon laughs.

Jody salts the popcorn, then tries some.

"Come on," Simon says. "What else?"

"He has shoes the size of rowboats."

"Tell me the scary part," Simon says.

"Uh uh," Jody says. "Let's color. Get the crayons."

"Tell me how he eats children for dinner."

"Simon!" Jody says. "That's disgusting."

He's right behind her on the way back into the living room. Jody puts the bowl of popcorn on the coffee table and props up her feet. Simon sits down so close to her he's nearly in her lap.

"When he's tired he covers himself with a tent instead of a blanket," Jody says.

Simon moves closer and twists a curl in his hair.

"He can chop down a tree with his hands," Jody says. "He can reach through the clouds and grab the moon."

She wishes she could go upstairs and climb into Andre's bed. Pushing up the sleeves of his sweater she feels a chill.

"You know how strong he is?" Simon says.

"How strong?" Jody smiles.

"As strong as thunder. You know how tall he is?"

"Taller than a mountain?" Jody says.

They work on a Mickey Mouse puzzle and are just finishing when Andre and Vonny come home. Andre's sweater has been folded back into the dresser drawer and the dishes have all been washed.

"Everything okay?" Vonny calls from the kitchen.

"Mommy!" Simon shouts.

Simon races into the kitchen and Jody picks up the empty popcorn bowl and brings it in.

"He's been great," Jody tells Vonny.

Andre is opening the refrigerator, looking for a beer. He can smell butter and whatever soap Jody bathes with.

"I'll bet somebody had popcorn," Andre says.

"Somebody did," Jody says.

Andre closes the refrigerator and looks at her.

"Did you bring back any candy?" Simon asks his father.

"Candy?" Andre says. "At this hour?"

"Damn it," Vonny says, looking through her pocketbook. "I don't have any singles."

"That's okay," Jody tells her. She has to walk past Andre to get her jacket. "You can pay me next time."

"Andre?" Vonny says.

He reaches for his wallet and counts out eight singles. He'd just as soon never go to a movie again if he has to go through this.

"Eight, right?" he says to Jody.

She wants him to tell Vonny it's too dark for her to walk home alone. She wants to make it only halfway across the yard before he stops her and slides his hands under her jacket.

"Eight's fine," Jody says.

Andre puts the money down on the table so he won't have to touch her. Jody rolls up the bills and slips them into her pocket. She hugs Simon good-bye and goes out the door while Andre's back is turned. She runs until she reaches the place in the yard where he might have held her. She stops there and closes her eyes before she runs the rest of the way home.

VONNY spends days preparing Simon. She tells him they're going to a party, but Simon knows what it really is. An introduction to kindergarten, which he will have to begin next fall. The yard and roads are slick with mud, so Simon wears his red boots, Vonny, her high laced boots and a rain slicker. When they go out to the truck the air is damp and their faces shine. Andre is waiting for them, one arm thrown across the length of the seat. Simon's deepest wish is not to be separated from his mother and have to go to school. It might be easier if he could go to the little schoolhouse in Chilmark, but kindergarteners have classes in the larger West Tisbury school. Yesterday Simon had a temper tantrum and kicked a hole in the wall by his bed. But there is no escape. He climbs up into the truck and lets Vonny strap him in.

Vonny and Andre have been arguing all morning. Though they will all be together today, Vonny is so anxious about the impending separation from Simon that she has a lump in her throat. Because of this she has been attacking Andre. In the past he would have ignored her; now he's fighting back.

"Could you open your window?" Vonny says.

Only one-tenth of her irritation is showing, but Andre gets the message. He slams the crank until the window rolls all the way down. Their driveway has been raked, but next door there are enormous ruts that make navigation impossible. Pools of water have collected, and there are small cyclones of mosquitoes above the muddy water. Vonny urged Mrs. Renny to direct all her visitors and deliverymen to their drive, but now they come face to face with some teenager's car, which screeches to a halt, then slides through the mud like a hydrofoil.

Andre sticks his head out the window and shouts. "Back up, idiot."

The teenager inches backward.

"Could you close your window halfway?" Vonny says.

"Maybe we shouldn't go at all," Andre says.

For Simon, a glimmer of hope.

Vonny pretends not to have heard Andre's comment. "I wonder if Matt will be in your class," she says to Simon.

Jody is running across the lawn. She stops and knocks on Vonny's window. When Vonny rolls her window down, Andre looks over for an instant and sees Jody's breath mix with the damp air.

"Sorry about blocking the driveway," Jody says. "Good luck at school," she calls to Simon, and then she takes off to catch up to her ride.

"Will you tell your friend I don't want her Romeos using our driveway," Andre says.

"Tell her yourself," Vonny says.

"My stomach hurts," Simon announces.

"Great," Vonny says to Andre, as though it were his fault. "She's not my friend, she's my babysitter," Vonny adds.

"She's my babysitter," Simon says.

"You could use a babysitter," Andre tells Vonny.

Simon looks up, worried.

"Daddy's making a joke," Vonny tells him.

The school, small by adult standards, is huge as far as Simon is concerned. Simon is in the middle holding his parents' hands, gripping his mother's as tightly as he can. Voices carry as older children run to class, their open coats flapping behind them. Vonny and Andre smile at each other over Simon's head. They're proud of Simon today, and they have no idea that each time he looks over his shoulder it's because he is certain bats are sweeping down the hallway behind him, their black wings blocking out the overhead lights.

Six children and their parents have been invited today. Six more will come tomorrow. They all crowd into a classroom that already holds thirteen students and the teacher, Miss Cole. When they form a circle on the floor, Simon inches onto Andre's lap. He can feel his father's heart beating. The teacher asks the visiting children to come meet the fish and the hamsters, but Simon doesn't move.

"Fish," Vonny urges him.

The other children have lined up to follow the teacher across the room.

"What color do you think the hamsters are?" Vonny asks, desperately she knows.

Simon hides his face against his father. Andre moves Simon aside, stands, then takes his son's hand. The fish tank is just below a window that overlooks the schoolyard. Andre crouches down and puts an arm around Simon's shoulders. There are two angelfish and a trail of neons. A catfish stirs up the green gravel as he searches the bottom for food. The teacher allows one small girl to feed the fish. While the others cluster around, the teacher approaches Simon and Andre. "I think you have the wrong classroom," she says to Andre. "The preschool is down the hall." She leans toward Simon. "When you're a big boy, you'll come here, too." She smiles.

Andre keeps one hand on Simon's shoulder. He knows without even looking that Simon's face has turned red, just as he knows the teacher was trying to be kind. This sort of kindness turns Andre's blood to ice, but he's careful to keep his tone friendly as he tells Miss Cole that they do have the right classroom since Simon will be five next November. Miss Cole thinks she is making it better by telling Simon how lovely it is that he'll be in her class. She doesn't realize that she's slipped into baby talk; she's cooing in a manner she'd never use with a larger child. Once Andre manages to drag Simon over to the hamster cage, Miss Cole offers him the honor of feeding them.

"I don't want to," Simon says.

Andre pours some food into his own hand and asks Simon if he'll reconsider. When Simon shakes his head, Andre feeds the hamsters himself. They're so overfed they barely notice the protein-rich kibble Andre drops through the mesh. One hamster burrows into a pile of cedar chips, waiting for noon, when the children leave. The other sits on his hind legs inside a blue coffee can, absolutely motionless.

THEY talk about it late at night, after Simon is in bed. Feeling guilty, they whisper, convinced that in imagining there is something wrong they are inviting trouble. Are they too quick to think he is defective? Are they blinded by their love for him, unable to see what is clear to everyone else? Seeing Simon in a classroom of children, some younger than he, has set off an alarm they can still hear. He is smaller than any of the others. They know that for a fact. They hold hands across the kitchen table and think that whatever might be wrong is probably their fault.

Jody sees the light turned on in their kitchen before she leaves at midnight and again when she's dropped off at three in the morning by a senior she certainly won't bother with anymore, even though he's sworn his brother can introduce her to Carly Simon, a singer Jody thinks her mother and Vonny both like.

Jody wonders when she sees their light. She thinks that couples awake at this hour are either making love or talking about divorce. She refuses to have a conscience. Vonny will just have to take care of herself. All the same, Jody can't sleep. She swears she can hear a woman crying. She sits up in bed, her knees pulled up. She hears the call of an owl. As she lies down to sleep, she feels she may have fallen in love with all three of them. She will always be outside what they have. She will always want it. That night Jody dreams of owls and skies filled with immeasurable light. She dreams that everything she touches falls apart and cannot be put back together again.

IT is late May. The water is calm, the air clean and sweet. Anyone would dread leaving the Vineyard on a day like this. On the ferry they count sea gulls and sailboats, and when the ferry docks at Woods Hole, Vonny and Simon walk down the wooden plank and wait for Andre to drive the truck down the ramp. Simon wears a shiny silver jacket Vonny's mother has sent him, and black-and-white striped overalls. Their pediatrician has made all the arrangements for a series of tests at Children's Hospital in Boston. It is far easier for Vonny to worry about how they will pay for all this without health insurance than to think about what the tests may reveal or whether they will be painful. They have promised to take Simon to the aquarium afterward, although Vonny worries that he won't be in any shape to go. Still, she has told him about the dolphin show and the three-story-high tank and Simon now alternates between mute terror and excitement, an awful combination. Vonny can practically see his emotions surface through his skin.

When Andre pulls the truck off the ferry, they run for it. Vonny is flushed by the time she lifts Simon inside. For a moment Simon forgets their destination and he argues with her so that Vonny has to carry him back out so he can get in all by himself. Vonny knows she should remember he is four years old, he is a big boy, no matter how he seems to her.

Over Simon's head, Vonny's and Andre's eyes meet. Andre has not slept well, and it shows. He has agreed to the series of tests, but he is still not convinced they are doing the right thing. There will be tests for irregular bone structure and hormone abnormalities. What is the worst that can happen? Hormone treatments that will cost more than they can possibly ever afford? A son who never is more than three feet tall? Death during surgery? They want to be assured that Simon's growth patterns fall within the normal range. Because the answer they want is so exact there is no room inside them for anything other than sharp, precise terror. Andre's fear makes him withdraw, from Vonny and Simon both. They sing songs on the way to Boston, but Andre pays attention only to the mileage. They share a packed lunch of sandwiches and Fritos and juice, while Andre, who insists he's not hungry, gulps a warm can of Coke.

Outside Boston, Andre pulls into a Mobil station. He gets out and pumps the gas at a self-service island. As he waits for the attendant to come take his money, every truck going south on 93 looks like freedom. He's been having trouble lately selling his bikes and their bank account is dwindling. If he's not careful he'll become the husband who goes for a pack of cigarettes and never returns. The father who steps out to fill up the truck with unleaded and then disappears. When he pays he counts out the bills slowly. He gets behind the wheel but, after pulling away from the pumps, he suddenly parks instead of getting onto the highway.

"I'll be right back," he tells Vonny.

The men's room is unlocked and not very clean. He washes his hands for a long time. There is a half-open window that doesn't alleviate the smell of urine and gasoline. He could hoist himself up and be out that window in no time. He has forty-three dollars, a MasterCard, and Visa. He had expected to hate Florida when they visited Vonny's mother two winters ago, but now he thinks of brown pelicans, of heat and melting tar. He could be riding solo, no helmet, no passenger adding excess weight. He turns off the water and runs a hand through his hair. When he walks out the door, he's still not certain he's going back to the truck. The traffic on 93 is deafening and the sky is a deep, cloudless blue. If he hitches straight through, he can be in Florida in two and a half days. He zips his jacket, then looks over at the parked truck. Vonny and Simon are gone. Were they ever there? Were they creatures he invented? He thinks of kidnapers, murderers headed toward western Massachusetts, people who will stop at nothing on a route straight toward evil. He is paralyzed. He is a spear of fire. Vonny and Simon round the corner, coming from the women's room on the other side of the station, and he can't be convinced it's really them. The relief he feels stings so badly he blinks.

Their pockets are stuffed with candy bars. The windows of the gas station are opaque and filled with the sky. It is Andre's moment to run for it and he knows it. But he slowly walks across the blacktop, shielding his eyes from the sun. After he gets into the truck and pulls the door closed, Vonny hands him an Almond Joy, already melting from the heat of her hand.

THE doctor greets them as though he's known them for years. They've been told most children fare better when only one parent accompanies them, so Vonny is to stay in the waiting room. Simon isn't talking, but he goes with Andre and the doctor, until they reach the door. Then he thinks *needles*, he thinks *metal clamps, blood, dark hallways, cold hands, strangers*. He runs back and throws himself on Vonny.

"Please," he says to her.

The word twists across Vonny's soul. She wants to sweep him into her arms and run out of the building. She wants to fend off the doctor with bands of electrified light. Instead, she puts her hands on Simon's shoulders and holds him away from her. She is a traitor. She smiles.

"I promise it won't take long," she tells him. "Then we'll go to the aquarium."

"I don't want to go to the aquarium." Simon's voice is hot and hoarse with terror. "I want to go home."

Andre says something to the doctor, then walks back to them. He squats down next to Simon.

"I'm going to be right with you," Andre says. "You're not going to be alone."

Simon looks at him warily. It's not Andre's blood that will be drawn today.

"Hey, guess what the doctor's name is," Andre says. "Dr. Fishman."

Simon laughs in spite of himself.

"Can a doctor be a fish?" Andre says.

"No," Simon says.

Andre stands and takes Simon's hand. It turns his stomach to do this. How can he do this so well?

"Can a fish be a doctor?"

"Nah," Simon says.

Andre looks at Vonny and nods. Simon is falling for it. Andre walks toward the door, and Simon follows along.

"Let's ask him if he sleeps in a fish tank," Vonny hears Andre say as they leave the waiting room. She can hear Simon laugh. Later, Simon will cry and there will be several times when he will want to cry, but will hold it in. Things will hurt him and he'll be afraid of things. And yet Vonny is able to read a magazine; she can drink coffee and watch a two-year-old work a puzzle while her son is taken from the lab to the X-ray department. How can she idly count the change in her purse, then phone to check on the times of the dolphin show? Why is it only later, in the darkened aquarium, as Andre and Simon watch the huge sea turtle, that Vonny has to look away from the Band-Aids lining Simon's arm?

A diver in a black wetsuit floats through the green shadows of the tank, rising above schools of fish, sharks, moray eels.

Why is it only then that she feels as if she is sinking?

Chapter Four

THE HOLE IN THE SKY

IT is possible to enter Manhattan without ever crossing a bridge, if you're not afraid to fly. Vonny takes New York Air from Dukes County Airport to La Guardia. When she manages to get a cab, she insists that the driver take her via the Midtown Tunnel. It is July and the back of her linen dress sticks to the plastic seat as she argues with the cab driver. Every time he says the words "Triborough Bridge," Vonny's heart flips over. Her internal temperature rises five degrees. The heat in New York is thick and damp. The cab driver is Israeli and such a good arguer Vonny has to offer him an extra ten dollars to take the route she wants. She does not trust him not to make a break for the 59th Street Bridge until they are ensconced in a traffic jam at the Midtown Tunnel toll booths. Only then does she allow herself to relax. Her knuckles, of course, are still white.

There has been good news about Simon, and Vonny should be happy. Certainly, she's relieved. All the tests Simon has had are negative. He has no hormone imbalances, no skeletal abnormalities. The decision is theirs—to wait and hope that he grows or to begin hormone treatments that may cost upward of ten thousand dollars a year, treatments the doctors cannot assure them won't be harmful. Only one of the doctors, the hematologist, who Vonny is sure knows no more than she does, has ventured to guess how tall Simon will be, suggesting five feet. If they're lucky. Their own pediatrician still believes that Simon's growth rate may increase.

In other words no one knows anything.

Guided more by fear than reason, they have decided against the hormone treatments. But Vonny cannot get rid of the knot in her stomach. The whole world seems dangerous. Anything can happen to Simon. A list of possible plagues haunts her. The older Simon gets, the less she can do to protect him. She cannot discuss any of this with Andre, who thinks she's overprotective anyway, but she has other fears about a very real issue Andre can't deny. Quite suddenly, they have no money, a zero balance in their savings account, a few hundred, already claimed by unpaid bills, in their checking account. That is the reason for Vonny's trip. It is not just the fifteen-hundred-dollar bill from Children's Hospital. Andre has not sold a motorcycle for months. It now seems likely that he'll have to work as a mechanic, not in his own shop this time, but as a hired hand, taking orders from somebody else. For days they have argued over who would be more humiliated if Vonny went to New York. To ask for money—or, as Andre sees it, to grovel for it—causes a man like Andre deep, immutable pain. It drives him even deeper into himself. Both of them have begun to wonder if he is a failure. On the night before Vonny was to leave she asked Andre outright if he didn't want her to go.

"You have to do what you think is right," Andre had said darkly.

"What is that supposed to mean?" she had shouted.

Because Andre refused to speak to her after that, Vonny has made her own decision and is about to spend her first night away from Simon. She has anticipated being away from him for weeks but, once she passes through the Midtown Tunnel, being alone has the power to erase even the most recent past. Simon and Andre both begin to fade. She has not been to New York for two and a half years and in that time the city has gotten bigger and noisier. It is so foreign that even the air looks different, turgid and faintly yellow. As she gets out of the cab her small suitcase seems too heavy. She can almost imagine that the cells that make up her body are dispersing, joining with the hot yellow air.

She has always been careful not to ask her father for anything, and unlike many of the women she knows she was happy to change her last name when she married Andre. Vonny's father, Reynolds Weber, married her mother during a burst of rebellion. In his case this meant rejecting his family and his family's money. The marriage did not work out. After the divorce, Reynolds began to manage several of his father's pie factories, and as soon as his parents died, Reynolds quickly sold out to a nationwide baked-goods conglomerate that kept the Weber name, but halved the amount of fruit in each pie. Since then, Reynolds has devoted himself to his second marriage and to collecting gold coins minted before 1900. Vonny has come to ask for five thousand dollars, which, though it is a price far less than any of these coins is worth, will save them from having to take out a mortgage on their house.

If she has ever been more nervous, she cannot remember.

She has not asked her father for anything since she was sixteen and desperately wanted an angora sweater that cost twenty-three dollars. She seriously thought she would die if she couldn't have that sweater and was surprised when she didn't.

She makes it past the doorman without collapsing, but she feels dizzy and has to hold on to the brass bar in the elevator. She plans to spend one night here, then go out to Long Island and stay for another night with Jill, her childhood friend, whom, although Vonny cannot quite believe this, she has not seen for three years. She has timed her arrival carefully, phoning her father's secretary for a two-o'clock appointment, in the hopes that Reynolds's wife, Gale, and their eleven-year-old son, Wynn, will not interrupt their meeting. It is a joke between Reynolds and Gale that they tried for Wynn longer than most people stay married, nearly ten years. Whenever Vonny is nervous about Simon's emerging independence, Andre says, "Do you want him to be another Wynn?" which is hardly fair since the only incriminating evidence against Wynn is that he is not allowed to take a bus by himself and that he is forced to wear scaled-down but otherwise identical versions of his father's wardrobe.

Vonny is let into the apartment by a maid named Odell, who clearly doesn't remember her and who asks that she wait in the hall. Along this hallway are four bedrooms, a maid's room, and offices for both Reynolds and Gale. Gale is a therapist whose specialty is rich young anorectics, whom she urges to eat. The one time Vonny peeked into her office she saw Limoges dishes filled with chocolate hearts and sweet dried apricots. From the doorway where she stands, Vonny can make out the dark couches and veined marble tables in the living room. The ceramic peacocks are still there, guarding the dining room doorway. The apartment is freezing, and Vonny's dress, still damp with sweat, clings to her back. Goose bumps rise on her skin. She has a moment of panic so severe she wonders if she has amnesia. Now that Simon and Andre seem like a dream she cannot imagine what she's doing here. What has she come to ask for? What can she really expect? She puts her suitcase down on a mahogany table, then opens her pocketbook and searches for a brush. When she turns to a gilt-edged mirror and brushes the lank hair away from her face she sees a tall, dark woman with severely cut hair who wears a beige dress, a thin gold wedding band, a pink ivory bracelet. The only part of her that seems familiar are her eyes.

Reynolds's sudden presence startles her. There is a moment

when they don't know how to greet each other. Finally, Vonny laughs and shakes her father's hand.

"This is a great surprise," Reynolds says, and Vonny is not quite sure if he means it's a pleasant surprise or a nasty one. The last time she brought Simon here he was eighteen months old, and Reynolds advised Vonny that she would have to pay for anything Simon broke.

She lets him guide her into his office, the place where he keeps his gold coins. It's impossible to hear any street noise up here. They might as well be in the clouds. A worn maroon-colored rug covers the parquetry floor and two easy chairs face Reynolds's desk. As Vonny sits across from her father, she feels like an unskilled laborer on an interview for a job which she is monumentally unqualified.

"I never leave the apartment when it's this hot," Reynolds says. He pours himself coffee from a silver pot, then, as an afterthought, offers Vonny some. Vonny nods, but what she'd give anything for is a cigarette. She has not had one since she began to try to get pregnant. Now she feels like asking her father to wait while she runs down to the drugstore.

"Andre and Simon doing well?" Reynolds asks.

"Very well," Vonny says.

"Mother still with her optometrist?"

"Delray Beach," Vonny assures him.

Reynolds has a lopsided grin that appears as he thinks of Vonny's mother safely removed to Florida. He is quite a powerful presence really. Vonny would hate to come up against a banker like him should they have to get a mortgage on the

house. She is certain that Reynolds would never grant a mortgage to self-employed people who have no regular income.

"Where are you staying?" Reynolds asks.

Vonny is tongue-tied. Surely he has seen her suitcase out
in the hall. If there is such a thing as a disinvitation, Vonny
has just received it. Quickly she says, "Jill's. Out on the Island."

"Sweet girl," Reynolds says.

Vonny does not bother to mention that this sweet girl now
has teenage daughters.

"I'll tell you the truth," Vonny says. She leans forward,
knowing she looks desperate. "I'm here for a reason."

"Are you?" Reynolds says.

Vonny can tell he has been waiting for this day. After so
many years he continues to view his first marriage as a noose
around his neck.

"Whatever it is," Reynolds says, "I'd prefer to get it over
with before Wynn comes home."

Vonny pushes her coffee cup away. Wynn doesn't quite
know who she is. At most he has seen her four or five times.
Once, when Wynn was five or six, Vonny called her father
Dad in front of him, and Wynn's head snapped up, his attention focused. Vonny realized he had never been told that his
father had been married before. She wonders sometimes if
he's figured it out or if he imagines she's an aunt or a distant
cousin. But Vonny understands what Reynolds is getting at.
He has erased the failure of his first marriage, which includes
erasing Vonny. It is the natural progression of denial. And yet

something in her curdles when he protects Wynn from her. She feels less like a beggar now than a thief. Before she was married, Reynolds and Gale took her out to dinner. Just before dessert Vonny noticed that Gale was wearing the ruby ring Vonny's grandmother had always promised her. Vonny excused herself, went to the women's room, and threw up. It does not make any sense; Vonny hates jewelry, it is nothing but a nuisance to her and yet she still wants that ring. Secretly she hopes that one day they may discover that the ring, which her grandmother bought in India, has been dipped in slow-acting corrosive acid that wears away flesh or that it carries a curse that robs the wearer of speech.

So far, Gale is still talking. Vonny can hear her now out in the hallway. And the quiet voice of a boy. Wynn. Reynolds grows impatient. But there is something more. He seems afraid of Vonny.

"What do you want?" he says.

"I need money," Vonny says, somehow thrilled by how crude she sounds.

"Absolutely not," Reynolds says.

It is amazing. He doesn't even have to think twice.

"May I tell you what I need it for?" Vonny says politely.

May I tell you how they stuck thirty-two needles into your grandson in one morning? May I tell you that if I can ever face my child and be this cold you have my permission to shoot me through the heart?

"I don't think I need to know," Reynolds says.

There is a brass letter opener on her father's desk. Vonny is mesmerized by its sharp, cold shape.

"You may like to think otherwise," Reynolds says, "but I don't owe you anything."

At home, Simon is probably waking from his nap and Vonny wonders if he'll cry when he realizes she's not there. Can it be that as a child she put her head on her father's pillow the way Simon does when he comes in to sleep beside her? Can it be that he held her hand as they crossed the street? It does not seem possible that she is to Simon as Reynolds is to her. A lizard stands inside this equation, blocking its probability. On his flickering tongue there is a gold coin that he will swallow whole if he has to. Even if he chokes.

"I need five thousand dollars," Vonny says.

"Earn it," Reynolds suggests.

Vonny's mother, Suzanne, swears she fell in love with Reynolds because of his looks. This makes Vonny nervous. She wanted Andre for the very same reason. When she thinks of falling in love with him she thinks of his dark hair and of clothes he used to wear, an aqua-colored T-shirt and a worn brown leather jacket. She thinks of the heat that rose up from his skin. And there was something more. It amazes Vonny now but she was attracted to his silence, to the way he really seemed to listen to what she had to say. Her mother has told her that the deeper attraction for her was how honest Reynolds was, how little regard he had for money.

It is terrifying how people can misjudge each other. Even more terrifying to think that an initial judgment was correct and that it is possible for someone to become utterly, unrecognizably changed. Vonny wonders if her mother would know Reynolds if she passed him on the street.

Gale opens the door of Reynolds's office. She freezes when she sees Vonny, but quickly regains her composure. She closes the door behind her and smiles.

"Vonny!" she says, and for a moment Vonny thinks Gale is crossing the room to embrace her. Instead, Gale goes to Reynolds, kisses him, then backs away.

"Wynn's home," she says meaningfully.

Although Vonny knows she is too young to have a heart attack, there is an awful pounding inside her.

"We're talking about money," Reynolds tells his wife.

"That's right," Vonny says. She doesn't make any attempt to control her voice when it breaks, even though she knows Reynolds recoils from anything remotely suggesting hysteria. "Are you giving me the money or not?" Vonny says. "Let's not waste our time, right? We don't want to do that."

"Calm down," Reynolds tells Vonny.

Vonny can feel Gale studying her. Perhaps she is changing her diagnosis.

"I'm perfectly willing to give you the five thousand," Reynolds says. He would hate it if he knew there was an edge of hysteria in his voice, too.

Vonny realizes that the one revealing piece of information she has about his childhood may not even be true. Suzanne has told her that Reynolds's father used to tie him to the bed when he refused to go to sleep. Vonny wonders how her grandmother could have endured the screams. The sound of Simon's cries makes her both stupid and fierce. She will do anything to stop them.

"But I have to get something out of this, too," Reynolds says. "I want you to sign an agreement disregarding the divorce settlement."

For a moment Vonny is confused. Has he forgotten she is not the one he divorced?

"I want to be free to make my own choices," Reynolds says. "It's my goddamn right to make my own choices."

Meaning Vonny will get nothing, rather than the fifty percent of his estate Reynolds agreed to when he was so desperate to end his marriage to Suzanne. Vonny has told no one how much she stands to inherit. Even Andre has no idea that his mother-in-law, who has lately joined her neighbor on her porch every evening to search the horizon for UFOs, managed to get Reynolds to agree to her terms.

When Vonny sees how carefully Reynolds and Gale are watching her, she knows she has them. For this brief moment they will do anything she asks to get her to sign. To test her powers, Vonny asks for a cup of tea.

Gale jumps up from the arm of the couch where she's been sitting and immediately calls into the hallway for Odell. Gale's haste makes Vonny wonder if she could ask for ten or fifteen thousand. Even push her luck and ask for twenty. Reynolds would scream at her, he might have to hold himself back from striking her, but in the end he would probably agree. She thinks of what all that money would mean to them. She thinks of fuel bills and college tuition and a closet full of new clothes. But something stops her. Something makes her idly cross her legs and wonder if Odell will remember lemon for the tea. How ridiculous to think she would be spending the night here. It almost makes her laugh.

Gale returns with the tea. There are both a plate of lemon slices and a small silver pitcher of cream. They will ply her with cream. Vonny knows they are equally kind to their cat, a sleek black thing whose name she has never managed to learn. As she drinks her tea Vonny wonders if she can get to Penn Station in the next twenty minutes and beat rush hour. The Long Island Rail Road will have her at Jill's before suppertime. Tonight Vonny will sleep two doors down from where she used to live. A long time ago her father made homemade apple pies, in defiance, she knows now, of the factory pies his own father produced. First he cut the apples on a wide wooden board. Then he squeezed lemon on the slices so they would not yellow as he made the dough. He turned butter and flour into crust and pounded it out until the kitchen table shook. He used only brown sugar, never white, and he preferred green apples to red. In every pie he made there were four apples, unpeeled, but carefully cored by hand.

Vonny is fairly certain Odell has been told to keep Wynn in the kitchen and, in a way, she's sorry. She would like to really look at him and see if there's anything at all familiar in his face. When she tells Reynolds she cannot agree to his terms, he tells her he expected as much. He thinks her decision has something to do with money, but it has more to do with the look on his face when he asked where she'd be staying that night. She is actually looking forward to the heat out on the street, to the long run through the cavernous station so she will not miss her train. She sees herself to the door, so eager to be gone from her father's house that she can barely contain herself until the elevator reaches the lobby.

On the way out to Long Island, Vonny wonders what she would do if Simon and Andre were both on the train and the underwater tunnel they sped through exploded. Which one would she save? She knows right away, the answer is Simon. Andre, she is certain, could take care of himself. And she does not see any point in clawing her own way to the surface if there is no one else worth saving. The surface is all illusion anyway. The tall buildings, the taxicabs, the train tracks through Queens are all reorganized dust. Vonny assumes she can get a mortgage on their house or, at the very least, a personal loan. Though she knows it is late in life to realize this, or even to care, she now sees that if she had been given her grandmother's ring she would now take it off her finger and let it drop to the floor, listening with great pleasure as it rolled to the rear of the train.

SIMON begins to miss his mother after his nap. It is not so much a thought as an ache, as though he has eaten too many sweets. When his father fixes his snack, Simon cries because there are no rice cakes, even though he doesn't even like rice cakes anymore. His mother always gives him orange juice, never cranberry. He gets his father so mad that he says, "Damn it, it's this or nothing," as he throws a bag of saltines on the table.

Afterward they eat in silence, chewing saltines and slices of cheese, not daring to look at each other. The windows are all open but the air is motionless, hanging heavily in invisible threads. Nelson has not moved from the ditch he dug that morning in the shadiest part of the yard. While Simon pours dog food into Nelson's bowl with a plastic measuring cup, Andre calls around to see if there's someone for Simon to visit so he'll be free to finish work on the Harley he hopes will cover Simon's medical bills. He tries the members of the defunct playgroup first, but Matt has already left for the beach and Kate's grandparents are visiting. Andre calls the Freeds as his last hope. Eleanor Freed doesn't have the faintest idea who it is she's talking to until Andre identifies himself as Simon's father. She is so startled by her surly neighbor's pleasant request she tells him to bring Simon right over, then instantly regrets it.

Simon is filling the dog bowl dangerously high. Pieces of kibble start to fall into the metal water bowl. The kibble expands in water, and when Simon reaches for the pieces they dissolve in his hand. Nelson is all right, but he never wants to play. To get him to chase a ball you have to make a big deal out of it. When he finally retrieves, he lays the ball at your feet, then flops down, exhausted. Nelson is really his mother's dog, and Simon begins to miss his mother all over again. Andre hangs up the phone and takes the measuring cup away before Simon makes any more of a mess.

"Let's go," Andre says cheerfully.

When they get outside, Simon runs toward the truck, but

Andre shouts, "Hey, wrong direction." Simon stops and looks back. He has to shade his eyes with his hand and he still can't quite make out his father's face.

"Over here," Andre calls.

Simon runs over to the shed and watches as Andre pulls out the bike.

"Let's test drive it," Andre says.

Simon's energy level rises one hundred percent. Andre and Simon both know that if Vonny were here Simon would not be allowed on the Harley. It is all Andre can do to get Simon to stand still so he can fit the helmet on and tighten the strap. He reminds Simon twice that he must hold on. He cannot let go of his father's belt for anything. Simon steps back while Andre kick starts the Harley. Then Andre reaches out a hand and helps Simon onto the rear of the bike. Simon's knees stick out; he holds on to Andre's leather belt with sticky fingers. It is less than a mile to the Freeds'. If they are lucky they will not meet up with the border collie who chases anything slower than the speed of light. Simon laughs and holds on tighter at every bump in the road. Halfway there, Andre remembers that the last owner of this bike was killed at a traffic circle in Eastham. He didn't pay any attention when the owner of the junkyard told him this, but now Andre breaks into a cold sweat. He slows down and takes the turn into the Freeds' driveway carefully. He unhooks the helmet and lifts Simon off the bike. Up on the porch, Eleanor Freed waves.

"Are you sure he'll feel comfortable here?" she calls to Andre.

"Oh, yeah," Andre assures her. "He'll do just fine."

Samantha Freed, now six years old, is attaching a white laundry rope to a magnolia tree. She pulls the rope and winds the other end around the trunk of an old crab apple. Simon reaches up and grabs his father. He vaguely remembers Samantha from last summer, but he's never actually played with her before, and his mother never just drops him off anywhere, she always stays with him.

"I'll be just down the road," Andre assures him. "By the time I come to get you, you won't want to leave."

"Stay," Simon begs his father, though he doesn't know why. He's not sure his mother would approve of this, and he's not sure he does either.

Andre leans down and gives him a hug. Samantha Freed pulls the rope so it is tight and about six inches off the ground. She wears polka-dot shorts and a blue T-shirt. She sits down and takes off her sandals and her socks.

"Just call if you want me," Andre says.

He makes Simon repeat their phone number. As he says the numbers, Simon squints in the sunlight to see what Samantha is doing.

"All right?" Andre asks.

"All right," Simon agrees.

Andre starts his bike, and when he waves Simon waves back. Eleanor Freed is potting plants. All of her window boxes are filled with pink geraniums. Samantha holds on to the crab apple tree with one hand. She has one foot on the ground, the other balanced on the rope. Simon begins to walk toward her.

"Don't sneeze or anything," Samantha warns him.

Simon holds his breath. It is cool under the trees. Simon can see that Samantha has a package of gum in her shirt pocket. There are two scabs on her knee. Samantha slowly lifts her other foot and places it on the rope. Simon holds his breath tighter. He would rather turn blue and fall down than sneeze.

Samantha concentrates on the rope. She moves her hand from the tree. She is standing on a tightrope, she moves first one foot, then the other. Her thin arms are straight out, crooked a little at the elbows. She walks almost the entire length of rope, then falls off suddenly. She sits on the ground, the breath knocked out of her, eyes shining. Simon walks over, so impressed he cannot speak.

"I almost made it," Samantha says. Her hair is tied back with an elasticized band. Small tangles have formed at the base of her skull.

"Good for you," Simon says, echoing exactly what his mother says when he almost does something well.

The soles of Samantha's feet are grass-stained from walking barefoot. Samantha takes out a piece of gum, unwraps it, and squashes it into her mouth. The smell of peppermint makes Simon's mouth water.

"Here," Samantha says.

She takes out another piece of gum and hands it to him.

"You want to play Care Bears?" Samantha says.

Simon nods his head yes. He has no idea what a Care Bear is. He is stunned by Samantha's sophistication. At this moment, he is quite convinced she knows everything that is worth knowing.

"You know what a Care Bear is, right?" Samantha says suspiciously.

"Right," Simon says.

Samantha gets up and slips her sandals on. Simon rolls the gum in his mouth into a ball.

"Come on," Samantha says. "They're up on the porch."

Simon follows her back into the sun. Two bears, one yellow, the other blue, sit on a bench. Simon has forgotten that he didn't want his father to leave. He has forgotten that thinking about his mother makes a lump form in his throat. When he stands next to Samantha his head is level with her chest. He's afraid that she'll think he's too little for her game, but Samantha allows him to be Birthday Bear, and it doesn't take long for Simon to figure out that in order to play the game all he has to do is make his bear talk and occasionally throw him over the porch railing so that he can be rescued.

AFTERWARD Andre will torment himself by wondering if he planned it. He could have kept Simon there with him, given him some Legos or a bag of marbles to keep him busy while he adjusted the clutch. He will wonder if the heat made him delirious; it must have been close to a hundred degrees in the shed. How furious was he that Vonny went off to ask her father for money? What can happen to a man who is left alone for just one day? He will almost believe that there is a dividing line between body and spirit, entities that inhabit the same space while having little to do with each other. He has problems with the clutch, and that sets him off. He pulls a chunk of skin off his thumb while tightening the flywheel with a wrench, and blood streams down his arm. It's nearly three when he finishes the job. He rolls the Harley out into the driveway, then goes inside for a beer. In a couple of minutes the beer is warm. A red-tailed hawk circles the sky. He hears tires on the road and he looks out the door, wondering if Vonny has come back early. He thinks she's a fool to go see her father when Reynolds has made it clear he wants nothing to do with her. He doesn't understand the need to connect with your parents. If he sees his own father once a year it's one time too many.

A BMW with New Jersey plates pulls into the driveway. One of Jody's boyfriends driving her home from Mad Martha's, the ice-cream store where she's working this summer. At least she no longer babysits for them very often. The kid wants to avoid the ruts next door, so he uses their driveway. Andre hates the kid after just one look. His parents have money, Andre can tell. He's got a tape deck turned on full blast, calling attention to himself. Van Halen. It figures. Andre sips the warm beer and feels his anger boil up inside him. When he was seventeen his father wouldn't even let him borrow his old Chrysler. He rode a bicycle until he could earn enough to get his first motorcycle. A scooter, really, which he modified. He has already decided he'll never buy Simon a car. He doesn't want him to grow up into this kind of kid, someone who pulls up in the driveway much too fast, able to swagger as long as he's backed by his father's money.

Jody gets out, her face expressionless. She's wearing blue jeans and a black sleeveless T-shirt. Her hair, which is longer than it was last summer, is pulled back in a silver clip. When the kid reaches and grabs her arm, Andre walks away from the screen door. By the time Jody allows this boy to kiss her good-bye, Andre is throwing his beer can into a plastic garbage bag. The tires spin as the kid backs up. When Andre hears the sound of metal on metal he can feel the crash inside his body. He runs to the door in time to see the BMW, now in first, try to pull away from the Harley. But there's no quick getaway. The Harley is stuck beneath the BMW's rear fender. Every time the kid shifts his car, he drags the bike with him. The kid gets out of his car and is trying his best to get the Harley unstuck as Andre runs across the lawn.

Jody, who was at the refrigerator when she heard the crash, drops her Diet Coke on the counter next to the cans of cat food. When she sees Andre tackle Gary, she pushes open the screen door and flies across the lawn. Andre has Gary down on the ground. Gary is swearing that it was an accident.

"Come on. Relax, will you?" he says to Andre. "My father will pay for the bike."

It is the wrong thing to say to Andre. Instead of making him realize he's dealing with a boy, it makes him want to shift the kid so that his back is up against the Harley's tire spokes. But he lets go and is standing up just as Jody reaches them.

"Stop it!" Jody screams at him.

When she says this to Andre, something vicious rises up in him. As soon as the kid attempts to get up, Andre moves toward him, frightening him into lying prone, his hands up over his face to protect himself. There is little pleasure in this sort of humiliation. Gary is a senior in high school in Livingston, New Jersey, here for the summer with his family. Andre feels as though he has just beaten Simon to the ground. Disgusted, Andre grabs the keys out of the ignition. He unlocks the BMW's trunk and takes out a tire iron, which he uses as a lever to bend the car's fender. The Harley will need at least three more weeks of work. Andre could kill the kid right here and now. As he struggles to get the bike out from under the car, the paint on the BMW's fender is gouged.

"You're scratching it on purpose!" Gary cries.

Meaning to scare him, Andre walks toward the kid with the tire iron raised. To his great surprise, the kid bursts into sobs. For a moment Andre doesn't know what he's doing or even how he got here in the first place. He cannot remember running across the lawn. He realizes that the sound he's hearing is his own blood.

"Don't you dare touch him!" Jody says. She cares nothing for Gary. She has known him for only two weeks, since the day he came into Mad Martha's for a frappe and wound up waiting all afternoon for her to get off from work. But her fury is real; she will defend Gary, even fight his battle.

"I have insurance," Gary says. He wipes his eyes with the cuff of his shirt.

"I think I will call your father," Andre tells him. "I think I'll have a talk with him. Come on," he says when Gary hesitates. "Who's your father, bigshot?"

"I'll get the money for you," Gary says. "Don't call my father."

Andre sees that the kid is shaking. He's sick of this game. "Get out of here," he tells the boy.

Gary looks at him carefully, not trusting him.

"Go on," Andre says, exhausted. "I don't want to see you back here again."

Gary runs to his car and gets behind the wheel. Andre turns to walk back home as the BMW pulls out of the driveway.

"You can't tell my friends not to come here!" Jody screams.

Andre keeps walking. He cannot bring himself to touch the Harley. He knows Vonny will use this against him, especially if she gets the money from her father. He is too irresponsible to take care of a motorcycle, let alone a family.

"Who do you think you are?" Jody shouts after him. She is in tears.

"Go back to your ice-cream stand," Andre calls back, without turning.

Watching him walk away, Jody feels something inside her break apart. She runs after him, and when she reaches him she hits him between the shoulder blades. Andre turns to her, shocked. His T-shirt is soaking wet and his throat is so dry it hurts. Jody is still crying and her face looks pulpy, like a piece of damaged fruit.

"You're disgusting," she says to Andre. She wonders if she's going insane. She hits him again, this time in the chest.

At first Andre just stares at her, as though she were from another planet. Then he grabs her arm and holds it so she can't move. Now Jody knows. They are both going crazy. She kicks at him, but Andre grabs her leg and she falls to the ground. Andre has never despised himself or another person so thoroughly. When he leans down and puts his arms around her, Jody stops crying immediately. It is the moment just before Jody gets what she wants. Andre tells her to be quiet. He helps her off the ground, then leads her across the lawn and takes her into the shed. They don't deserve clean sheets, pillows, a fan in the window. As soon as the door to the shed is closed, the heat is unbearable, they both feel faint, but they are no longer thinking anyway. There isn't even time to take off their clothes. Andre unzips Jody's jeans and pulls them down, to her thighs. If her back were not supported by the rough wood behind her, Jody would fall down. After all this time, they can't wait another minute.

When Andre has allowed himself to think about her he has imagined kissing her slowly, watching her take off her blouse. Now, he doesn't even look at her. If he did he would see that her eyes are closed. She cannot bear it that she is thinking of Vonny. She will not think about Vonny. All those high-school boys Jody has been with are meaningless. She knows absolutely nothing. She only knows that if she looks at him, if she sees how angry he is, she will have to stop this. So she looks at the ceiling. She doesn't move, except for an involuntary shudder when he pulls down her underpants. She is melting in the heat. Something is wrong with her nervous system. Sounds echo. When Andre pulls down the zipper of his fly she can feel the zipper slide along the row of metal teeth. Her shoulder blades are slammed up against the wall as he enters her and, for a moment, she is weightless. She is on the verge of weeping, but she won't. She tightens her arms around his neck, she pulls at her jeans so she can wrap her legs around him. Andre has one hand under her T-shirt, the fingers of his other hand push into the flesh of her bottom. They are going to regret this for the rest of their lives. Deaf, dumb, and blind, the only part of them that seems real is their desire. Hundreds of times Jody has gone over how she would appear to him once they were together. She thought she had everything planned. How her neck would seem longer if she arched it, how she would manage everything so neatly. Now, her mouth is all over him. When he finally kisses her on the mouth, groaning, Jody dissolves. The molecules that hold her together split apart. She is only one more arc of heat and her skin turns black and blue, and days later she'll stroke the bruises Andre leaves on her, bruises he'd be shocked to discover, since he never meant to hurt her.

VONNY can hear the Southern State Parkway inside Jill's kitchen. She realizes that as a child she never once noticed the sound, although the hum of the parkway must have snaked through her dreams, leaving her with the sense that traffic

always led away from the house where she lived. Jill, who
hated the suburbs, came back when she and her husband discovered they couldn't afford to live anywhere else. She would
move in a minute, but now Jill is trapped. Her daughters actually like it here. The younger one, who is twelve, is now at
ballet. The oldest, Melissa, sits across the table from Vonny
drinking Lo-Cal iced tea with lemon. Melissa's blond hair is
pulled into a French braid and she looks a lot like Jill at
sixteen. Jill was four months pregnant when they graduated
from high school, and Vonny was the one who set up Jill and
Brian's first date, so she has an uneasy feeling of responsibility.

On this visit, Vonny feels closest to Melissa. With her pale
pink nail polish and purple sneakers, Melissa seems more rec-
ognizable than Jill, who no longer looks anything like the girl
she used to be. Jill has never visited Vonny in Chilmark. Once,
before Vonny met Andre, Jill came up to Boston, wept for an
entire weekend, then went back home to Brian and her two
young daughters. Things are much better now, Jill assures
Vonny. Jill talks about excruciatingly personal things in front
of Melissa, whose presence makes Vonny back off from giving
her true opinion. Her opinion is that Jill continues to do what
she's always done: sell herself short. She has convinced herself
that she is stupid. Vonny wonders if, after all these years, they
are really friends. They talk on the phone, but see each other
only on Vonny's infrequent trips to New York. Jill has met
Andre twice, seen Simon only once.

After dinner, when they leave Brian and the girls to take a

walk around the neighborhood, Vonny has the urge to put her arm around Jill. Instead, they walk so close their shoulders touch. It is dusk and they can smell cut grass. Children are calling to each other in backyards. They walk to the high school, where the darkening sky is reflected in tall arched windows. Jill takes a cigarette and a lighter out of her pocket and recounts what has happened to some of the people they used to know. She goes through four divorces, a nervous breakdown, and a list of girls, women now, who have recently gone back to school.

"How did we get old so fast?" Jill says.

"You've been saying you're old since you were seventeen."

"Well, I was," Jill insists. "I am. Only now I have fat thighs to prove it."

"You don't," Vonny says.

"You look the same," Jill tells Vonny.

When Vonny laughs, disbelieving, Jill says "Really. If anything, you look better."

They sit down on a curb so Jill can have another cigarette before they walk home. They used to do this every night in the summertime, waiting for boys, getting away from their mothers. They can see Jill's younger daughter, Kerry, riding her bike down the street. When Vonny and Jill were in high school, girls who were almost thirteen didn't ride bikes, or play ball either. They combed their hair and fought with their mothers and swore they would never forget what it was like to be young. They have forgotten, and they know it. They wish they still lived next door to each other. They wish they could still tell each other their secrets. Jill used to tell Vonny about her affairs, but recently she stopped. They both realized it was the same story, over and over again. If they met now as adults they would not even like each other, let alone be best friends.

The lights along the Southern State are turned on, reminding Vonny that tonight is Illumination Night. She's purposely avoided it after what happened last year and now she wonders if she's made a mistake. She could be in Oak Bluffs now. She could be with Andre, who she hopes doesn't go without her.

As they walk back to the house, a miniature schnauzer runs off a porch and follows them, barking, until Vonny turns around and shouts, "Boo." When the schnauzer takes off, they double over with laughter.

Kerry has parked her bike and is sitting on the cement stoop in front of the house.

"Do you wish you were that age again?" Jill asks.

"You bet I do," Vonny says.

"No, you don't," Jill says. "You were miserable."

"I was not," Vonny insists.

"I remember you better than you remember you," Jill says. "You were."

Jill's girls share a room so Vonny can have Melissa's bed. There are pictures of Bruce Springsteen all along the wall, and Vonny feels as though she's being watched. The sound of traffic makes it difficult to sleep. She thinks about her father and the day he left. He was thoughtful enough to pack up his boxes and move after midnight, so Vonny wouldn't see. She saw anyway. A rented van was in the driveway parked behind Suzanne's car. Vonny had had supper and stayed late at Jill's. She can no longer remember if they were nine or ten, but she knows they made a tent out of sheets, supplied themselves with flashlights, cookies, Thermoses of water. They had made a vow to always tell each other the truth, but when Jill asked, "Don't you feel terrible about your father?" Vonny made a sour face and said no.

When her father drove away in the van, Vonny watched from the window; then she went out in the backyard. There was a cherry tree in bloom and Vonny sat between it and the willow tree Reynolds had planted the week Vonny was born. Later, the willow had to be cut down—its roots were interfering with the sewage tank—but on that night its leaves were silver, stars attached to twigs. All that week Vonny slept on a roll-away bed in her mother's room. Her mother was afraid to be alone, and Vonny was too. If her father could move out, anything could happen. Houses could catch fire, homes could be wrecked, children could wander into any one of the identical houses on their block and never be missed.

When she wakes in the morning, in Melissa's single bed, Vonny doesn't know where she is. After a shower and breakfast, she still feels oddly unconnected. Jill drives her to the airport, then asks her to stay a few more days. Vonny is suddenly terrified that something may happen to Simon if she doesn't get home quickly. She leans over and gets her bag out of the backseat.

"I miss you," Jill says.

Vonny hugs Jill and swears she'll come back to visit soon, an empty promise that makes them both grin. She gets out and waves, then goes to buy her ticket. She runs her pocketbook and suitcase through the metal detector and has a coffee until her flight is called. It's a little too crowded on line. Vonny is behind a family, and just as she is about to walk from the ramp onto the plane, something happens. She leans against the wall and lets the people behind pass her. Her legs will not move. Her skin is cold. She is not quite sure why but she knows that if she walks into the plane she will die.

Your heart is beating much faster than a human heart.

The flight attendant at the door is watching her and Vonny is certain that whatever is happening to her shows. She has read somewhere that the average time for an ambulance to get to you in New York is three and a half hours. By that time, she will be dead.

"Are you all right?" the flight attendant asks.

The flight attendant, who has come to stand near Vonny, is blond, with a smooth southern accent.

"Oh, sure," Vonny says. "A bad ankle."

You can tell she believes you.

"Do you want to lean on me?" the flight attendant asks.

Vonny smiles and leans on her shoulder. "I love Boston," the flight attendant says.

"Me, too," Vonny says.

You're a dead woman, you might as well make conversation.

During takeoff, Vonny is amazingly calm. Her heart stops racing. After five years of not smoking, she asks the young man next to her for a cigarette and lights up as soon as the No Smoking sign is turned off. The sky is filled with thin, spidery clouds. Vonny feels nothing at all. She doesn't think about Simon or Andre or her father, but of the cool perfection of the clouds. When they prepare for landing Vonny notices a purple streak in the far horizon. A dangerous color for this time of year. She shuts her eyes and imagines flying right into that color. She gives in to it, lets her energy go. By the time the plane sets down, she is limp. She has to force her legs to work. She manages to get out of the plane. She knows she is almost home, and yet she is convinced she is lost.

You might think you have contracted some sort of madness, but it has descended upon you too quickly. You walk slowly. You don't dare run.

Out by the parking lot, Simon waves to her from Andre's shoulders. Against the blue sky, Simon's hand is like a flag, and Vonny follows it blindly. When she reaches them, she lets her bag drop to the ground. Simon leaps into her arms:

"I'm double-parked," Andre says. He wears sunglasses so she cannot see his eyes. He jangles his key chain in one hand.

"Did you get me something?" Simon asks.

Andre picks up Vonny's bag and she points to the side pocket where there is a stuffed animal Vonny bought at Jill's local drugstore. A small yellow chick that squeaks. Andre tosses the chick to Simon, then starts walking toward the truck.

"Yippee," Simon says as he makes the chick squeak.

"My father said no," Vonny tells Andre. No one could tell there was anything wrong with her, even though her legs feel as though she's just run a marathon. "He won't give us the money."

"That figures," Andre says. He is sick of summer and all this heat.

"What is that supposed to mean?" Vonny says.

"I wish to Christ you would stop saying that to me," Andre tells her. "Don't turn everything I say inside out."

They have reached the truck. When Simon climbs into the truck, Andre and Vonny are face to face. Andre looks away.

"He hasn't had anything to do with you for years. I don't know why you expected it to be any different now," he says, cruelly he knows. "How's Jill?" he asks, wanting to back off, to be on safer ground.

They both get into the truck. Vonny fastens Simon's seat belt as he examines his new stuffed animal.

"She says she'll come visit," Vonny says. "Her daughter wears purple sneakers. She reminds me of Jody, only a little less sullen."

Andre starts the truck and backs up too fast. He just misses a Jaguar with New York plates. Last night, he checked on Simon once an hour. Even when he heard Simon's deep, sleepy breathing, he still was not comforted. He has the wild urge to tell Vonny everything, right here and now. He promises himself that if he can just drive home without saying anything, it will be all right. He can no longer be certain of what really happened. He is angry, as though he's been tricked. If he isn't careful, he'll start blaming Vonny. She wasn't there; she had to go ask her father for money when they both knew it was hopeless.

They do not talk to each other on the ride home. Vonny tells Simon about the airplane and promises one day he will go on one. Simon announces that Samantha Freed can walk a tightrope. Vonny smiles, then looks over at Andre, curious.

"He went over for the afternoon," Andre says, a defensive edge in his voice. He holds the steering wheel tightly. Vonny looks beautiful to him, but extremely far away. "Eleanor Freed invited him."

Having been reminded of Samantha, Simon now looks at his new toy with distrust. He had forgotten that what he really wanted was a Care Bear, just like Samantha's.

"An idiot friend of Jody's ran over the Harley," Andre says.

"Oh, great," Vonny sighs.

"Is it my fault?" Andre says.

Simon looks down at his shoes. There are scuff marks all over the toes.

"I didn't say that," Vonny says. She is exhausted. She doesn't care if it's his fault or not.

Andre clamps his mouth shut and turns down their road. When they pass by the Freeds', Vonny sees that there is indeed a tightrope stretched beneath two trees. High above, where the branches of the trees do not meet, there is a circle of intensely blue sky. Vonny puts her arm around Simon's shoulders and pulls him close. She has missed him terribly. She doesn't want to let him go.

When they park in the driveway, Vonny sees Elizabeth Renny outside feeding birds. She no longer needs her canes. Startled by the sound of the truck, Elizabeth Renny spins toward them.

"I see you're much better," Vonny calls across the lawn.

Andre grabs Vonny's bag, then walks up the porch steps. Nelson is at the door, whining to be let out.

"Much better," Elizabeth Renny calls.

When Nelson is let out, he runs to Vonny and jumps on her. She laughs, then pushes him away. As she walks toward the house, her legs tremble. All she has to do is keep going.

It is cool inside, you know that for a fact. You will feel better once you're inside. Today you will hang laundry out on the line, but tomorrow, when it is time for you to pick up your son at his new friend's house, you will get only halfway down the road, then have to run back home. Your legs will be rubber again. You will feel yourself being sucked into the sky. You will tell your husband that you've turned your ankle, and of course he won't doubt you. When he gets into the truck and drives down the road to get your son, you will sit at the kitchen table until you stop shaking. You will actually feel the circle closing in until you know exactly where you are safe. In less than a week it will be impossible for you to get past your front door.

By then, the grocery and the post office will be as unreachable as distant planets.

Chapter Five

THE GIANT OF CHILMARK

THE Giant of Chilmark sells zinnias and eggs in the summer, pumpkins and chrysanthemums in autumn. None of his customers ever sees him. They buy his goods from a roadside stand made out of rough planks of pine. They comment on the difference between country and city life as they slide their money through a slit in the top of a coffee can. Cowed by good faith, people are usually honest, paying for their squash or bunches of flowers, making their own change. A few times a year, teenagers pocket the money they find in the coffee can. Local children occasionally steal eggs with which they gleefully pelt each other. The Giant sees the remains, bits of cracked brown shell and streaks of deep yellow, along the center of the road. When it grows dark he carries a bucket of water up from his house and washes away as much of the dried eggs as he can. Crows will take care of whatever is left.

Contrary to the reports of the delivery boy who brings groceries and chicken feed, the Giant is not an old man. He is not eight feet tall, although he has to crouch at certain points in his house so that his head won't graze the ceiling. His is an old house, built for a shorter man, the Giant's grandfather, Edward Tanner, who was five foot six. The Giant, who drinks coffee every morning from a blue-and-white Staffordshire cup his grandfather brought with him from England, is twenty-four years old. Most people in Chilmark haven't seen him in so long they've forgotten he ever existed. A few old women remember his grandfather Edward Tanner well; they were kissed by him on summer evenings.

The Giant arrived in October. It was a rainy, wood-scented night and his grandfather was drinking beer and polishing his boots. When there was a pounding on the door, the Giant's grandfather had the urge to jump into bed and pull the quilt up. Something told him not to open the door. He'd had quite a few angry husbands come looking for him, and although he was old for that now, there were other scores unsettled. He owed a little money and he had never believed in taxes. He had the feeling it was someone official because of that sturdy knock.

The Giant was out there, swallowing rain. He was ten years old and already six feet tall. When Edward Tanner opened the door all he saw was a tall man in a black overcoat.

"Don't come looking for me unless you're looking for trouble," Edward Tanner said. He held his boot up, menacingly.

The chickens in the henhouses were clucking like mad. It

was raining so hard all the sweet potatoes in the garden were unearthed and washed away.

"Grandpa?" the Giant said in a high tentative whisper. It was as though a hidden ventriloquist were throwing a child's voice into this man's shape.

"Don't kid a kidder!" Edward Tanner said. He could not have been more afraid if a ghost had appeared at his door.

"It's me, Eddie," the Giant said in his sweet boy's voice, and Edward Tanner the elder fell on the floor in a dead faint.

There is such a thing as rotten parents, and the Giant's parents were as rotten as they come. They might have had problems even if their son hadn't been a giant, but Eddie's height put an end to their marriage. The Giant's father was nearly forty when Edward Tanner's nineteen-year-old daughter, Sharon, who was easily persuaded, followed him off the Island. In fact, their marriage lasted longer than Edward Tanner had predicted. The Giant's parents were together for eight years before the Giant and his mother were deserted in southern New Jersey.

Sharon set out to find another man and dragged her son around four states before she found what she wanted at a naval base in Rhode Island. She figured Eddie was her punishment, and she preferred him to stay well out of sight. When her boyfriends came over he hid in the hall closet and prayed that night's sailor hadn't worn a coat. Finding a giant in the closet when you're merely reaching for a hanger is enough to give even a strong man a heart attack. The Giant knew what he was from the time he was two. He had seen pictures of himself in books. He was the creature beneath the bridge who devoured goats. He was the owner of the harp who fell asleep at his own dinner table. One morning he would wake and find his head through the roof, his arms and legs akimbo out the windows. Vines would grow over him. Birds would perch in the crook of his elbows.

The Giant went to school until the fourth grade, but when they moved to Rhode Island he didn't bother with it anymore. He couldn't take the merciless teasing and there was no one to check up on him. Sharon was gone more than she was home. To fill up his days, the Giant began to make pictures, at first using pencils and tubes of lipstick and eye shadow stolen from his mother's purse, later saving enough money for cheap watercolors and brushes. Because he wanted to keep his painting from his mother, who'd only laugh at him, and because paper was scarce, the Giant worked at miniatures. A whole year's worth of his paintings could fit in a rubber boot. An entire state, New Jersey for instance, could be reduced to the size of a strawberry. Painting one perfect, tiny face or a tree filled with flowers might take him an hour. If he was lucky, he would not finish before he went to bed and would then have a reason to wake up in the morning.

The Giant often caught Sharon staring at him, as though she were disgusted by him or, worse, afraid. She may have kept him just to spite her father, whom she alternately adored and despised. She urged her boyfriends to use the one photograph she had of Edward Tanner as a dart board. But sometimes she took the thumbtacks out and brought the photograph down to show the Giant. The Giant's grandfather was sitting on a chair in his living room. He looked directly into the camera and he seemed annoyed. When she had lived with him Sharon had dreamed of burning down the house and escaping to New York. Now she described each room lovingly. She had, after all, named the Giant after her father. And, the Giant knew, she was capable of changing her mind with startling quickness, for no apparent reason. When she was kind, offering him a chocolate or cooking him dinner, he never trusted her. When she was awful, he knew it wouldn't last. He had learned, early on, that he must be careful. He couldn't afford to have fits of temper. Not with Sharon. Once she had borrowed a car from one of her boyfriends and had taken the Giant with her on a picnic. The Giant was nine years old, and because Sharon was being so nice to him, he felt a little too comfortable. On the way home they drove along 95. The Giant was in the passenger seat holding a paper bag in which there were still some sandwiches and cupcakes. He had saved the best for last, a chocolate cupcake with rainbow-colored sprinkles. He reached into the bag, but when he pulled it out the cupcake broke into pieces. All he could think about was how much he wanted that cupcake. He forgot himself. He forgot who he was with. He let out a wail and kicked the dashboard.

"Oh, for God's sake," Sharon said to him. "Don't be such a baby. Take another one."

"I don't want another one," the Giant had said.

"Take another one," his mother told him.

"No," the Giant said. "I won't."

When he kicked the dashboard, Sharon reached over and grabbed his leg. The car swerved out of its lane.

"Are you a moron?" Sharon shouted. "Do you want to ruin this car and get me in trouble? Take another cupcake. Now."

The Giant looked at the sprinkles sifting over the car seat and started to cry.

"I won't," he said.

Sharon pulled the car over onto the shoulder of the road. It was nearly rush hour and crowded.

"Get the fuck out," she said.

The Giant stared at her.

Sharon leaned over him and threw open the door. She gave him a shove.

"You heard me!" she said.

When the Giant put his hands on the seat to steady himself he left streaks of chocolate frosting on the upholstery.

"Do it!" Sharon said, and she pushed him halfway out of the car. He wouldn't let go of the door, so she slapped his hands, and as soon as the Giant loosened his grip, she pulled the door closed.

She stepped down hard on the gas. Without bothering to look at oncoming traffic, she pulled into the highway, cut off a station wagon, and kept right on going. The Giant followed her, running along the side of the road. He kept right on running, even when he didn't see the car anymore. His eyes and throat were filled with tears. He was screaming

"Mommy" over and over again until it wasn't even a word. Up ahead, a car was pulled over on the shoulder, black exhaust rising from the tailpipe as it idled. The Giant wasn't certain it was the right car until he got up beside it and saw Sharon inside, crying.

The Giant stood on the side of the road and wiped his face with his shirtsleeve. He was so hot that his hair was soaking wet. Sharon got out of the car and walked around to him. Every time a truck went by the earth shook. Sharon kept crying and didn't even try to hide it.

"Look, I don't want you," Sharon said.

There was goldenrod along the side of the road, and a flat tire someone had left behind.

"Can you understand?" Sharon said.

The Giant had a stitch in his side from running so fast. Every time he breathed he could feel the stitch tighten.

"I'm a person, too," Sharon said. "You know?"

The Giant was so grateful to her for not driving on without him that he almost started crying again. He didn't care what she said to him. He didn't care what she thought of him. What he wanted more than anything was for his mother to hug him but he knew it was too much to ask.

"Get in the car," Sharon said to him. "Just get those goddamn sprinkles off you before you sit down and ruin everything."

Sharon started staying out more often after that, and the Giant never asked where she was going or when she was coming back. He learned to cook, he set his own bedtime, he washed his clothes in the bathroom sink. He was so used to being alone that when Sharon disappeared for good, it took a week before the Giant realized she wasn't coming back. He wasn't really surprised, he didn't feel much of anything, but he couldn't sleep. He kept checking the light bulbs in the apartment to make sure they wouldn't burn out and leave him in the dark. He slept during the day, in a chair by the window, and when he ran out of food, he put on an old black overcoat that used to belong to his father and went out to buy groceries at a local market. He knew his voice would betray him, so he pointed to what he wanted. Hot dogs and rolls, a carton of milk, mustard, M&Ms. He found his grandfather's address in a drawer beneath a black nylon slip. He still wonders if his mother left thirty dollars in the sugar bowl on purpose or if, in her hurry to cut her losses, she simply hadn't bothered with it.

The Giant, who has lived on his own since his grandfather's death five years ago, sometimes forgets the sound of his own voice. The chickens he raises for eggs are great-great-grandchildren of his grandfather's stock. He has continued to paint and some of his miniatures are so small he needs to use a magnifying glass for the more detailed work. He mail-orders paints and the heavy cream-colored paper he prefers. The farmstand and the inheritance of his grandfather's life savings—eight thousand dollars kept in a metal strongbox in the chicken coop—allow the Giant the luxury of avoiding other people. He knows he has missed out on many things: owning a car, friendship. Mysterious things like movie theaters and hardware stores. He has never been to Lucy Vincent Beach, which is less than a mile from his house. He can live with these small losses. He despairs only when he considers his chances for ever falling in love.

Jody hears about him again from one of the boys who used to steal eggs. It is Jody's senior year. She has managed to persuade her parents to let her stay on until graduation. The idea of going back to Connecticut, even for a weekend, makes her sick. She is thinner than last year and much more careful. She has not made love with anyone since Andre, but high-school boys still vie for her even though she barely talks when she dates them. She is now included in a group of boys and girls whose common interests are fast cars and cutting classes. She often drags her friend Garland along, not because she feels sorry for Garland, who has fewer dates, but because she wants a chaperon. She has decided to remain true to Andre, even though he has deserted her. Whenever she calls and offers to babysit for Simon, Vonny says she's much too busy with her pottery to go out. Jody is certain this is a lie. Andre is the one who doesn't want her around, not that Jody intends to let that stop her. She can wait, she has time. And if a boy wants to help her pass that time, fine, but when he takes Jody out, he gets Garland, too.

They're on their way to Edgartown, and Garland is forced to sit in the backseat next to Rosellen and Carl, a couple who can't keep their hands off each other. When Greg, the boy driving, starts talking about the Giant, Jody doesn't believe him. She flips down the sun visor, looks at Garland in the small mirror, and rolls her eyes.

"You people think off-Islanders will fall for anything," Jody says.

"It's the truth," Greg says. "There were two nights when he tried to get me and I outran him both times. He's almost nine feet tall, you know."

"Creepy," Rosellen says. She makes herself shiver.

Greg glances over at Jody to see if she's impressed by his battle with the Giant. She takes out a comb and fixes her hair. As they pass by the farmstand she can see coffee cans filled with yellow chrysanthemums.

Carl untangles himself from Rosellen so he can lean forward. "Manute Bol of the Washington Bullets is seven foot six," he says to Greg. "You want me to believe this guy's a foot taller?"

"Are you calling me a liar?" Greg asks him.

"Hell, no," Carl says. "A bullshitter."

"Oh, yeah?" Greg says. He makes a quick U-turn, tires screeching. He's still trying to impress Jody, and it's still not working. When they're parallel to the farmstand, Greg makes an even sharper U-turn that throws Jody up against the car door. Then he pulls right up to the farmstand. The motor idles loudly. The Giant's house is set in a hollow behind a grove of locust trees, and all they can see of it is a slightly tipped chimney. Already the boy in the back seat is losing his nerve.

"We're never going to get to Edgartown this way," he says.

"Got the guts to take something?" Greg goads his friend.

"Come on," Carl says. "What do I want with flowers?"

"Get the eggs," Greg says. "We'll attack the farmstand, then the Giant will have to come out."

"They're ridiculous," Garland says to Jody. "Grow up," she tells the boys.

"Well?" Greg says when his friend hesitates. Greg grins, then leans over the seat and pushes down on the door handle so that the back door swings open. Rosellen screams. Carl quickly grabs the door and slams it shut.

"Not me," he says. "You won't catch me out there."

"Then you believe me," Greg says. "Right?"

Greg is hoping he won't have to get out of the car to impress Jody. The truth is, he's shaking, just as he did when he was twelve and the Giant and some old man called out to him as he stole some eggs and an already decaying pumpkin. At least this time he has not peed in his pants. But of course, he has not seen the Giant yet.

"Let's get out of here," Garland says.

The sky is no longer quite so blue. The locust grove throws shadows on the already dark moss. They have all begun to whisper. As Jody places her pocketbook on the floor near her feet she is making a bargain with herself. If she doesn't see the Giant, she'll keep her mouth shut. If she sees him, and survives, she'll tell Vonny everything. Andre will hate her at first, but he'll get over it.

Jody snaps her door open.

"Hey!" Greg says. He tries to grab her arm, but Jody is already out of the car.

"Get back here!" Garland calls.

The weather has turned chilly. When a car passes wind rises up. The earth is dark and rocky, but a path has been worn from the side of the road to the farmstand. Jody keeps her eyes on the path in front of her. As she gets closer to the farmstand she can smell the rough pine boards and the slightly sweet odor of rotting vegetables. Jody would rather face a Giant than Vonny, but she will go to Vonny if she has to. She never breaks the bargains she makes with herself.

Greg is probably a liar, although he's honking the horn like a madman to get her attention. If there is a giant he certainly won't be caught sleeping with that horn honking. Greg doesn't let up on the horn until Jody reaches the farm-stand. And although he gets out of his car and watches her, he doesn't have the courage to go after her.

Now Jody sees that the bunches of flowers are different shades of yellow, from gold to pale ivory. The stand fronts a dark, cool shed in which there are melons and squash. Jody reaches past the tin of money for a basket of brown eggs. Either she is so nervous her hands are hot or the eggs are still warm. Would she really break up a family? Maybe it would be a relief to everyone involved. Maybe Vonny wishes she were back in Boston. A confession might be an act of mercy. Jody follows the path down into the hollow. In the basket, the eggs hit against each other. She can no longer hear the idling motor of Greg's car or traffic up on the road. The grass here is oddly soft and pale; it has never been mowed. She can see the house and it's much too small for an alleged giant. All she has to do is get a glimpse of him and she can tell Vonny everything. She walks down to the house, which has a fresh coat of gray paint. The foundation is made of brown and red stones. The door, at which visitors never knock, is the color of blood. Jody peeks in the front window. Her breath is coming hard and it's difficult to see; the window is old glass, the kind that distorts. She thinks she sees a stone fireplace, a blue couch, an old wooden table. She can hear the chickens now, and she follows their clucking behind the house. There is a sunny fenced-in area with several chicken coops. The chickens whose eggs Jody has stolen are red bantams. Their feathers shine in the sun. When a rooster crows the sound raises bumps along Jody's arms and legs. She looks to the side of the henhouses and sees him. He has been frozen, unable to move or even breathe since she walked down from the house. He sits in a metal chair, a cup of coffee in one hand, a newspaper on his lap. He wears beige slacks and a white shirt. His hair, which he washed in the kitchen sink, is still wet and combed back, drying in the sun. The sleeves of his white shirt are rolled up. From where Jody stands it is impossible to gauge how tall he is, but the old workboots he wears are huge. He is, by far, the most beautiful person Jody has ever seen. He makes everyone else seem deformed. Unsteadily, Jody bends down and, still looking at him, she places the basket of stolen eggs on the ground. Then she turns and runs. She nearly loses her balance climbing back up the hollow. The Giant wishes he could help her, but he dares not stand up and let her see him for what he is. So he watches helplessly. A teenage boy comes to the top of the hollow and throws two sharp rocks at him, but the Giant remains where he is. At last she makes it up the slope. When she is gone, the Giant gets up and slowly gathers the eggs.

*   *   *

Here you are. The sky is blue and it is October. Your child, who will soon be five, has started school more than a month ago and you have not once driven him there. You have not been inside his classroom, you have not watched him on the playground. In the morning, you pack his lunch and smile. You fix bags of crustless sandwiches, iced raisin cookies, carrot sticks, seedless orange wedges. You wave from the back door like the best of mothers.

You have read about force fields in science fiction novels, and now this force you thought existed only in fantasy has sprung up around you. If you come close to the force field, say walk out on the porch, a knot the size of a walnut forms in your throat. If you break through the force field by placing one foot on the porch steps, you are jolted back. You can feel the force field enter your body. You cannot go any farther. If there were a string of electrons that shocked you each time you tried to leave the house you could not be any more trapped. If you're not careful you might begin to believe in evil spirits. What is free will if you can't walk down your own road, if the idea of going to the market makes you so nauseated you have to lie down? You would trade your soul for a cigarette, which unfortunately you can't have because you can't get to the store. More than anything you fear that the circle will continue to close in on you. Can anyone exist on a couch? Can anyone be broken down and then stored in a wineglass, a teaspoon, a thimble?

Every day you tell yourself this day will be different. This is the day when you will kiss your husband good-bye and drive your child to school. You will admire his paintings taped to the classroom walls. You will chat with the other mothers out in the parking lot. On the way home you'll roll all the windows down and cold air will sting your cheeks. You will stop at a store you have never been to before and buy a pack of cigarettes. If the sun is out you will park on a bluff above the beach. There will be no tourists at this time of year and it will be just you, only you. You will drive home the long way and honk the horn to let your husband know you're home.

Since this day has not yet come, and since you still cannot leave your house, you will spend hours tying to figure out the cause of the force field. As a child you were like a little adult; if you could have gotten a driver's license at the age of eight you would have driven clear to California. You have lived alone and with lovers in both the city and the country. You have had a child on a November night when the moon was orange and there was a foot of new snow. Of course, you were always afraid of bridges. If you try hard you can remember other times you were afraid, once on a crowded subway in Manhattan, another time when a boyfriend in Boston gave you a wrong address and you sat on an unfamiliar doorstep, a sudden terror making it impossible to move. When you were pregnant you had a morbid fear of slipping on ice or mud and crushing your baby. You will soon see that rehashing the past is worthless. It doesn't matter what the reason is, there is a force field around you.

Unfortunately, you are married to a man who doesn't be-

lieve in fear and who has, you can tell, already thought of
leaving you. You keep your fears secret and when you are
certain no one is home you will try to get past the force field.
You will try to do what you are most terrified of: getting into
the truck and driving somewhere. You will be sick all that
morning. You will have three cups of coffee, then regret it. At
last you will take the keys off a metal hook beneath a kitchen
cabinet. Your heart will begin to pound and you are nowhere
near the force field yet. When you open the back door you
will hear a malevolent hum. You step out onto the porch and
find that your lungs feel tight and sore. This makes you wonder if perhaps there is no oxygen in the force field. All you
have to do is get past it, so you run. As you run you realize
that the force field is not a long, vertical space, reaching from
earth to sky. It is as wide as an ocean. It goes on forever. You
are still in the thick of it when you get into the truck. You
start the engine anyway, and hold one foot down on the
clutch, even though your legs are almost too heavy to move.
You get to the end of the dirt driveway, and then, suddenly,
you cannot breathe. You throw the truck into reverse. If
someone was standing behind you, you'd run him down without thinking twice. You see now, you will never make it. You
don't even know where it is you will never make it to because
you have forgotten to plan a destination. When you park the
truck, it lurches. You pull the keys out of the ignition and cut
a long thin line along your palm with the sharp edge of your
house key.

   Then you run. You can feel the vibrating power of the force

field recede. You can feel your legs growing stronger. In the kitchen, you bend over the sink, then drink a glass of cold water. It is nine thirty in the morning, and when you look out your window you will be amazed to see that the sky is still just as cloudless and blue as it was before you walked out the door.

Simon has actually begun to look forward to going to school. He is the hamster monitor all this week. He makes certain that no crayons or puzzle pieces are dropped through the wire mesh into the cage and, most wonderful of all, he will be allowed to take the hamsters home for the Columbus Day weekend. His parents have already said yes.

The other children in his class don't seem to notice that Simon doesn't look like the rest of them. As far as they're concerned, the only thing that makes him different is that he's very good at sharing. But out in the playground, some of the older boys have a nickname for him, Thumby. Even though Simon doesn't realize that this is shorthand for Tom Thumb, the name makes him uncomfortable. He keeps to himself on the playground. Once he's back in the classroom, Simon helps build roads out of blocks, he finger-paints and traces his hand on construction paper. A little girl named Tara, who is almost as small as Simon, has chosen him for a friend. In return, Simon lets her fill the water bottle for the hamsters. Though Tara is not half as interesting as Samantha Freed, whom Simon has not forgotten though he won't see her again till next summer, Simon always sits next to Tara at story time.

Today the story is one of Simon's favorites, and he knows it by heart. A small wizard named Fisher teaches a wolf good manners. The wolf, who looms above Fisher, sits in a wooden chair with milk dripping down his face. He wears a dunce cap while Fisher concocts a potion to turn the wolf into a gentleman. The children are hysterical when they see a picture of Fisher holding his nose as he prepares the potion in a blender, adding strawberry juice, cucumber peel, half a cup of salt water, one slice of pizza. Fisher is so tiny he has to stand on the table to reach the wolf's mouth. Simon wonders what sort of potion he could prepare to make his parents happy. If he thinks about his parents too long he will begin to believe that what has happened to them is his fault. His parents act as though they were strangers. When Simon has a tantrum they don't yell at him, they simply look tired and give in. Is it his fault that his mother cries as she cooks dinner? Is there some mistake he has made that has driven his father away?

After school, he and Tara race to see who can get to the parking lot first, but as soon as Simon sees his father he stops and Tara wins the race. When Tara calls good-bye Simon doesn't hear her, and she yells, "Say good-bye to me, Simon." Simon waves and considers ingredients he might use: orange soda, vanilla ice cream, a bluebird's feather, Red Zinger tea. Simon used to run to his father when he saw him in the parking lot. Now, he's more careful. He walks. After Simon has climbed into the truck he asks if they can stop at the market.

"What for?" Andre asks.

"Stuff," Simon tells him.

They stop at Alley's store and Andre follows Simon up and down the aisles. Andre pays for the orange soda and ice cream and picks up a pack of cigarettes for Vonny at the counter. While waiting for his change, he keeps one hand on Simon's head. Simon needs a haircut, and although his hair is still silky, it's starting to change, becoming a bit coarser, less like a little boy's. On the way home, Andre asks about the hamsters and Simon tells him that on Friday he has to be picked up early so they can load the cage and the supply of hamster food into the truck. The ice cream is melting. As soon as they are in the kitchen, Andre puts it right into the freezer. Simon hangs up his jacket, puts his lunchbox on the table, then lets Nelson out. It takes a long time for Nelson to pick himself off the floor and Simon has to whistle several times to get his attention. Though he's been practicing, copying the older boys on the playground, Simon's whistle is still more breath than sound.

Andre can hear Vonny out on the sun porch. Sometimes she just pretends to work, but Andre hears the squeaking of the wheel as she throws a pot. At first he thought she somehow knew he'd been unfaithful. He has heard this can happen; you smell betrayal on the other person. It is not so much that he regrets what happened with Jody, but more that it seems to have happened to another person. He has questioned himself ruthlessly: Does he want to be with her again? What he really wants is for him and Vonny to have just met. He wants that first night, when she came to his apartment and did not leave for three days. He wants to make love without talking. He wants to not feel so disappointed.

He has tested Vonny, bringing up Jody's name, and getting no reaction. When Jody phones to ask if they need a baby-sitter, Andre listens carefully and doesn't even hear suspicion in Vonny's voice. One week he convinces himself that what has gone wrong between them has something to do with Vonny's father's rejection. The next week he guesses that worrying about Simon's height has caused the rift between them. Always, he wonders if Vonny is disappointed, too. He has had to take a part-time job at a garage in Vineyard Haven. It is not what he planned for himself and, he is certain, it's not what Vonny had hoped for. At work he barely speaks and he knows if he weren't such a good mechanic he'd have been fired by now. He and Vonny never discuss the job. He disappears every morning and once a week brings home a check.

For a while he wondered if he was overreacting because he was so humiliated by his job. He's tried to believe Vonny. She twisted her ankle. She has a headache. She doesn't want to go out in the rain. He no longer believes her. He knows that she's lying when she tells him she visited a friend while he was at the garage in Vineyard Haven. He's checked up on her, and neither Jane nor Peggy has seen her since the summer. Each time they phone Vonny says she's too busy to talk. Andre has been unfaithful, and she's the one who's lying. When he realizes that Vonny has not left the house for two months, he feels a surge of fear. He tries to tempt her, offering to take her to the movies, to a hotel in Boston for the weekend. He braces himself for her excuses. He sees that when she smiles at him she's trying to charm him, as if he were an idiot who doesn't know her any better. He's afraid that if he confronts her, she'll accuse him of sleeping with Jody. So he waits, hoping to catch her in a lie.

As Simon drags a chair over to the freezer to get the ice cream, Andre walks out to the sun porch thinking, Please lie to me. Vonny has finished a vase that she sets on a terra-cotta slab to dry. She wears a yellow smock over her sweater and a pair of worn blue jeans. There's clay under her fingernails and stuck to the soles of her sneakers. She looks up at him and smiles as he stands in the doorway.

"How was your day?" Andre asks.

"Great," Vonny says. She gets up and kicks off her sneakers so she won't track clay through the house. "I didn't even hear you pull up. Is Simon in the kitchen?"

"Why don't we drop him over at Matt's tonight," Andre says. "We'll go out to dinner. The Menemsha Inn," he suggests.

Vonny wrinkles her nose. She wears her hair pinned up, exposing the slope of her neck.

"I'd just as soon stay home," Vonny says. "I'm defrosting chicken."

Chicken which, Andre remembers, he bought last week when Vonny couldn't go shopping because she felt feverish. As they walk through the living room they hear the hum of the blender, and Vonny runs to the kitchen to check on

Simon. She sees him mixing an orange-colored milkshake and laughs in spite of the mess. Simon is both bewildered and pleased to hear her laughter.

"What is this?" Vonny asks.

"A snack," Simon says. "It's for you guys."

Vonny and Andre exchange a look. It is the sort of wordless communication that used to make Simon feel excluded. Now, he's delighted. When they drink the milkshake in tall glasses, Simon watches them carefully. Unlike the wolf who turns into a gentleman, his parents undergo no immediate transformation. But that night when Vonny puts him to bed she reads him two stories and kisses him three times. Even Andre has a feeling of hope. While Vonny is washing the dishes he comes up behind her, puts his arms around her, and kisses her neck. He can feel her body bend toward him. Near midnight, when they make love, Andre believes that he can stay away from Jody. His marriage may not be ruined after all. But afterward, Vonny is shaking. She won't let him touch her.

"What's wrong?" Andre says when she sits up on the edge of the bed.

"Nothing," Vonny insists. "Too much coffee."

He can't let this go. "I mean about leaving the house," Andre says.

"I don't know what you're talking about," she tells him.

"You haven't left the house in weeks," Andre says. He considers saying months but is afraid of pushing her too far.

"You're crazy," Vonny says.

She gets out of bed and takes a cigarette from the pack on the bureau. She wonders how long she can go on with this charade. Once he discovers what is wrong with her, he will leave. Of course she's imagined him leaving before, but she always thought she and Simon would be together. Now, she knows she couldn't be the one to keep Simon. She can't take care of him. She can't even drive him to school. It is devastating to realize how much she needs Andre.

She blows out smoke in choppy streams.

"I'm worried about you," Andre says.

"I don't have to take this kind of crap from you," Vonny says. She stubs out her cigarette, pulls on a blue nightgown, and leaves him. She goes downstairs in the dark and doesn't turn on a light until she reaches the kitchen. She knows she made a tactical mistake and she hopes he'll fall asleep. Tomorrow she can charm him. She'll try to go with him when he delivers her pottery to Edgartown.

She hears his footsteps on the stairs. She feels sick to her stomach. She takes a frozen chocolate cake out of the freezer and tears open the box. Andre comes into the kitchen, wearing only jeans.

"*I'm* crazy?" he says to her.

Vonny knows it's best to ignore him.

"Prove it," Andre says. "Let's see you go someplace right now."

"It's three A.M.," Vonny says. She is calmly cutting chocolate cake. She is certain this is the end. The force field is vibrating outside the door. She licks the knife. "Want a piece?" she asks him.

"Go on," Andre says. "Let's see you leave the house."

"You're going to wake up Simon," Vonny tells him.

Andre goes to the back door and flings it open. He doesn't have to be doing this. He could be on his way to Florida. He could run away with a seventeen-year-old girl who really loves him. If only Vonny would walk right past him, out into the yard, and snidely say, "See, you were only imagining things." She is up against the counter. He can see through her nightgown.

"Leave," Andre says. "Show me I'm wrong."

Vonny despises him. She walks across the kitchen, then, shaking worse than ever, goes out the door. There are no stars and no wind either. Vonny keeps going even when the pressure of the force field clamps down, hard, pushing her breath out. Andre watches her walk through the dark in her nightgown. She turns back toward him. Her face is as white as the moon.

"Come back," Andre says.

When Vonny doesn't move, Andre goes outside and runs down the porch steps.

"There's something wrong with me," Vonny says.

Andre is afraid she'll move away when he puts his arm around her, but she doesn't. She stands with him in the center of the force field, until, together, they carefully make their way back.

ELIZABETH Renny's house is much too crowded. The two boys, Jody's brothers, will have to sleep in the storage attic.

Jody's mother will sleep on the couch. It is the Columbus Day weekend, and when they arrive they're exhausted. Laura had forgotten to make a ferry reservation and they waited in line for three hours in Woods Hole. Laura is not herself lately. She and Glenn have now been legally separated for five months, and the separation is not at all what she expected.

As soon as they get into the house, Keith, who is ten, and Mark, thirteen, race up to the attic to search for bats. Laura embraces her mother, then gasps when she sees Jody.

"You're so grown up!" Laura says in a voice that's more accusing than she means it to be. She hugs Jody, then stands back to appraise her. "Wow," Laura says.

Jody has made lasagna for dinner and Laura and the boys can't believe she can cook.

"She's been a great help to me," Elizabeth Renny says.

Jody looks down at the table and smiles. She can't understand why all this attention pleases her, but it does. Her brothers, who are not yet settled enough to be obnoxious, watch her but do not speak. Their typical behavior when meeting a grownup. After dinner, the boys go upstairs. They set up their Gobots sleeping bags, then scuttle through the attic, checking out all the corners with their flashlights. Jody is in the kitchen, washing dishes. Her mother is watching, astounded that she even knows what liquid Joy is.

"I'm going to faint," Laura says.

"Will you stop?" Jody laughs. "Go sit down. Don't bother me."

Laura goes into the living room where her mother is drinking oolong tea with sugar and lemon.

"I don't know what you've done, Mother," Laura says to Elizabeth Renny. "She's a different person."

"Hardly," Elizabeth Renny says. "Just a year older."

Each time Elizabeth Renny returns the cup to its saucer there is the faint clicking sound of china. Her first impulse, when Laura suggested this visit, was to say no. Now she's nervous. More so, when Laura continues to compliment her.

"You've done a great job," Laura tells her. "If I had been forced to deal with Jody's acting out while Glenn and I were separating, I wouldn't have made it."

Laura has fair skin and the same pouty mouth Jody has. Occasionally, her little-girl's voice creeps in, so that some of her sentences are marked by a slight whine. "But I don't really think this is the right place for her. Life here is not what I want for Jody."

Laura wanted desperately to get off the Vineyard and into the world, in her case, Boston College. Elizabeth Renny vaguely remembers how hurt she was at the time. They had been close and then quite suddenly they were enemies. By the time Elizabeth Renny's husband died, five years after Laura went off to school, they could not have a conversation without enormous effort. It seems impossible that this woman, who is forty-one years old, was her baby girl. It seems just as impossible for Elizabeth Renny to imagine that she herself was ever a married woman, that every night, for twenty-eight years, she wrapped one arm around her husband's shoulders before she fell asleep. She should feel some sympathy for Laura—they have both lost husbands, both have had to deal with adolescent daughters—but she feels none. Who is Laura, with her ruined marriage and ill-mannered boys, to insist Jody fill out college applications? Elizabeth Renny feels that Jody has a right to mess up her life any way she chooses. She considers Laura a selfish mother, which is not to say she doesn't wonder if she's equally selfish, if perhaps all those times when Jody climbed out her bedroom window at midnight, Elizabeth Renny wasn't somehow going along with her, balancing carefully on the pitched roof.

"Jody is the one who'll have to decide where she'll live," Elizabeth Renny says.

"Of course," Laura says.

"You have to think about your life now," Elizabeth Renny says.

"That's exactly what I'm doing," Laura snaps. "That's what I'm trying to do." She laughs. She leans forward, to her mother. "I have my whole life ahead of me now," she says to her mother. "Isn't that true?"

Elizabeth Renny's failing vision softens her daughter's features. Laura's face is pale and formless. As a child she had beautiful skin that always seemed flushed.

"Can you come closer?" Elizabeth Renny asks.

Laura is puzzled, but she gets up and walks toward her mother. She stands in front of Elizabeth Renny's chair, unsteadily. She doesn't quite know what to do with her hands, so she crosses them in front of her.

"I feel silly," Laura says.

Upstairs, the boys are thumping around like monsters, scaring each other in the dark.

"Please take my advice," Elizabeth Renny says. "Don't make a fuss about Jody."

"God, Mother, I think I know how to act with my own daughter," Laura says.

Elizabeth Renny wishes this had been true for her, but she never knew how to act. She is still worried about offending Laura; whatever she says will be wrong. Later, when Elizabeth Renny has gone into the parlor for the night, Jody comes into the living room and helps Laura make up the couch with worn pink sheets.

"We miss you at home," Laura says casually. "I guess you know I'd like you to come back and finish your senior year. Maybe apply to school in Boston. Or in Connecticut, if you want to stay at home and commute. Your father has to pay your college tuition whether he likes it or not."

"Mom," Jody says.

Laura bites her tongue. She cannot believe that her husband is annoyed at the amount of child support he has to pay. If she isn't careful she'll badmouth him so horribly Jody will simply turn her off, the way the boys do.

"I'm not trying to pressure you." Laura pulls a pillowcase over a down pillow. "I'd just like you to come home."

Jody reaches for a thin cotton blanket. "I guess I'll stay here," she says, not daring to look at her mother.

"I'll bet it's too cold for us to have a picnic tomorrow," Laura says quickly. "I can't remember the last Columbus Day weekend when we had good weather."

Laura and Jody each take a corner of the blanket. From

her hospital bed, Elizabeth Renny sees the blanket balloon up in the air, then settle over the couch. Elizabeth Renny doesn't often think about winter or her blind eye anymore. There are birds, she knows, who live their whole lives in the dark, who drink from night-blooming flowers, guided by scent alone. When she first lived in this house she often left dishes of honey on her windowsills on summer nights. Each time she did, the honey would disappear by morning. It may well have been squirrels or mice she was providing for, but she has always preferred to believe night birds found those porcelain bowls.

SIMON is awakened by the sound of the metal exercise wheel turning. He rises up through sleep like a swimmer, frightened by the creaking. He has forgotten that the hamsters' cage is on his dresser. Now he learns the hamsters' secret; they may hide during the day, but at night exercise is their mission. On Tuesday Simon will no longer be the hamster monitor; this weekend is his farewell. Simon pulls a chair over to the dresser. One hamster runs on the wheel, the other perches on the coffee can, waiting his turn. Either they don't see Simon in the dark or they don't care, not even when he presses his face closer to the glass.

The night-light is on and a stream of light from the hallway filters beneath the bedroom door. The house is so quiet it's almost frightening. Simon knows his parents are asleep. He has begun to have hopes for them. Sometimes, he walks into a room and finds them deep in conversation. They look up at

him, as though they're surprised to see him. He is certain that
by the time his birthday comes things will be all right again.
He may even get the rabbit he wants. By taking care of these
hamsters he has tried to prove that he is ready for his own
pet. He has cleaned the hamsters' cage twice, washed their
lettuce, doled out their food pellets with a thimble. If he gets
a rabbit he will train it to sleep on his pillow; he will make
it a collar out of pipe cleaners and beads.

He measures out a little more food for the hamsters and
lifts off the wire mesh on top of the cage. The hamsters look
up briefly as he pours the food inside, then continue as though
Simon didn't exist. He watches them a little longer, then gets
down and pulls the chair away from the dresser. The window
shade is up, and on his way back to bed he sees there is a full
moon and stops to look. The sky is dark blue and the trees,
though they have all turned color, look black against the sky.

Simon is falling asleep on his feet. He wears one-piece flannel pajamas with a zipper and plastic feet, and the warmth
makes him even drowsier. The moon, the turning of the exercise wheel, the fan of light beneath his door, these things all
may be a dream. Out in the yard next door there is a giant.
He has blond hair and a dark jacket that is too short at the
waist and wrists. The Giant stops near the pine tree, and
Simon notices that he has to duck so his head will not hit the
lowest branches. Simon rubs his eyes, but the Giant is still
there. What is under his arm? A harp that speaks? A sack of
gold? Simon watches, hypnotized. He is motionless, the way
he is when he studies an anthill. The hamster on the exercise

wheel is slowing down. The clock on the living-room mantel chimes four times. If Simon were not so tired he would stay up and watch the Giant, but the yard is dark and it's difficult to see, so Simon gets back in bed and pulls the covers up. In the morning, he will not be able to remember what he has dreamed and what he has actually seen. When he goes to check the hamsters they will be sleeping. Next door, Jody's brother Keith will stumble over a basket of brown eggs as he runs out to the car to get his robot collection. The eggs will fall down onto the grass, unbroken, and will remain there until Jody kneels down and gathers them, stretching her night-gown over her knees to form a white hammock.

Chapter Six

THE SAFE PERSON

SIMON's rabbit is a white lop-ear named Dora. After just one month she is already trained to use a litter box and only occasionally chews on quilts or jumps on the table to eat out of the sugar bowl. It was pure good luck that when the rabbit was let out of its wicker basket Nelson didn't even lift his head. He still ignores Dora, except for moments when an uncontrollable urge to chase her strikes him. Then, Nelson's claws clatter on the floor, but as soon as the rabbit stands absolutely still, Nelson stops and casually looks over his shoulder, making certain no one has seen him acting like a dog.

Vonny had expected to hate the rabbit, but she finds she likes her. The rabbit seems affected by the force field, too. One day Simon leaves the door ajar and Vonny finds the rabbit on the doorstep, terrified by the cold open space stretching out in front of her. Vonny picks her up and can feel the rabbit trembling. She puts Dora up on the kitchen table and pours her a small dish of sugar. Lately, Vonny has found that she can leave the house, she can go almost anywhere, as long as she is with Andre. She has no idea why, but when she is with Andre the force field dissolves. By early December not only can she go with Andre to Simon's school, she can walk down the hallway to Simon's classroom with him. Andre begins to believe Vonny's been cured. He's delighted when Vonny calmly helps him pack so that he can deliver a motorcycle to Providence. But at the door, as he's about to leave, Vonny panics and begs him not to go.

From where Jody stands on her grandmother's porch it looks to her as though Andre is leaving for good. She has not kept her promise to herself to tell Vonny, and, for a moment, it seems she won't have to. Jody stands perfectly still, waiting for Andre to run to her and grab her by the arm. She's almost relieved when it appears that Vonny has persuaded him to stay.

What has stopped her from trying to break up their marriage is the basket of eggs the Giant brings to her once a week. At first, she dreaded his gift. She wanted him to reveal himself, to harass her outright if that's what he meant to do, to frighten her on a dark night. She did not feel safe even in her own bed. She can't figure out what he wants. What does he think he's buying with these eggs? Maybe he doesn't expect anything in return. Growing braver, she wakes early and waits in the kitchen, hoping to catch him in the act, but she's always too late. She thinks she hears him at night when it is only raccoons rattling the garbage cans. The winter is rainy; with slick patches of ice rather than snow, and the Giant doesn't leave footprints. Were it not for the eggs, she would think he had never existed in the first place.

Twice, when it was her turn to get behind the wheel in driver's ed., Jody drove past the farmstand, but it was boarded up for the winter and she couldn't see the Giant's house from the road. Both times she got yelled at for speeding, and now Mr. Davis, the driver's ed. teacher, always says "Stay alive at fifty-five" directly to her when the class begins.

Lots of the kids Jody knows have already applied to colleges; on Saturdays they study for SATs. On Saturdays Jody walks to the market, orders, then waits around until she can get a ride home with the delivery boy. Sometimes she goes to Garland's house in the afternoon and they watch movies on the VCR or lie on Garland's bed and smoke cigarettes. It is amazingly easy for Jody to keep secrets while listening to Garland pour out her heart. This trait makes Jody feel awful about herself; she is allowing Garland to think they are best friends when Garland doesn't even really know her. Garland does things by the book. She knows she's going to work for her father after high school; she will probably marry Rob Norris, if she can get him to talk to her. If a giant was bringing her weird presents in the middle of the night, she'd call the police and have him arrested. Or she'd tell her father who, because he owns a hardware store, would probably set the largest steel trap he could find.

Jody has been invited home for Christmas by both parents and she doesn't want to go. She doesn't want to hear her mother complain about her father. She doesn't want her father to give her a too-expensive bracelet just because he feels bad that he never sees her. She knows from her brothers that her father is involved with someone and Jody especially doesn't want her father to have to tell his girlfriend to get all her stuff out of his apartment so that Jody won't happen upon red nail polish in his bathroom or a silver belt hanging in the closet next to his ties. She writes letters to her parents during social studies and tells them she can't possibly leave her grandmother alone at this time of year. There's some truth in this. Jody has found a box of Christmas ornaments in the attic. There are blue glass balls and a silver angel. She lugs the cardboard box downstairs.

"These are all dusty," Elizabeth Renny says when Jody places an ornament in her hand. She remembers buying them, when Laura was ten or eleven, at a Woolworth's in Hyannis.

"I'll dust them," Jody says.

Jody rips a worn T-shirt in half and sits cross-legged on the floor. The cats, certain that she has unearthed a box of new toys for them, have to be pushed aside. Jody has bought what she thinks is the perfect gift for her grandmother: a sack of safflower seeds. She's caught her grandmother mournfully watching the few birds who gather this winter to eat her bread and seeds. The cardinals, always so easy to spot against snow and ice, have not returned, and Garland's father has promised Jody that cardinals can never resist safflower seeds. Presents from Jody's family have already arrived: a wool sweater and silk shirt from her mother, a gold bangle bracelet from her father, plastic earrings in the shape of goldfish from her brothers. She knows she should have waited to open her presents until Christmas. Now she will have nothing. Her grandmother certainly can't get to a store and Jody has seen her trying to read mail-order catalogues. But each time she tosses them aside, annoyed that she can't read the small print.

Elizabeth Renny has not celebrated Christmas for several years. She does not consider getting a fruitcake and a scarf from her daughter once a year cause for celebration. Now she begins to sing "White Christmas" in a high, wavering voice. Jody puts down the Christmas ornament she's polishing, listens, then applauds.

"I used to think I could sing," Elizabeth Renny says.

"Sing something else," Jody says.

"Oh, no," Elizabeth Renny says. "I only make a fool out of myself once a night."

She picks up a glass ball and holds it up to the light. Her reflection wavers and looks liquid. She could swear it was only moments ago that she was the same age as Jody. She and her sister Maureen, who has been dead for eighteen years—longer than Jody has been alive—always hung up red stockings the night before Christmas. In the morning they would find little gifts that brought them a ridiculous amount of pleasure: ribbons, dried fruit, bottles of ink, tortoiseshell combs for their hair. Elizabeth Renny has wrapped two of these combs, both of which are edged with silver filigree, in white tissue paper. Though they are a far cry from the purple plastic things Jody uses, the combs are to be Jody's Christmas present.

Elizabeth Renny used to wear her hair long. Before she began to go blind, her reflection sometimes scared her. As a child she had been terrified of old ladies; she would hang on her mother's skirt when an old aunt came to visit. Now she realizes that she herself looks ten times worse than her aunt ever did. She wonders if the little boy next door imagines she's a witch. She cannot remember if she ever called her aunt a witch to her face, or if she just thought it so hard it seemed as though she'd said it aloud. Tonight, her reflection is almost beautiful, it shifts in the light, turning silver and then deep blue.

THAT night the tree is dropped off in the yard. The two men who pull up in a battered truck are landscapers who sell Christmas trees each winter and who promised Jody they would deliver. Well, deliver they have, right on the lawn, but they will not carry the tree up the porch steps. Simon and Andre are in the shed, gathering hidden presents to take inside and wrap, when the truck pulls away.

This Christmas they have something to celebrate. Since Simon's examination at Children's Hospital he's grown two inches and has moved up a clothing size. Under their tree there are four pairs of new overalls, a snowsuit, and two sweaters—one patterned with reindeer, the other with black cats. Vonny and Andre can't bring themselves to deny him anything these days, and Simon is often surprised by their leniency. Before Andre can stop him, Simon has run next door, waving and calling to Jody. Andre wishes he had grabbed hold of his son before he made his getaway.

Jody is wearing jeans, a heavy green sweater, and high boots. She and Simon gaze at the tree, admiring it. Only a few days ago, in a store in Edgartown, Andre picked up a silver chain, planning to get it for Vonny. Attached to the chain was a small bell. When he lifted the chain the bell's chime was distant, a sound you'd have to be very close to hear. As soon as Andre realized the necklace was the perfect present for Jody, he quickly put it down and bought Vonny a pair of blue enameled earrings he knows will look great when she wears her hair up.

"Hey, Simon," Andre calls across the yard. He will do almost anything not to have to go over there. "Hey, Jody," he calls as an afterthought.

Jody looks up and waves without enthusiasm.

"This tree is bigger than ours," Simon tells her.

"It didn't look this big when I picked it out," Jody says.

Jody grips the tree by its trunk and tugs. Branches scrape along the ground, but the body of the tree doesn't budge.

"Maybe the Giant can help you with it," Simon says.

Jody stares at him.

"I think I might be getting a Care Bear for Christmas," Simon announces.

"What giant?" Jody asks him.

"I don't know," Simon says.

They stare at the tree; though their breath turns smoky in the cold, there's no chance that this will be a white Christmas.

"Giants are never around when you need them," Jody says.

Simon nods. "They're afraid of people."

"Let's go, Simon," Andre calls. They plan to stash their presents in the kitchen cabinets while Vonny wraps presents on the sun porch. Andre has spent the past few days running deliveries for Vonny—during the week before Christmas she sells more pottery than she does the whole rest of the year. He made excuses for her to the shop owners who asked why they no longer saw her: she was working overtime to complete her orders, she had a sore throat, a headache, she was leaving on vacation. This year Vonny was terrified that she wouldn't be able to go into a store to do any Christmas shopping. Andre had to wait for her outside each shop, parked right in front in case she needed him. He timed her; she could not last more than six minutes in any of the stores before she had to run back out to the truck. He's not supposed to know what she bought him, but when she came out of the shoe store the box she had was so big it could only contain a pair of boots.

"My dad can help you," Simon tells Jody.

"That's okay," Jody says. "I'll manage."

"Dad!" Simon yells. He flaps his arms up and down when he yells, as if winding himself up.

Andre puts his hands in his pockets and walks across the lawn.

"You sure must like Christmas trees," he says to Jody, careful to look not at her but at the tree.

"This can't be the one I picked out," Jody says. It's amazing how she can make her voice sound absolutely flat.

"Come on, assistant," Andre says to Simon. Andre directs Simon to the top of the tree and tells him to hold the branches so he'll think he's helping. Then Andre lifts the tree and drags it up the steps.

"You don't have to do this," Jody tells him.

"I know," Andre says. "But I'm already doing it."

Jody grabs some long branches and helps guide the tree through the door. It will be a mess, Jody can see that already; she'll be sweeping pine needles off the floor all evening. Elizabeth Renny calls out for them all to be careful not to strain their backs. Then she gets her pocketbook and fumbles in her change purse.

"Let me pay you something," she says to Andre, handing him a five-dollar bill.

Andre backs away from her and shakes his head no. If Simon hadn't run over he would have let Elizabeth Renny herself struggle with the tree just so he could avoid Jody.

"Then let the boy have it," Elizabeth Renny says when Andre refuses her money. "He helped."

Simon takes the money without hesitation.

"Thank you," Andre says to him meaningfully.

"Thank you," Simon tells Mrs. Renny.

Simon runs out the door before anyone can decide that the money should be returned. Elizabeth Renny is not certain why, but she feels unwanted in her own kitchen. She can feel something pass between Jody and Andre and yet she takes a coat off the hook and follows Simon out onto the porch. She pulls the storm door closed behind her, and in giving them a moment alone, she becomes a co-conspirator.

"What are you going to buy?" Mrs. Renny asks Simon. "A dump truck?"

"Nope," Simon says, balancing on the last icy step. "A bed for my rabbit."

Inside the kitchen, Andre and Jody's hands burn from pine needles.

"Look, I'm sorry," Andre says.

"That's okay," Jody says, without the slightest idea of what she means.

"It's not," Andre says. "If I was a different person," he begins, then stops himself. It is meaningless to say, or even think such things.

Jody can tell he's nervous. He keeps looking over at her grandmother, who is just on the other side of the door, keeping Simon busy.

"I've been planning to go over and tell her all about it," Jody says now.

Andre doesn't say anything, he doesn't move an inch, yet she can tell he's panicked.

"But I decided against it," Jody says, deciding as she speaks.

"Well, good," Andre says. He's broken into a sweat.

"Dad," Simon calls from the porch. Elizabeth Renny turns

to them, an apologetic look on her face. You can keep a boy like Simon engrossed in conversation for just so long on the night before Christmas.

"Merry Christmas," Andre says to Jody.

He can picture the silver chain around her neck, hear the way the bell would echo as she leaned to pull on her boots or as she turned on her side in bed. He feels off balance and as Elizabeth Renny comes inside he gives her a quick, totally unexpected hug before he pushes the door open. Then he stomps down the steps, swoops Simon up, and runs across the lawn. Simon lets his head swing back and he screams with delight. Clouds cover the moon as Simon bounces up and down in his father's arms. Inside, they march in place until all the ice on their boots flies off and scatters. Nelson beats his tail on the floor to greet them. Simon unzips his jacket, tosses it on a chair, then runs into the living room to find his mother.

"Don't look!" Vonny cries.

From the doorway, Andre can see Vonny stuffing wrapped presents under the couch. Simon stands nearby, hands covering his eyes. The rabbit is curled up on one of Andre's old sweaters on the coffee table; one ear twitches in her sleep.

"I saw!" Simon chortles, hands still over his eyes. "I saw a Care Bear!"

Vonny looks up at Andre and smiles. After Simon has gone to bed, Andre will have to go out and search whatever stores are still open. They had hoped he would forget about Care Bears, but since there will be plenty of times in his life when he will be disappointed, they might as well get him what he wants.

THE Giant does not know how other people fall in love. Do they experience insomnia? Loss of appetite? Do they hear ringing in their ears? The Giant falls asleep easily in his large wooden bed, for breakfast he has cereal and toast, he can hear a single drop of water leaking from the kitchen faucet when he is clear across the house. His life has not altered: he takes care of the chickens, cleans his house, paints his miniatures. The only difference is, once a week, very late at night, he walks three miles with a basket of eggs and doesn't return until the sun comes up. The walk there, though sometimes so cold he has to wear two pairs of gloves, is always beautiful. The road shimmers with ice; the bark of oak trees turns to rough silver. But the walk back is terrible, endless and dark. When he comes home, the Giant collapses and sleeps until noon.

The Giant cannot stop thinking about love. Though he barely remembers his father, he knows what passed for love between his mother and her boyfriends. The desire he saw seemed brutal and mean, but whenever he overheard his mother talking with other women he wondered if he had missed something completely. She described her romances as if she were a swooning girl, she showed off the gifts her boyfriends brought, offering her neighbors chocolates from boxes tied with ribbons, gently taking a pair of cheap earrings out of a cardboard box, flaunting them as though they were gold.

The Giant studied his mother carefully when she dressed to go out on a date or to a bar to look for somebody new. She applied her makeup slowly. She changed her clothes three or four times until she got it right. Often, as she was leaving, she yelled at him to make himself scarce in case she brought somebody home. But the way she looked as she stood at the door, ready to go out, mesmerized the Giant and he could not move. Something delirious shone out from her; the night was filled with mysterious and endless possibilities. The Giant has never imagined any such possibilities for himself. Who would want him for a lover? Who would not run from him? Even when he's alone, he cannot delude himself into thinking he is like everyone else. Chairs are too small for him. China breaks in his hands.

The Giant knows that his grandfather loved him, but that gives him little comfort. His grandfather liked defective things. If a table was broken it was all the more a treasure, a sweater without a patch was an unnatural object, what good were planets when there was such a thing as a falling star? The Giant realizes he was lucky to be loved as a child. He knows what it's like to be afraid of thunder and have someone's hand to hold. What he does not know about is passion, although he is beginning to think passion has less to do with uncontrollable urges than with hope. When the blue light of dusk appears the Giant feels what may be desire. Wanting to be with the girl with the gray eyes makes him feel both stronger and weaker than he is.

He has told himself that he takes the eggs to Jody's house

without any expectations, but that is not exactly the truth. He is fairly certain that the elation he feels when he walks into her yard is not something normal people feel. He has begun to do stupid things. He forgets the coffeepot on the stove and returns to find it sputtering, the coffee boiled down to a rubbery black coating at the bottom of the pot. He goes out to the farmstand in broad daylight to repair some loose boards and allows himself to be seen by several motorists, some of whom, he is sure, will be back to gawk with a carload of disbelieving friends.

On Christmas Eve the Giant goes out to the henhouses at dusk, his throat thick from the blue light. The temperature is dropping, and, because the earth is still warm, fog rises in unexpected places, spilling out from beneath the henhouses, encircling ferns. The Giant feeds his chickens and on the way out of the henhouse finds an egg he overlooked that morning. He takes the egg from the straw and puts it in his sweater pocket. Inside the house he lights a fire, then places the egg on the table and gets his paints. He takes a pin and makes a tiny hole in the shell, then raises it to his mouth and sucks out the raw egg. He uses acrylics, and paints carefully with the finest brushes he has. He holds a magnifying glass above the egg and he stops working only once, when his fingers cramp and he has to put down his paintbrush and open and close his fist several times.

When he is finished, the Giant is so hot that he doesn't bother to wear a coat and he doesn't feel the cold as he walks to Jody's house. It has taken him longer than he'd planned to paint the egg, and it's nearly dawn when he gets there. He goes to the back porch, which is covered with pine needles. Then he does something so stupid he can't believe it: he puts his hand on the doorknob. When he shifts his hand to the right, the doorknob turns. He quickly pulls his hand away, but the door opens. The Giant holds his breath, ducks, then goes inside. His pulse is so wild he can't believe the noise doesn't wake anyone. He puts the egg on a white saucer left on the kitchen table. The egg rolls back and forth, then is still. The Giant has painted the scene of their first meeting. Tiny chickens peck at the dust as a girl holding a basket of eggs flees, her hair streaming out behind her. In a chair near the henhouses, the Giant has painted himself. He wears a white shirt, as he did on that day, but in his painting his heart is visible, and he clasps his hand to it, as though wounded.

Having walked all this way in the cold, the Giant is now hypnotized by the heat in this house. If he lets his eyes close he will fall where he stands. Two cats surprise him and rub their arched backs against his legs. They follow the Giant to the kitchen doorway. He can see the Christmas tree, and the opened presents beneath it. The cats pace back and forth in front of him. When the Giant reaches down and strokes the white cat's back, she turns up her face to him and mews. He cannot be as stupid as this, and yet he doesn't want to leave and begin that cruel, dark walk back home. He knows he is breaking the law, knows people wake early on Christmas morning. But he doesn't move, even when he hears a thud above him, then footsteps. Jody is coming downstairs, a wool cardigan over her nightgown. She sees him and stops on the landing, rubbing her eyes. She tells herself she won't be scared unless he makes a move toward her. Then she will turn, run upstairs, and lock herself in the bathroom. But the Giant is the one who turns and runs. Panicked, he forgets to duck and hits his head on the top of the kitchen doorway. The crash is so loud his pain is audible. The Giant reels backward, stunned. Jody holds on to the staircase banister. In the center of the Giant's forehead is a deep gash.

"I don't want to scare you," the Giant says.

"Okay," Jody says. "Good. Don't scare me."

The cats won't leave the Giant alone. They troop around in front of him before darting into the kitchen, in the direction of their food bowl.

"I wanted to bring you a present," the Giant says helplessly.

"Why?" Jody says.

The staircase is curved and short; Jody leans her head under a low beam and puts one hand on a rafter to steady herself.

"I don't know what I'm doing here," the Giant tells her.

"Be quiet," Jody says. "My grandmother's asleep in the parlor."

The Giant is embarrassed. He thought he was whispering.

"What's your present?" Jody says, narrowing her eyes. "You?"

The Giant looks at the floor. He is a fool.

"No," he says, and he does whisper this time.

Jody realizes that she's shivering. She wraps her cardigan tightly around herself.

"You can't just walk into people's houses," Jody says, more gently.

"You're right," the Giant says.

The Giant is afraid to look at her, and Jody can tell he has no idea how beautiful he is. She feels as though she has trapped a firefly in a mason jar, and she does not want to take the top off the jar.

"Well?" Jody says.

"Well?" the Giant says, puzzled.

"Are you coming upstairs or not?" Jody says.

The Giant draws back. A blue rope of veins stands out along his neck. Jody knows she is feeling all the wrong things. She should be scared, at the very least feel as if she's courting danger. She wonders if the power of his wanting her has made her temporarily insane. She leans forward, stepping on the hem of her nightgown.

"Hurry," she tells him.

The Giant follows her up the stairs. He is afraid to ask questions. He has lost the ability to speak. The cats run after them, until Jody shoos them away. He sees her bed and is paralyzed. He stays in the center of the room, the only place where he can stand up straight, until Jody tells him it's all right for him to sit on her bed. It is just before dawn and yellow lines cut through the sky, but the bedroom is dark. Jody takes off her sweater and sits on a wooden chair. She pulls her nightgown over her head. For a second she's afraid

that making love with him may be impossible, he may be too
big. But she goes and sits down next to him. She can feel the
Giant shivering and she expects him to be too shy to look at
her, but when she turns to him he's staring at her.

"What's your name?" Jody says.

The Giant laughs.

"What's so funny?" Jody asks, vaguely hurt by his laughter.

"It's a strange time to ask me my name," the Giant says.

Just to make certain that he's real, Jody touches his cheek,
then moves her fingers down his neck until she reaches the
first button of his shirt.

"Eddie," the Giant says.

His name suddenly sounds like the oddest word in the
world; it's as though he's never heard it before. He cannot
believe he has the nerve to touch her; he holds her so that his
hands fit over her ribs. Jody unbuttons his shirt and presses
her breasts against him. The Giant makes a noise that he has
never heard come from inside himself before. Once he starts
to kiss her, he doesn't know if he can stop. Jody lies back and
the Giant leans next to her. He is thinking too much and not
at all. He is afraid to put his workboots on her clean sheets.
He is afraid he will hurt her. He has never been with a woman
before and he knows she'll be able to tell.

The Giant moves away from Jody. He sits up in the dark.

"What?" Jody whispers. She sounds frightened and out of
breath. She props herself up on her elbows.

The Giant takes off his sweater and his shirt, then bends

down and unlaces his boots. He pulls his boots off, then stands and finishes undressing. When he folds his clothes and puts them on the chair his hands are shaking. He lies down next to Jody and pulls her close. At least, he thinks, she cannot see him in the dark.

When Jody comes downstairs, Elizabeth Renny is in the kitchen making coffee. The painted egg is still in the saucer on the table, and Jody picks it up and holds it in the palm of her hand. Elizabeth Renny squints, but to her the egg looks like a blue globe, just another Christmas ornament. Jody returns the egg to the saucer, and as Elizabeth Renny gets herself a cup of coffee, she notices that Jody smells like soap and straw.

Upstairs, the Giant opens the bedroom window, climbs out on the ledge, then drops to the ground soundlessly. There is ice on the telephone wires. Ice is coating all the trees. It is still early enough so that no one notices a giant running down the road, grinning like a madman, absolutely unaware that this is the coldest Christmas in fifty years.

When you call your mother in Delray Beach on a snowy Wednesday morning the first thing she tells you is that it's eighty-five degrees and that her husband is out picking oranges from their tree at this very moment. You have waited to call until your son and husband are out of the house because you are certain this will be a difficult conversation. "Mom," you say when you can get a word in, "there's something wrong with me."

*There is silence on the other end of the wire. You can prac-
tically feel the Florida heat.*

*"I'm having real problems going out of the house," you
will tell her.*

*Your mother will laugh so hard that at first you will think
she is choking. "My God," she will finally say. "I thought
you were going to tell me you had cancer. You can't go out
of the house? Honey, in Florida people don't go out of the
house the entire summer long, and nobody thinks anything
of it. It's so hot the sun would fry you like an egg."*

*You could get out of it now and talk about the weather
but you have come this far. You tell her the rest. You can't
drive, you can't be alone, you have strange physical symptoms: sweating hands, a racing heart, a knot in your stomach
that feels like a tumor. The idea of a plane ride makes you
physically ill. You cannot go to a supermarket or a movie
theater without your husband, and even then you have to sit
in an aisle seat in case you cannot control the urge to escape.
You have avoided your friends so often, making up lame excuses, that they no longer phone you. You can tell by a smack-
ing sound that your mother is pursing her lips. "When did all
this come on?" she will say. If you tell her right after your
last visit with your father, she will launch into a tirade about
how he tried with all his might to ruin her life. "After I was
on an airplane," you tell her. "Maybe I'm crazy," you'll say,
expecting her to insist that you're not. She will murmur
"Hmm," thinking it over. You will tell her that you are terrified your son will discover there's something wrong with*

you. When your mother asks if you're hiding it from him, you'll admit that you are. "Then he'll never know," your mother will say. "You never did."

You will sit down then. You will consider hanging up the phone.

"What?" you will say, and your mother will say. "You heard me." Now she will tell you that after her divorce she didn't go out of the house for two months. For nearly a year afterward she ordered deliveries from the market over the phone, and your best friend's parents drove you anyplace you had to go. At the time you had assumed your mother was busy, but now that you think of it, you're not sure doing what. Your mother tells you that her terror of leaving the house lasted almost three years, and then one day she got into her car, drove to the corner, and just kept going.

"Don't ask me how it started or how it stopped," your mother will say. If she intends for this to be comforting, it isn't. This is awful news, an illness that may be hereditary, and more than ever you fear you'll contaminate your own child. Your mother surprises you by asking if you want her to fly up and visit. You tell her that you have to get over this by yourself, meaning not with her. You begin to wonder what else she has hidden from you and if as a child you in fact knew more than you do now. Before you get off the phone your mother will tell you that you are definitely not going insane. "Yeah, sure," you will say, in that same sullen voice you used with her when you were a teenager. Your mother will tell you that she has recently watched a TV talk show

about your disorder. "What you've got is panic attacks," she will say, quietly, so you know that her husband has come into the kitchen with his just-picked oranges. Your mother will not let you hang up until you promise to call a hospital or a clinic, and you promise, but it will be a week before you actually make the call.

They will refer you to their expert, who will not understand a word you're saying at first because your voice will break. As soon as you tell him you can't leave your house alone he will begin a litany of your symptoms. He will know every-thing about you and you have said less than four sentences to him. Sweaty palms, he will say. Rubbery legs, a racing heart, a barrier you can't cross. He insists that this is not mental illness. When he tells you that you have agoraphobia you will be elated to find a name for what's wrong with you. Of course you didn't believe your mother, but now a total stranger has told you you're not insane. Since you are too far away to join the therapist's treatment program, he will refer you to a mail-order course and a reading list. He will tell you that you can modify your behavior, that you can fight this and win. When he asks if you have a safe person, you don't understand, and your son immediately comes to mind. You think of him asleep in bed, how safe he must feel, surrounded by stuffed animals, content to know you and your husband are right down the hall. When the therapist explains that a safe person is someone you can rely on, someone in whose presence you can manage things you can't do alone or with anyone else, you realize that your safe person is your hus-

band. This realization jolts you. No matter what you think of him, in your heart of hearts you trust him more than anyone else on earth.

Later, when your husband comes home, you will wrap your arms around him so tightly he will be momentarily afraid that some tragedy has happened while he was gone. You will tell him there is a cure for what you have, you will plan all the things you can't do now but will as soon as you're cured. You will want him all that evening, and when your son goes to bed, you will make love to your husband and weep when it is through. All that week you will wait for the postman's truck. You will sit by the window. You will watch the snow, alternately feeling terror and hope. When the postman's truck appears you realize that you will have to wait until your husband gets home for him to bring in the box that is addressed to you.

Sitting in the shed with the kerosene heater turned on high, Andre is supposed to be working on a Ducati, a bike he wanted so much he met its inflated price. Instead, he's reading one of the books on Vonny's reading list that he picked up for her at the library. It's a book about panic attacks, and the truth is, he's feeling vaguely panicked himself. They have already gone over several of the chapters in Vonny's behavior modification program and it's clear there is no magic prescription. Vonny has to practice, setting up a series of small goals for herself, using techniques such as focusing and relaxation, something Andre doesn't even believe in. He's got the urge for a beer, but he doesn't want to go into the house just yet. He can tell this phobia program is going to be a pain in the ass. It would be easier just to go to the market or pick Simon up at school than to go through all this modifying with Vonny. He's been reading everything he can get his hands on and he still doesn't understand why Vonny can't just climb behind the wheel and drive somewhere. And, when he allows himself to admit this, he's not a hundred percent certain he wants her to.

Since her panic attacks began, Vonny has been entirely dependent on him. Andre understands this much: he is her only safe person. Once a phobic can go places with a new safe person, the cycle of dependency will begin to break down. Andre feels a weird hot jealousy when he tries to imagine who that other safe person might be. He feels betrayed already. He switches off the heater, zips his jacket, and carries the books to the house. As he lights the stove to heat some coffee, he can hear Vonny's relaxation tape droning in the living room. Andre opens the cabinet looking for sugar and can't find the sugar bowl. He pours a cup of hot coffee, tosses the grounds in the trash, then tears open the refrigerator. There is no milk. He slams the door shut, then drinks his coffee standing up, at the counter. Vonny turns off her tape recorder and comes into the kitchen. Andre isn't certain if he's imagining things, or if she looks scared right here in her own kitchen. They're supposed to drop Simon off at a school friend's house, then go out so Vonny can practice her driving. Her goal is the parking lot before the cliffs at Gay Head. Andre would rather stay home, take a shower, and watch TV.

"Ready?" Andre says to Vonny.

"I guess," Vonny says. "Ready as I'll ever be." Which means, Andre knows, that she's terrified. After two weeks of practice, Vonny can once again go to the supermarket, as long as Andre is waiting outside the door. Twice she has dropped off boxes of pottery, but her heart was pounding so hard afterward she has refused to go back to Edgartown. Now, while other people are fixing their dinners, they will be driving back and forth, measuring Vonny's symptoms each time to see if they're lessening.

"Simon," Vonny calls as she gets her coat and his jacket from hooks near the door. Her face is flushed, with excitement or fear Andre can't tell, Simon is to have dinner at his friend Tara's and Vonny has made turkey sandwiches that she and Andre will eat in the truck during a break. Vonny goes to the foot of the stairs. "Simon!" she calls.

Up in his room, Simon is reading a book he knows by heart to Dora, the rabbit. He has recently asked Andre to make a sign for his room on which is printed DO NOT DISTURB.

"All right!" Simon calls to his mother.

He continues to read to the rabbit.

Vonny wonders if everyone is conspiring against her to keep her from driving. She goes into the kitchen but doesn't sit down for fear she won't get up again. She is, she knows, well practiced at avoidance.

"Can't you do something?" Vonny asks Andre.

Andre goes to the kitchen doorway and yells, "I'm going to count to three."

Simon slams his book shut, gives his rabbit an apologetic look, then storms downstairs.

"I just wanted to be alone," Simon says as he takes the jacket and backpack Vonny hands him.

It amazes Vonny that her five-year-old wants exactly what she is most afraid of. If there was ever a time when she wanted to be alone, she can no longer remember it. She imagines that she does not exist without another person there to perceive her. She imagines her skin is dust, her bones a puzzle that needs expert hands to piece together.

"Look, we don't have to go," Vonny says.

"Will you guys make up your minds?" Simon says, clearly disgusted.

Andre puts a hand on Simon's back and guides him to the door.

"Is Mom coming or not?" Simon asks him.

Vonny grabs the bag of sandwiches, then goes to the door and puts an arm around Simon. He is surprisingly solid when she pulls him close. As they walk outside, Simon forgets himself and holds her hand. They listen to the radio on the way to Tara's. Vonny kisses Simon good-bye, then watches as Andre walks him up to a yellow house with green shutters. When the door opens, Tara's mother waves at Vonny, but Simon goes inside without looking back. Vonny knows that children have to declare their independence. She watches him run into the house, and the last she sees of him is his blue nylon backpack. It's cold in the truck, and Vonny feels a chill. Andre gets back in and slams the door shut. Vonny clears her throat.

"I'm supposed to drive," she tells him.

"Right," Andre says.

He gets out and Vonny slides over behind the wheel. Andre is not at all comfortable at the prospect of having someone who panics drive him around. He fumbles with the radio, looking for a good station. Vonny puts the truck in gear and steps on the gas. She has not driven for almost five months and she doesn't remember the clutch being so stiff, the steering so loose. Tonight, with Andre beside her, the force field shouldn't be activated, but Vonny can feel a wave of anticipatory panic just beneath her chest. She knows she's supposed to breathe deeply, even put her hand on her belly to make certain it rises as she inhales. She does this at a stop sign and feels somewhat better.

After Chilmark center the road is uphill. To the right there are marshes flooded with water, and beyond, the harbor at Menemsha. Tall reeds make it impossible to tell where you could walk and where you would sink like a stone.

Vonny makes a left turn onto the less traveled Moshup's Trail, a road that leads along the ocean. She begins to feel something in the pit of her stomach. A wire being pulled tight. The Indians named this road after a legendary giant who wanted to go beyond Gay Head to a place called Noman's Island. At low tide he dropped huge boulders into the ocean, but then, they say, he grew tired. He could not bring himself to leave his island. The end of the earth, Vonny thinks. The last rock before an ocean with no floor. When the panic rises again, this time into her throat, she pulls over to the side of

the road, just as she's read she's supposed to do, waiting for
her panic to subside before she tries again instead of simply
giving up.

Andre's watching her, but he doesn't say anything. He
reaches down for the paper bag with their supper, takes out
a sandwich and begins to unwrap it.

"Do you have to do that?" Vonny says.

"If I want to eat I do," Andre says.

Vonny switches off the radio and listens instead to the wind
and the crackling sound of plastic wrap. The sky has grown
dark. She is thirty-four years old. She is afraid of an empty
road.

"Get out," Vonny says suddenly.

Andre stops unwrapping the sandwich.

"Correct me if I'm wrong," Andre says. "But aren't you
the one who double-wrapped the goddamned sandwiches?"

"Get out," Vonny says.

"Don't be so nervous," Andre tells her. "I'm not letting
you drive if you're nervous."

Vonny laughs meanly. "It's not up to you to let me do
anything."

"I didn't mean it that way," Andre says.

"Okay," Vonny says, sounding very calm. "You can
drive."

Andre tosses his sandwich into the bag, gets out, slams the
door tightly, then walks behind the truck. Vonny can feel the
wave building inside her. It is more like fury than terror. She
will not live this way. She will not count seconds, miles, steps.

If the force field kills her, let it. Let Andre raise Simon, let him marry again, someone younger, someone who is not afraid of the dark. A stewardess. A race-car driver. A circus acrobat.

Vonny can see Andre in the rearview mirror as he walks around the truck. He is a streak of black, the shadow who covers her shadow. Her leg, which is so weak, now does the most amazing thing. It moves, and slams down hard on the gas. Before Andre can reach for the door handle, Vonny throws the truck in gear and takes off. She heads toward the horizon. The panic rises higher, into her brain. She looks briefly in her rearview mirror and sees Andre standing there. The bag holding their dinner lurches and everything spills on the floor. Cigarettes fly off the dashboard like shrapnel. When she checks the speedometer and sees she's doing sixty-five she feels a rush of excitement, or terror—she can no longer distinguish the symptoms. Her heart is pounding and her hands are sweating, but she feels deliciously light-headed. She knows that this is how it can be. Somewhere in her throat Vonny makes guttural noises, as though she were moving the car by sheer will. She is alone in the world and she loves it. She has no fear of getting lost because there is nothing to get lost from. When she hits the force field, Vonny slams on her brakes. As her panic starts to take over she tells herself there is nothing to be afraid of. She has driven a quarter of a mile on a winter evening and left her husband behind. She makes a U-turn.

When she pulls up beside him, Andre throws open the

door, reaches in, and takes the keys out of the ignition. Vonny's eyes are shining. She won't let go of the wheel.

"Are you crazy?" Andre shouts. He pulls her out of the truck. He walks away, then turns back to her. "Don't ever do that to me again," he says. His voice sounds thick. "Are you listening to me?" he asks.

Vonny puts her head back and strains to see the sky. Tomorrow she will begin slowly, getting into the truck and just sitting there, then backing down the driveway. She has been advised to set small goals and she understands now that it may be weeks before she can make the turn out of her own driveway. She will keep rolls of Life Savers in her coat pockets; she'll make certain to have a map and a full tank of gas. The next time she comes to this stretch of road it will be early in the morning, and she'll be ready.

Chapter Seven

SPEAKING TO STRANGERS

ALL spring Elizabeth Renny watches her neighbor drive up and down in her driveway. The spinning of tires in the mud and gravel creates a comforting hum as Elizabeth Renny hangs out sheets on the clothesline, fills the bird feeders with seed, attacks the unruly lilacs, already turning blue, with a hedge clipper. Occasionally, Elizabeth Renny waves, but mostly she ignores her neighbor. There is no polite way to ask Vonny what on earth she's doing other than making deep ruts in the driveway and wasting a lot of gas.

Elizabeth Renny has recently done something awful. She has changed her will and left everything to Jody. Of course everything is not all that much: a small savings account, her personal effects, and whatever the sale of her house may bring. Her lawyer arrived at the appointed time but before he allowed her to sign the papers he asked, "Are you certain you want to do this?" three times. Laura had been the beneficiary, with the understanding that upon her death the three grand-children would share whatever might be left. Elizabeth Renny agrees with her lawyer, there is nothing fair about this new will. She has decided that she has the right to do the wrong thing. It is, after all, her money, her house, her death.

She has not mentioned any of this to her daughter or to Jody and she plans to keep it this way. Revising her will has changed something inside her. She no longer believes she can cheat death by deciding the hour and manner herself. She wants to see how Jody turns out, and now, when it is almost too late, Elizabeth Renny wants to wake up in the mornings. She is an old woman who may soon be completely blind. And she wants her life. She can feel everything inside her slowing down. It's an odd feeling, as if time had shifted. She knows she is dying, and it seems a ridiculous death, caused not by accident or disease but by this slowing down. She has the childish fear that when she no longer exists nothing around her will either. Birds, trees, sky, all of it will evaporate at the hour of her death. She has never thought much of herself and now here she is, convinced the world is contained within her.

She decides to get her house in order. She hires a junk man to clear out her cellar and throws out old beads and chipped saucers. For a week Jody spends every day raking the yard, and Elizabeth Renny still is not satisfied. Although a wood-pecker is living in the pine, she wants the half-dead tree cut down before it falls on her house. She wants this place to be worth something when it's sold. She walks over to the idling truck and surprises Vonny, who quickly shifts into neutral and grabs the emergency brake.

"I didn't even hear you," Vonny says.

"I guess you know every inch of this driveway by now," Elizabeth Renny says, giving her neighbor the opportunity to explain what she's been doing all these weeks.

Vonny laughs, explains nothing, and takes a cigarette from the pack on the dashboard.

"I'd like to have the pine tree cut down this year," Elizabeth Renny says. "Unless you're opposed."

"Not at all," Vonny says.

"Good," Elizabeth Renny says, and then, purely out of politeness she adds, "Come and have tea with me sometime."

"I couldn't," Vonny says quickly, feeling her panic level rise. She has not yet been in anyone else's house without her safe person.

"Well, of course," Mrs. Renny says. "You're busy."

As Mrs. Renny slowly walks back across the lawn, Vonny has the urge to run after her. She desperately wants to be able to go to her neighbor's house for a cup of tea. Why is she so terrified that she will have an attack in front of the old lady? How can she be so certain that the force field will rise up like an iron gate if she makes one move to follow her neighbor? She feels like a child, unable to take care of herself. Though she takes care of Simon she is only pretending to be an adult. She is the one who needs someone to hold her hand. She knows the fury children feel when they need a parent desperately, and it's a bitter taste in her mouth.

At night Vonny dreams she is a child again. She is in her own backyard, searching for treasure. Though the sky is dark, a black metal lantern beside her casts its yellow light. She digs effortlessly in the dirt, then gets down on her hands and knees. When she looks into the hole she sees her grandmother's ruby ring. It does not surprise her in the least to discover that the ring is worn on a hand rising up through the earth. The hand is white. It wants her.

Vonny is sweating when she wakes up. Her T-shirt and underpants stick to her body. When Andre wakes, an hour later, Vonny is at the window, studying the distance between their house and the house next door.

"You okay?" Andre says.

Vonny nods. The last time she looked at the lilacs there were only buds. Suddenly, there are leaves.

"Sure," Vonny says.

Andre gets out of bed, pulls on a pair of jeans, then goes to stand behind her. In the past month Andre has felt closer to Vonny. He knows that when he works at the garage in the morning, she is waiting for him. Sometimes when he pulls down the driveway he sees her dart away from the window. Her image is distorted through the glass, ghostly and comforting at the same time. Awful, but this has cured him of Jody. And, he can tell, Jody has been cured as well. Now when she sees him she calls out, "Hey, Andre!" then smiles, as though she's been foolish.

Andre and Vonny go back to bed and make love, quickly, in case Simon wakes. Vonny finds herself listening to the sound of a plane somewhere overhead. She is already thinking about the moment when the truck makes the turn out of the driveway. When that moment comes, Vonny is at the back door, waving. Nelson has followed the truck to the road, and when he returns, Vonny lets him inside and wipes his paws with a towel. It is the last week in May and still muddy so Vonny pulls on high boots. She slips a black sweater over her head, then puts on a raincoat and ties the belt. Standing by the door she smokes a cigarette, then she sits down at the table and listens to house noises. A loose shutter slaps against some wooden shingles. Water flows through metal pipes. Nelson clicks across the floor, puts his head on her knee, and softly whines. She strokes his head and tells him he's a good boy.

Vonny thinks of her dream, then remembers standing in the backyard with her father while he pointed out Sirius. Her father told her sailors used to chart their course by the red star, but that somehow the star had turned white as any other. It astonished her to learn that a star could change color. She feels a surge of loss, as though she'd just been notified of her father's death. She reaches in her pockets and makes sure she has everything she needs: a roll of Life Savers, cigarettes, matches, her keys. She snaps on Nelson's leash and walks to the back door. It smells wet outside. As soon as Vonny pushes open the door Nelson strains at his leash. He has picked up the scent of the tomcat who is lurking in the yard. Using Nelson for protection is no good, Vonny can see that. She takes off his leash and locks him in the house. She stands on the porch and eats two wild-cherry Life Savers. She has the urge to run all the way and get it over with, but she knows she's supposed to take it slow—stop and wait till she can try again—if she has to.

THE wood railings of the porch are rickety and need to be replaced. As she walks down the steps her throat tightens. She tells herself she alone has created the force field, she alone can get rid of it. She begins to walk across the yard. Halfway to her neighbor's house, Vonny's panic level lurches and begins to rise for no reason at all. Level one is the beginning stage—sweaty hands and a fluttering stomach. Ten is an all-out attack. She is already at a five without knowing why. The stimulus for her attacks can be outrageously trivial. There may have been the caw of a crow. A car somewhere down the road may have sped by a little too fast. Her level rises quickly. She has an overwhelming desire to run. She is a fox who will chew her foot off in order to escape from a trap. She leans against the pine tree and decides to count to fifty. If she still has to run after that, she will. She counts too fast. She can smell the spicy pine. Her raincoat is too warm. She feels in her pockets and counts the keys on her key ring. She still has the key to her mother's house in Florida. In her mother's garden there is ginger, sage, and lemon mint. There is an orange tree, and a rock garden filled with succulents.

She realizes that she has counted to a hundred. The only symptom she has left is a burning in her stomach. Since she is just as close to Mrs. Renny's house as she is to her own, she slowly walks forward. She will not think about the fact that eventually she will have to walk home. If necessary she will call the police to escort her. She knocks on the door two times. She does not know what she will do if Mrs. Renny is not home. She begins to count again and reaches twenty before Elizabeth Renny comes to the door. Mrs. Renny blinks in the sudden light.

"I can't stay," Vonny says. She tightens the belt of her raincoat.

"That's fine," Elizabeth Renny says. She is extremely confused. She decides they must have made an appointment she has forgotten.

"I may not be able to stay," Vonny amends.

While Mrs. Renny puts up water for tea, Vonny looks out the window to gauge how close her house is. Mrs. Renny asks what sort of tea she wants. Vonny says English breakfast, but winds up with oolong. Mrs. Renny serves pound cake, not homemade, but good all the same.

"Would you like to take that raincoat off?" Mrs. Renny asks.

"Oh, no," Vonny says. She takes a bite of cake. "There's something wrong with me," she says, and then quickly shuts up, horrified by her own words.

Vonny's mail-order course suggests that phobics tell those around them what is wrong. No one will slam the door shut in her face, no one will stare at her as though she were insane. And, this is the part that troubles Vonny, if they do they aren't worth much.

"Then by all means keep it on," Elizabeth Renny says, imagining Vonny must have some sort of skin disease.

"I have panic attacks," Vonny says in a voice that is certainly her own. "I can't go anywhere without Andre."

Elizabeth Renny, who was raised to believe troubles should be kept to oneself, slices more cake. Vonny cannot seem to stop talking.

"I can't believe this has happened to me," Vonny says. "At my age."

Elizabeth Renny, who would give anything to be Vonny's age, feels more confused than ever.

"You're afraid to leave your house?"

Vonny nods, then gets up and clears the table. Andre will not be home from Vineyard Haven for perhaps another hour. Her house looks a little farther away.

"But you're here," Elizabeth Renny says, puzzled.

"Well, yes," Vonny says. The walk over here, which seemed so monumental, now seems an insignificant accomplishment. "I'm supposed to practice and try to go a little farther every day."

Elizabeth Renny can tell this is serious. One minute Vonny looks just fine and the next her face seems to crumble. Elizabeth is suddenly reminded that she can walk down that road anytime she wants to. There are better things to be afraid of than a country road bordered with scrub pine and oaks.

"Walk with me down the road," Elizabeth Renny says.

Vonny turns to her. Her back presses up against the sink so that a wet line forms on her raincoat.

"I'm very slow," Elizabeth Renny warns Vonny. "I'm definitely not a jogger."

"I can't," Vonny says.

Mrs. Renny gets up and takes a thin sweater draped on the back of her chair.

"Seriously," Vonny says, "I can't."

Mrs. Renny takes her house key from a dish on the counter.

"I may not get any farther than my own house," Vonny says.

"I don't know why I bother to lock the door," Elizabeth Renny says.

Vonny walks out onto the porch and waits for Mrs. Renny. It takes Elizabeth Renny a long time to fit the key in the lock and she's afraid Vonny will know there's something wrong with her eyes, but when she turns Vonny is practicing her deep breathing.

When they set off they walk slowly, their feet sinking into the mud as they cross the lawn. They walk past Vonny's house and down the driveway.

"What if I have to run?" Vonny says.

"What a wonderful thing," Elizabeth Renny says, "to be able to run."

Mrs. Renny has to stop three times, and each time she does Vonny focuses on a small patch of the road, counting ants and stones. She knows concentrating on something outside herself is supposed to keep her in the present and prevent her from imagining, and possibly triggering, a panic attack. If she has an attack she knows the first thing to go will be her legs. Who will carry her home? Who will save her?

"Can you see the magnolia from here?" Elizabeth Renny asks.

Vonny realizes that they are almost to the Freeds'. Their house is never opened before Memorial Day, so the Freeds never get to see the tree at its peak. Windows are boarded up with shutters, nailed closed in case of storms. The porch swing has been taken down and stored in the garage.

"Yes," Vonny says, "I can see the tree."

It's filled with purple-and-white flowers. Soon, Elizabeth Renny can see a blur of violet and white, like clouds spread out in front of her on the road. She used to wait for her husband right here to come home from work on summer evenings. She used to hold her daughter by the hand. When a car passes by, Vonny guides Mrs. Renny toward the side of the road. Vonny's raincoat flares out behind her as she helps Mrs. Renny over the ruts. They are up to their ankles in mud, but they have a perfect view of the magnolia here.

It is a beautiful day and much warmer than anyone expected. Andre has all the windows in the truck rolled down when he reaches the bend in the road just before the Freeds' property. He thinks he must be dreaming when he sees Vonny and Mrs. Renny standing by the side of the road. How is it possible for Vonny to be so far from home without him? Andre steps on the brakes and lets the truck idle. It takes a while before he realizes that Mrs. Renny has just become another safe person. He takes a deep breath. He knows he should be glad. He watches them, unnoticed, but not so very far away from the saucer-shaped flowers that by Memorial Day will have scattered across the unmowed lawn.

THEY never talk about the future. Sometimes, when they're together, they get up to lock the doors or pull down the window shades at the exact same time, as though they could somehow protect themselves. There is no protection. Jody knows the reason why she is always the one to come to his house, she knows why they will never go to a movie together, and why they will never have friends. She has seen the way people who stop at the farmstand peer down into the hollow. She has done it herself.

Falling in love with the Giant is like falling into a pool of water. The world turns inside out and dissolves. When they are in his house, Jody truly forgets what he is. The rooms are small enough to make anyone seem clumsy, and the two of them spend a great deal of time in bed, where it is possible to forget anything. She remembers how impossible their future is at unexpected times: when her metal gym locker at school slams shut; when she takes blue sheets out of his closet; when she kisses her grandmother good-bye and runs down the road to the place where he is waiting for her, hidden in the dark.

She cannot have friends anymore. She cannot tell Garland who it is she loves and she cannot lie to her, so Jody avoids her completely. It is even harder not to talk to Vonny, although now when Vonny comes to visit it's to see Jody's grandmother. Vonny and Elizabeth Renny go for walks several times a week. Once while Vonny waited for Mrs. Renny she studied Jody carefully, then announced, "You're in love."

"Uh uh," Jody said.

"Yes, you are," Vonny said. "You look like you're all lit up."

"I'm on a diet," Jody said. "Maybe that's it."

Vonny lowered her voice. "You're not pregnant, are you?"

"God, you sound like my mother," Jody said.

"Oh," Vonny said, wounded.

"I'm on the Pill, all right?"

"That's your business," Vonny said. "Forget I asked."

"Look," Jody had said, "you don't have anything to worry about anymore."

"What was I supposed to be worrying about before?" Vonny asked.

They could hear Elizabeth Renny in the parlor as she closed a bureau drawer.

"Nothing," Jody said, meaning Andre.

"I see," Vonny said.

Could it be that they never had anything in common other than loving the same person? Vonny is no longer reminded of the girl she used to be when she looks at Jody. She sees another woman. One she hardly knows.

Before she left, Vonny gave Jody a quick hug. "Don't be a stranger," she said.

"Sure," Jody agreed, but they both knew that was what she had become.

The one person Jody can discuss the Giant with is Simon. At first she avoided him, but every time Simon saw her he ran across the lawn. He wants to know everything. It amazes Jody that someone as small as Simon can be so precise. What size shoe does the Giant wear? Is he tall enough to reach the sky? Exactly how tall was he when he was five years old? Jody is not certain if Simon really believes there is a giant or if he thinks they share the same dream. She tells him the Giant was already as tall as full-grown man by the time he was ten. She tells him the Giant can reach through the clouds. It gives Jody an odd sort of comfort to talk about the Giant, even when she's turning him into a story. Every now and then she tells Simon a bit of the truth. Chickens in the Giant's yard are red; rows of lettuce and peas have already begun to sprout in his garden; his house, which he always paints gray, is on South Road, but hidden from view by the tilt of the land, by locust trees whose leaves are shaped like feathers.

All that spring Jody sleeps in the Giant's bed whenever she can. She leaves her grandmother's house on Friday night and doesn't return until Monday morning. They do not try to guess what will happen to them. They do not ask each other how long this can last. During the last week of school, Jody cannot talk above a whisper. Her hair becomes threaded with knots. She hides her cap and gown up in the storage attic. Graduation day is marked on her calendar as the last day of her life. She will be propelled into some kind of future. What she feels for him becoming a fevered recollection. She keeps the end of the term secret, hoping he won't notice her anguish.

Finally, she tells the Giant she won't be able to see him on the weekend.

He doesn't ask why.

"Aren't you afraid I'll be seeing someone else?" Jody says. "Maybe I'll never come back."

"I can't force you to," the Giant says.

"Yes, you can," Jody says, "if you really cared."

The Giant sits up in bed, facing away from her. Jody looks at his back and knows she has hurt him. She is horrible. She is a beast. She has never seen anything beautiful before seeing him.

"It's graduation," she says. "My family's coming."

"I wish I could be there," the Giant says.

"You won't be missing a thing," Jody says.

LAURA and Jody's brothers arrive at the house late Friday night. Jody's father and his girlfriend, Robin, are staying at the Kelly House in Edgartown. Laura knows this and the more she tries to hide how upset she is, the more it shows. She has brought two large suitcases with her, with eight changes of clothes. She has had her hair frosted, and Jody doesn't risk telling her that if anything the blond streaks make her look older. Just Jody's luck, graduation will be the first time her mother meets her father's girlfriend, who is twenty-eight years old.

As soon as Laura walks into the house Jody sees that her mother's eyes dart around too quickly. Laura hands her a box

wrapped with rose-colored paper. Inside is a graduation present, a dress bought in Boston. Jody thanks her mother, and
when Laura shrugs Jody can tell her mother is on the edge of
something. Mark and Keith have picked up on her tension
and are making things worse. They bicker nonstop and manage to do the exact opposite of everything they're told. Jody
has made pot roast for dinner, but nobody eats.

"I refuse to say one bad thing about your father," Laura
says to her children.

"A fine idea," Elizabeth Renny says.

"That bastard," Laura says as soon as the boys have gone
upstairs.

Laura bends her head and tears roll onto her plate.

"Don't cry, Mom," Jody says.

"I'm not," Laura snaps.

Jody looks across the table at her grandmother.

"Let's hope she has an affair with a man twenty years
younger than Glenn," Elizabeth Renny says.

Laura laughs, and her voice breaks. "You know he'll blame
me for the fact that Jody's not going to college."

The closest Jody can get to disappearing is to carry the
plates to the counter. She scrapes them clean and piles them
up on top of each other.

"You can't stay here forever," Laura tells her.

"Not everyone is meant to go to college," Elizabeth Renny
says.

"Oh, sure," Laura says. "You'd just as soon she stay here.
Just like you wanted me to stay without ever caring what it
was I wanted."

They both know this isn't true, but Elizabeth Renny wonders if it's her fault that Glenn is sleeping with a twenty-eight-year-old girl.

"I'm sorry," Laura says.

For the rest of the evening they act as though nothing is wrong. But when Jody goes upstairs, it is all she can do not to climb out her window and run to the Giant's house. She forces herself to get undressed and put on her nightgown, then goes to brush her teeth. When she pushes open the bathroom door she sees her younger brother Keith crouched over the toilet, vomiting. Jody goes over and puts a hand on his back. She can feel him shudder through his thin pajamas as he strains, then vomits again. She keeps one hand on his back as he stands and flushes the toilet.

"I must have eaten something weird," Keith says, but Jody knows he has eaten nothing at all.

"Mom's driving you crazy," Jody says. It seems odd to her that they should have the same parents.

"Yeah," Keith says. Then he adds, defensively, "She's okay."

Because he's forgotten his own, Jody lends him her toothpaste and toothbrush.

"Do you want to sleep in my room?" Jody asks. She knows from babysitting for Simon, it is sometimes easier for kids to fall asleep when you pretend to sleep with them. But Keith is eleven and already past those sorts of tricks. His arms are too long for his body. One day he will be taller than his father. He shakes his head no, but Jody can tell that the dark hallway that leads to the attic spooks him.

"I left my gown in there," Jody tells him.

She knows he's relieved that she leads the way down the hall. Their footsteps echo on the wood. The door has been painted so often, Jody has to push hard to get it to open. Inside, their brother Mark sleeps heavily, his face pressed against the dust surrounding his sleeping bag. Jody gets her graduation gown. It sways on the wooden hanger. She fiddles with the plastic protecting the gown until Keith has slipped into his sleeping bag. He closes his eyes so tightly lines fan out from his eyelids.

"Good night," Jody whispers, but Keith pretends to be asleep.

In her own room, Jody hangs the gown in her closet, then closes the door. She sits down in front of her mirror without turning on the light. She will never dye her hair blond or try to look younger than she is. She will never be fast asleep while someone she loves is frightened and sick or live with a man she doesn't love anymore just because she's afraid of living alone. Jody gets into her bed wishing she could tell Laura everything and knowing she won't, though she's not certain whether she's protecting her mother or herself.

At a little before nine, Jody puts on the pink-and-white sleeveless dress her mother has bought for her. Along the hem there is a line of white lace, meant to show. Laura makes her two boys comb their hair with water. She rushes them through breakfast, but then they all have to wait for Elizabeth Renny to finish getting dressed, and while they're waiting skirts and slacks wrinkle and collect cat hairs.

"Shit," Laura says as she studies herself in a mirror.

"Mother," Jody says.

"What?" Laura says. "I'm allowed to curse. I'm a grownup."

She tells Jody to turn around and fixes her hair, pinning up strands that have fallen from the tortoiseshell combs. Jody's brothers have been sent out to wait in the car. It's a perfect June day, not one cloud in the sky. Elizabeth Renny struggles with her zipper, then holds on to the overstuffed arm of the couch as she slides her feet into her shoes. She feels light-headed and proud of Jody but she's worried about whether she'll last through graduation and manage to get to the restaurant where they're all to have lunch.

"All ready?" Jody says to her grandmother, surprising her by coming up on her right side.

Elizabeth Renny takes Jody's arm and walks outside with her. Jody helps her into the car, then gets into the back with her brothers. The box with her cap and gown rests on the floor beside her feet. Laura drives a little too fast to the high school. Cars are parked all along the Edgartown-Vineyard Haven Road. The air buzzes with the hum of the P.A. system, now being tested. Jody's brothers are wearing suits and white shirts and, worst of all, ties. They shift uncomfortably as Laura pulls up and parks.

"Help, I'm being strangled!" Jody's brother Mark says, holding his tie straight up in the air and letting his tongue dangle out of his mouth.

Keith laughs nervously.

Once they're all out of the car, Jody wants to get away from them as quickly as she can.

"I'll meet you afterward," she says.

Laura comes around and straightens her collar. "Whatever happens," she whispers, "don't make me sit next to your father at lunch."

Jody nods and walks across the parking lot. The graduates have all flocked together outside the gym. Boys let their black capes swirl around them as they shake hands and sneak cigarettes. Garland waves Jody over and helps pin on her cap.

"Can you believe we made it?" Garland says. "Free at last."

Jody feels awful about avoiding Garland for so long. She hugs her and pins Garland's cap over her blond braids. She wants to tell Garland she's in love, but in broad daylight, here behind the gym, the word *giant* itself seems ridiculous. Hers is a secret that belongs to the night, to empty roads, to a bed pushed up against the wall.

The graduates are told to form two straight lines.

"Oh, my God," Garland whispers. "This is it."

When the band begins to play, Jody feels a lump in her throat. She follows right behind Garland. They cross the small street, file past the tennis courts and across the field. When it's Jody's turn to go up onto the wooden platform the sun beats down on her black gown. As she gets her diploma and shakes the principal's hand there's some scattered applause in the audience. Jody walks along the aisle and sits between Garland and a boy she knows from biology. Her brothers whistle and call out her name and Jody turns, scans the audience till she finds them, then waves. She sees her grandmother looking straight ahead, directly into the sun, and her mother, sitting on the edge of her chair, shielding her eyes with the graduation program. Jody looks toward the back row and finally spots her father, wearing a beige suit and sunglasses. Jody supposes that the woman next to him is Robin. They both look tan, as though, for them, summer had begun a long time ago.

Beyond the rows of chairs something is moving out of the trees, beyond the baseball field. The day is getting hotter and Jody squints. A man walks through the waves of heat. He wears black slacks, a white shirt, and a black tie. His blond hair is combed back neatly. Jody feels her stomach tighten with desire. From this distance he doesn't even seem tall. He stops halfway across the field, in the middle of the diamond. Jody knows that if you added together all the people he's seen in the past ten years it would not add up to the crowd he now faces. She is not good enough for him, she doesn't deserve his love, and what's more she knows that if he takes one more step toward the crowd, it will kill her to have to give him up.

After the ceremony, her father is the first to find her. He pulls Robin behind him, and when he reaches Jody he puts his hands on her shoulders and kisses her on each cheek.

"My beautiful daughter," he says to Robin. "Now all we have to do is convince her to go to college."

Robin laughs and congratulates Jody. Jody smiles, but she looks past Robin.

The Giant is walking slowly through the field. Jody can't tell if he's about to search for her or make his escape.

"I've been looking forward to meeting you for ages," Robin says.

When Jody looks up and meets her eyes, Robin takes a step backward. Then, feeling silly for having been stung by the cool glance she's received, Robin laughs and says, "I love graduations."

Jody's brothers run toward them, then stop short. Behind them is Laura, annoyed because Elizabeth Renny is so slow in getting through the crowd. She wanted to be the one to get to Jody first.

"Jody," Laura calls weakly, then waves.

Jody waves back. He is closer now. In the sunlight he seems like a stranger. He looks blindly into the crowd. Jody wants to call out his name. Instead, she bites her tongue.

"You actually made it here," Laura says to Jody's father. "What a surprise."

"Not today," Glenn says to her. "All right?" He lightly kisses Elizabeth Renny. "You look great, Mom."

Laura snorts when he calls her mother Mom.

"We'd better go," Glenn says. "We have reservations."

"I love seafood," Robin says.

Everyone turns to her, as though surprised to see her.

"Well, I do," Robin says.

Jody's brothers gladly accept their father's offer to ride with him and Robin into Edgartown. They make certain to avoid looking at their mother so they don't have to see the murderous glances she shoots them.

"How about you?" Glenn says to Jody. "Drive over with us."

The Giant is walking toward her. Several people have turned to stare at him, but the Giant doesn't seem to notice. Jody does not begin to know how to introduce him to her family. She has never imagined them existing in the same universe.

"Holy shit," Jody's brother Mark says. "Get a look at that!"

"Mark!" Laura says, ready to lecture him until he grabs her sleeve and tugs. Then she turns to see what he's pointing at.

Jody has hoped that one day the Giant would agree to meet her grandmother. She has imagined her grandmother sitting on the porch, feeding the birds, late in the afternoon. He would not have seemed so unusual to her since, Jody knows, her grandmother can barely see. Elizabeth Renny would have tilted her head when his shadow fell across her, blocking the sun. She would have lifted her face toward him when he spoke.

He is only a few feet away. He waits to see if he should come any closer. She cannot ignore him. She blinks, but there is still a glare of light that comes between them. She cannot see his face, but he still takes her breath away.

Jody waves, and the Giant walks over. Elizabeth Renny sees his white shirt.

"This is Eddie," Jody says to her family.

"Oh," Elizabeth Renny says. "I knew an Eddie when I was in high school."

"Congratulations," the Giant says to Jody formally.

Jody wants him to bend down and kiss her.

"Everybody ready?" Jody's father says loudly. "Let's go."

The Giant is holding a small box that he puts in Jody's hands.

"Good to see you," Jody's father tells the Giant. "But we've got to get a move on. We've got reservations." Jody is so stunned by her father's insincerity that she shifts and puts her foot in a rut. Her high heels buckle and she loses her balance. The Giant reaches out to steady her, but thinks better of it and backs away.

"We're going out to lunch," Jody says to the Giant. "I'm sorry."

"That's okay," the Giant says. "I've already had lunch."

Jody knows he's trying to make her feel better, but she can't stand how awful her family is. She can't stand herself.

"I'm sorry," she tells him.

"Really," the Giant says, "it's okay."

"I remember my graduation day," Elizabeth Renny says. "It rained buckets."

"Come on, Mom," Laura says, as though she were talking to an idiot.

Jody's father insists she go in his car. Jody's eyes refuse to focus as they walk toward the road. She has no appetite. She has no courage.

Once they're inside the car, Glenn leans over and pushes down the buttons so all the doors are locked. Jody sits in the back, between her brothers.

"This is how you get back at me, isn't it?" Glenn says.

He turns the key in the ignition too hard and the engine screeches, then turns over. Robin puts a hand on his leg.

"Don't be so hard on her," Robin tells him.

"You don't know anything about me!" Jody says to her.

"I'm trying to help," Robin says.

"Don't," Jody tells her. "You can't."

Jody turns and strains her neck to see out the rear window. She can see the Giant. He is farther and farther away, walking back the way he has come.

"Believe me," Glenn says, "you're not staying here another day."

"Are you asking me to move in with you?" Jody says coldly, knowing that will shut him up.

"Don't talk back to me," Jody's father says. "Don't say anything at all."

In the backseat, Keith is crying.

"Stop yelling," Jody tells her father.

"You've got it all wrong," Glenn says. "I'm the one who tells you what to do."

No one goes out for lunch. They drive back to Elizabeth Renny's house in silence. As Laura is packing Jody's belongings she breaks two fingernails. She leaves the trunk upstairs to be picked up later and carries two suitcases down to Glenn's car. Jody's two brothers play an edgy game of catch on the lawn, but Jody is instructed to wait in the car while her father goes into Elizabeth Renny's house to phone ahead and reserve a room at the inn for her. Her parents have already decided—in the morning they will take her back to Connecticut until they can decide what to do with her next. Jody sits in the backseat of her father's car, still wearing her cap and gown. She opens the box the Giant has given her and finds a gold pin that once belonged to his grandmother. She pins it on her dress, underneath her black gown. When it grows dark tonight it will be the easiest thing in the world for her to walk out of her room, toss her hotel key on the grass, and just keep walking.

SAMANTHA Freed's parents are worried. Every day Samantha bolts her breakfast and disappears. Though she only goes down the road to Simon's house, they think about that missing girl, Jody. They have never liked Simon's father and now they don't trust him either. His hair is too long, for one thing, and he's involved with motorcycles.

And there is something more that troubles them. Not that they believe the awful gossip about a giant, but they have a sudden fear of aberrations. Though Simon has grown almost four inches since they've last seen him, they are convinced that he is still not right. He is not right for Samantha. Hal Freed insists that is exactly why Samantha is so interested in him: she can boss Simon around. She has found someone to look up to her.

Though it will not be easy for her to say what needs to be said, Eleanor Freed decides to take a walk down to Simon's house. When she gets there the children are out in the yard, surrounded by stuffed animals, one of which, a much-loved poodle named Alfred, Samantha has insisted on giving to Simon on the pretense that she is too grown-up for such things. Simon's father is examining a red motorcycle out by the shed. The children don't notice her, so Eleanor Freed rounds the shed, surprising Andre. He throws a wrench into a grease-covered box of tools and stares at her.

"Eleanor Freed," she says. And when he continues to look at her blankly she adds, "Samantha's mom."

She can tell the children get no supervision over here.

"Oh, sure," Andre says. "That's who you are."

There's no point in attempting to have a conversation with him, so Eleanor says she's come for a visit with his wife.

"My wife?" Andre says, puzzled. Vonny never has visitors.

Eleanor Freed looks up and sees Vonny at the screen door. She's greatly relieved to be able to leave Andre and walk across the yard. On her way, she calls hello to Samantha. Both children look up. They wave, then quickly return to their game.

"Those kids are oblivious," Vonny says, opening the screen door. They have been neighbors every summer for five years, and this is the first time either has been inside the other's house.

"To tell you the truth I'm concerned about them," Eleanor says. "I think they may be too close."

"Oh?" Vonny says.

"Simon's a terrific kid," Eleanor says.

Vonny feels herself retreat from Eleanor, as though she's been insulted.

"Just a little too short," Vonny says.

Andre comes in and lets the screen door slam behind him. He washes his hands at the kitchen sink with strong green soap.

"I'm taking the bike down to the shop to do a little work," he tells Vonny. Vonny knows the truth—he just can't resist the urge to drive the bike one last time before it's crated and sent on to a buyer in Delaware. Andre takes the keys to the truck out of his pocket.

"In case you need them," he says.

"Are you kidding?" Vonny says. Although she's gotten as far as the end of their road, with Andre waiting for her in the driveway, she isn't ready to drive by herself. "I'm not going anywhere."

Vonny sounds anxious and Eleanor Freed's not surprised that there are problems in this marriage.

"All right," Andre says. He knows he sometimes pressures Vonny, alternating between wanting her to be instantly cured and enjoying her dependence. When he passes Vonny he puts a hand on her shoulder and leaves it there for a moment. "I won't be gone long."

"Do you mind if I smoke?" Vonny asks Eleanor Freed after Andre's left. "I'm quitting next month."

"Go ahead," Eleanor says. She sits down near the window so she can keep an eye on Samantha.

"Look," Vonny says now, "if you don't want your daughter to play with Simon, why don't you just say so."

"You're offended," Eleanor Freed says.

"Of course I am," Vonny says. "What do you want me to do? Show you his charts to prove to you he's growing? Promise you your daughter won't be friends with a freak?"

"You think I'm saying he's not good enough for her," Eleanor says. "That isn't the way I meant for it to sound. Maybe it's that girl disappearing. Next door."

"Jody," Vonny says.

The police have been here twice, the first time late at night, when Vonny and Andre were already in bed. Since then, Vonny has been next door several times, but Mrs. Renny refuses to discuss her granddaughter. When she asked Andre if he was upset he said, "Of course I'm upset. Shouldn't I be upset when someone I know vanishes?" That was when Vonny understood that something more than a note left under his pillow went on between them. If he had said "we" rather than "I" she might never have known. She has always believed that if she ever discovered that her husband had been unfaithful she would leave him, if not within the hour, within the day. She is beginning to believe in second, and even third, chances.

Behind the hedges the children can hear their mothers saying good-bye at the door. As Eleanor crosses the lawn, they decide to scare her and charge her from behind.

"Oh, my goodness," Eleanor says. "What monsters are these?"

"It's us!" Samantha shouts.

"It's only us!" Simon echoes.

Vonny looks out and sees the children following Eleanor

down the driveway. She's still angry and considers calling Simon back. Then she thinks better of it. Why should she ruin Simon and Samantha's friendship to please Eleanor Freed?

At the edge of the driveway, the children stop.

"Well, come on," Eleanor Freed says to her daughter. "Time to go."

"Not yet," Samantha says. She has a whine in her voice that Eleanor knows means trouble.

"She can stay for dinner," Simon says.

"Please!" Samantha begs.

They stand close together. Eleanor can tell that separating them will be a long process. She doesn't have the energy to put her foot down, so she agrees. As long as it's all right with Vonny.

"It is!" Simon insists.

"No later than seven," Eleanor Freed warns Samantha. "You'll wear out your welcome."

Simon and Samantha sit in the driveway after Eleanor leaves.

"Does your mom ever make pizza?" Samantha asks.

"Not too often," Simon says. He's drawing a tic-tac-toe board in the dirt with a stick. He knows that Vonny is defrosting chicken for dinner and he doesn't want to reveal the menu to Samantha. He's afraid she'll change her mind about staying.

"I wonder if the Giant has a kitchen," Simon says.

"Are you kidding?" Samantha says. "There aren't any giants."

"There are," Simon says. "Really."

"Really really?" Samantha says. She's a little confused because her father has told her there are no giants, monsters, or ogres, yet she knows Simon doesn't lie. They will soon be looking for trouble, but it does not seem that way to them. They don't even plan to go look for the Giant, they are, quite suddenly, doing it.

They wait at the end of the driveway, giving Samantha's mother enough time to get home, then they peer over their shoulders. Once they're sure Vonny's not looking, they take off like lightning. As they run, the wind moves through their hair. They jump over ruts in the road, there since last winter. It is difficult to remember a time when it wasn't summer. Difficult to remember, as they pass Samantha's house, that their mothers have told them not to go any farther than their own dirt road. Not ever. They turn onto the paved road and run until their legs hurt. Simon knows from Jody that the Giant's farmstand is off South Road. They run until Simon says, "My heart is beating too fast." Samantha slows down and lets Simon take his time. Occasionally they forget that they have a destination and stop to look at rocks and centipedes. The day grows warmer, then grows hot. They do not know enough to bring a Thermos, they do not know that in real life people get hot, tongues begin to burn, feet drag after the first two miles.

Long before they reach the Giant's house, Samantha and Simon realize they are scared. They are doing something so bad that their voices crack when they speak. It is too late to turn back, so they hold hands and don't mention the fact that they are thoroughly lost. Simon's face is hot and flushed. He tries to believe Samantha when she tells him they're almost there, forgetting that he's the one who's supposed to lead the way. He waits in the tall grass while Samantha asks a man changing his tire if they are on the road to Edgartown. They know they are not supposed to talk to strangers, but now that they have begun they can't seem to stop being bad. When they finally do reach the farmstand they have blisters on their feet. They walk behind the farmstand and stop when they see the roof down in the hollow.

"That must be his house," Simon says.

The wind is hot and up on the road the asphalt has begun to melt.

They both wish they were back home.

"There are no giants," Samantha says firmly.

"Yeah," Simon agrees, even though he has seen the Giant with his own eyes.

"We don't believe in him," Samantha says. "Right?"

Simon moves closer to Samantha. His head reaches the height of her shoulders.

"Right," Simon says.

NEAR dinnertime, Vonny begins to fix chicken and rice. Andre should be home soon and Vonny assumes that Eleanor has taken the children back to her house. They have left behind their stuffed animals and there is still an indentation in the grass in the spot where the children had knelt.

Vonny turns down the fire under the rice and covers the pot. Then she phones Eleanor and asks that Simon be sent home.

"Simon?" Eleanor says. "What do you mean? They're at your place."

Vonny quickly hangs up and runs outside. She calls for the children and claps her hands as though calling for the dog. Her voice grows sharper, and she can feel the edges of the force field. When she runs back inside the house the phone is ringing. Eleanor Freed. Vonny tells her that the children are missing.

"Hang up," Eleanor says. "I'm calling the police."

Vonny hangs up, then grabs the keys to the truck. The metal bites into the palm of her hand. She is having trouble seeing, but she jumps into the truck and manages to get the key into the ignition. When she tears out of the driveway she can feel her head fill with blood. She has no idea where she's going, but she's going there fast. If she spoke to someone now her words would turn to glass and cut right through him. She thinks of Jody, missing for nearly a week. She thinks of maniacs and roadside graves. She winds open her window and screams out their names. At the end of the road she pauses, not to see if there's oncoming traffic, but because she doesn't know which way they would have gone. She makes a left turn, cutting off a car whose horn echoes behind her. She's not looking at the road, but along the side, into bramble bushes and ditches. The truck weaves over the double yellow line, but she drives faster. She hears a siren but doesn't slow down until the nose of the police car is touching the bumper of the truck. Then she stops. When the cop walks up to her window she's crying.

"My son is missing," she tells him.

She has to tell him this three times before he can understand her.

The officer insists on seeing her license, which of course she doesn't have. He walks back to the car and radios into the station. While she's waiting Vonny imagines that she will explode. She considers taking off, but knows he would only catch up to her and pull her over again. When the cop comes back he is apologetic. Eleanor Freed has reported the children missing. Still he tells Vonny not to speed. What good will it do if you have a head-on collision before we find your son? Vonny bites her tongue and nods. The force field has begun to flicker around the truck. She tries to count backward and can't. She puts the truck in gear, waits for the cop to drive off, then begins to drive, more slowly at first. She calls out Simon's name through the open window. Her voice is hoarse, like a frog's.

As soon as you find him you can collapse. You can let the force field take over.

She presses her foot down harder on the gas.

JODY has slept fitfully ever since she's come to the Giant's house. She stays awake all night, then falls asleep in the morning, lulled by the clucking of chickens in the yard. She has finally convinced the Giant that they have to leave, at least for a while. In three months Jody will be eighteen and her parents will have no legal right to run her life. Since she has been in hiding Jody has twice waited till after dark before walking down the road to a pay phone at the gas station. She called her grandmother and apologized for disappearing and, just last night, she made two reservations on a flight from Boston to San Francisco.

She has taken her life into her own hands. No one can tell her who to love. Naturally she is upset. Anyone in her situation would shake each time a car passed by on the road. That is why the Giant has agreed to go away with her. He does not want to lose her, but each time he thinks of leaving his chickens his throat gets tight. Who can he ask to take care of them while he is gone? The postman? His closest neighbor, a half a mile away, a man he has never spoken to? The Giant cannot imagine anything worse than disappointing Jody. He has always tried to please, even as a child, and it embarrasses him now to think that there were times when he slept with a brick on his head, when he cinched his belt tight, thinking he might cut off his blood supply and, if not shrink, at least not grow any taller.

When Jody is kind to him, the Giant is completely undone. Kindness has always had a peculiar effect on him. When he was fifteen and unmistakenly a man, he had a fever of a hundred four. As his grandfather perched on the edge of his bed and poured alcohol on a rag to wipe his neck and chest, the Giant began to weep. His grandfather sat him up and pounded on his back, thinking he might be choking. Now, the Giant regrets all he never said to his grandfather. His grandfather cried each time he wrung the neck of one of his chickens, and before they had that particular chicken for supper, the old man offered up a small prayer. He gave each chicken a name more suited to a sailor than a hen: Mighty, Primo, Good Sam, Gunther.

Late in the fall, when the afternoon light was thin and pale, the Giant liked to watch his grandfather search the vegetable beds for cabbage that had not yet frozen. His grandfather wore a navy-blue jacket, which, although it is too short for him, the Giant likes to wear sometimes. There are still some cough drops in the pockets, and the odor of tobacco and sweat is trapped in the lining.

The Giant does not want to go to California. He doesn't want to leave home. He did not exist before he came to this island, and he's afraid he will cease to exist if he leaves. Jody sleeps, but the Giant sits in the shade of the yard committing this place to memory. He falls asleep in a lawn chair and when he wakes, near suppertime, he has a crick in his neck. He gets up, stretches, then gathers some strawberries to replace those in the farmstand buckets. He walks past his house, checks to make sure no cars are passing, then climbs up the hollow. Carrying buckets of strawberries, he starts up toward the farmstand. He sees the two children from the corner of his eye. He is much more aware of the speeding car, the flash of silver as the sun is reflected in the side-view mirror. Probably he is more frightened and surprised than they are, but it is in his nature to freeze when startled. He feels an immediate kinship with the little boy who, although he opens his mouth wide, doesn't move an inch. The little girl is the one who screams when she sees him. What comes out of her mouth is like an electric current rather than a noise, and it fills the Giant with shame.

Strawberries fall out of the tin buckets onto the ground, then roll down the hill as the little girl runs away from him. The air is warm and thick, the shadows green as apples. The Giant feels the impact of the car as though he were the one who had been hit. He runs to the little girl while she is in the air. It seems as though she is in the air forever, suspended in the blue sky. The Giant drops his pails. He passes the little boy and tells him to run into the farmstand. No one should see this. The little boy opens and closes his mouth like a fish, but he does what he's told. By the time the little girl hits the pavement, the Giant is beside her. He kneels over her on the blacktop as the car screeches to a halt and pulls over onto the shoulder of the road. Dust rises into the air and comes down like rain. The driver gets out, but before he can move, the Giant yells for him to drive up the road and call an ambulance.

The Giant knows you're not supposed to move injured people, but he can't stand to see the little girl lying in the road. He picks her up and carries her to the grass. When he tells her to open her eyes she does, briefly, but long enough for him to see that her eyes are blue. He does not move when he hears sirens, or when the ambulance arrives. He stands and backs away so that the paramedics can gather around her. They check her quickly, then carry her into the ambulance. Three police cars pull over. The dust that rises up now is like a wave; it catches in the leaves and in the folds of the Giant's clothes.

Vonny knows that whatever has happened has something to do with her as soon as she sees a police car parked sideways, blocking the road. She sees the force field, visible for the first time.

It is a deadly brown film. It can cover you. There is heat inside of it, radiating out in thick, dark lines.

Vonny is sweating as she steps down on the gas. She breaks right through the force field, and as she does it explodes into bits of white light. She pulls over, leaves the truck running, and jumps out. Her heart hurts as she runs to the ambulance. She pushes a paramedic aside and sees Samantha. She begins to cry. An awful sort of crying, one that has very few tears and burns her throat.

"The other child," she says to the paramedic.

It is impossible to understand her because her throat is held in a vice. The paramedic looks at her stupidly, then gets in the back of the ambulance and pulls the doors closed. Vonny runs to the nearest police officer.

"My little boy," she manages to say.

She has grabbed the policeman's hand and her grip is frightening. The hand of a madwoman.

"Just relax," the policeman says. "There's no little boy."

The ambulance turns on its siren and pulls onto the road.

Jody is at the window of the Giant's house, terrified that her father has sent the police here to look for her. She wears one of the Giant's old white shirts and nothing else. She sees Andre's truck up on the road and she tears at the curtains, but she can see no farther than the sunlight, the blue flashing lights, the green leaves of the locust trees. Beyond these trees, the Giant sits, slumped, his head in his hands. He knows this is his fault. He can scare a little girl so badly she will run in front of a car. He can ruin someone's life. How can anyone love him, he wouldn't even want that love. He cannot imagine anything other than the little girl up in the air, caught between clouds.

Vonny will not let go of the policeman. "My little boy," she insists. These are the only words she knows.

The Giant remembers the other child. That he could have forgotten the boy makes him despise himself even more.

"I didn't want him to see any blood," the Giant says.

Vonny turns to him. The way she looks at him sets the Giant's skin on fire.

"He's in the farmstand," the Giant says.

Vonny runs and goes inside. The sound of her own pulse fills her head. It is pitch dark and the air smells like dirt and wood. She wills her pulse to stop pounding; if she can't see at least she can hear. She follows the sound of his crying and finds Simon in a corner, crouched down among spiderwebs and turnips. Vonny sinks down next to him and pulls him onto her lap. She kisses him on the top of his head and along his neck. She can feel his ribs through his T-shirt as she holds him in the dark.

Chapter Eight

THE LOCUST TREE

HE packs his suitcase and gives the chickens away, carrying each one to the closest farm, depositing them at midnight to blend in with his neighbor's stock. Yet even after the tickets to California come in the mail he continues bringing strawberries and lettuce up to the farmstand. If he acts as though nothing is about to change maybe nothing will. But on front porches and at grocery checkout counters people are talking about him. They say he's eight feet tall, and he's growing. He has become an old man who wears rags and snaps the heads off live chickens with his teeth. Already there is a joke being told. How many giants does it take to roof a house? One, if you slice him real thin.

For a while there was a slow parade of traffic. Sometimes five or six cars were parked on the shoulder of the road. They waited for the Giant, but he only came out at night. A week after the accident, a police car drove up and an officer got out and directed traffic, urging rubberneckers on. The assigned officer, Hammond West, knew old Eddie Tanner and, as a boy, sometimes did odd jobs for him. They didn't get along too well, and as a man Hammond avoided old Eddie, but he remembers seeing the Giant lumbering after his grandfather, a bag of seed or flour over his shoulders. It tears Hammond West apart to think of the line of tourists and troublemakers who will be waiting for the Giant if he has to come down to the courthouse to sign an affidavit for the inquiry. It makes him brood over his mother and father, both of whom were deaf. To Hammond, they always seemed perfectly normal, unless they had to deal with officials. His parents were afraid of tax assessors, meter readers, clerks at the Department of Motor Vehicles. Something as minor as a meeting with one of his teachers would send his mother and father reeling. The strongest memory he has is of them dressed up, walking into town, holding hands, growing smaller and smaller against the horizon until they were no bigger than dolls. And so he has convinced his boss, who's twenty years younger than he is, to let him take down Eddie's grandson's eyewitness account. Hammond waits until traffic has thinned out; then he takes off his sunglasses and walks down the path and into the hollow where, he judges, it's at least ten degrees cooler.

What makes knocking on the door a whole lot harder for Hammond is that he knows the Giant has the girl in there. The Giant doesn't know how lucky he is that his girlfriend's father is a loudmouth. When his daughter wasn't found in twenty-four hours Jody's father started name calling, saying he was going to bring in some real cops from Hartford. He started shouting about some guy who was a giant that his daughter had gotten mixed up with, and that pretty much closed the case. It's not that the department stopped looking for Jody, just that they understood why she ran away. Since the accident, they've stopped referring to Jody's father as the asshole from Hartford. They're starting to think about pulling the Giant in for questioning. Hammond loves some of these cops like sons, he's treated them like sons. Maybe that's why he takes off his badge and slips it into his pants pocket before he knocks.

It takes a while for the Giant to answer the door, about the same amount of time as it takes for Jody to run into the bathroom and hide in the tub.

"I'll bet you don't remember me," Hammond says when the Giant opens the door. "Hammond West."

"West," the Giant repeats, but the name means nothing to him. He blinks in the sunlight, he's in a cold sweat, certain he's about to be arrested for something. "How's the little girl?"

"Not as good as anyone would like her to be," Hammond says.

The Giant meets Hammond's gaze for the first time. Hammond straightens up and, without realizing it, stands on his toes to gain a little height. "We thought it'd be a whole lot easier if you wrote down your account of the accident instead of having to come in."

"All right," the Giant says. "I'll mail it to you."

"Sorry," Hammond says. "I've got to see you write it out in your own hand." He looks past the Giant into the house. "I wouldn't mind something to drink."

The Giant doesn't say anything, but he moves away from the doorway, and Hammond follows him inside.

"I remember your grandfather real well," Hammond says, after the Giant has gotten him a glass of ice water.

Each time Hammond takes a gulp, ice cubes hit against each other in his glass. He sits across from the Giant, watching him write out his account of the accident. There's a pair of white sling-back shoes near the bed and a tube of some kind of makeup—lipstick or eye shadow—Hammond can't tell. "He was a nut about chickens," Hammond says. "Wouldn't even sell one."

Hammond finishes his water and walks to the sink to rinse out his glass. The henhouses are all empty. The only sound, inside or out, is the scraping of a pen as the Giant writes.

"I'm glad I'm not young," Hammond says. He picks up the Giant's affidavit and looks it over. "Better sign your name," he tells the Giant, then he bends down and countersigns. "Boy, if I was young and caught harboring a runaway underage girl I don't know what I'd do. But I guess I'd be smart enough to send her packing. Hey, I might pack up and go with her."

The Giant looks pretty pale to Hammond. If he faints it will be like a tree falling.

"If you've got that girl from Hartford I have to see her," Hammond says. "I have to know she wants to be here."

The Giant nods and gets up. Hammond follows him across the room. The Giant opens the door to the bathroom and Jody glares at him from the bathtub. She is wearing jeans and a sweater that's too big for her. Her arms are wrapped around her knees.

"Are you crazy?" she says to the Giant. "Don't let that guy see me."

The Giant closes the door.

"I guess I'm satisfied," Hammond says. "I probably won't even remember seeing her for a couple of days." At the door, Hammond stops. "Don't blame yourself about the little girl," he tells the Giant. "She might have been just as scared if it had been me who popped out of those trees."

After Hammond is gone the Giant cannot stop staring at the front door. That night he cannot eat and his eyes look glassy. He begs Jody to walk down to the pay phone and call the hospital, and when she returns Jody tells him that the girl is recovering nicely. In the morning, he makes her call again, even though she may be spotted in daylight. This time she tells him that the girl has been discharged. Jody is lying, and she can tell the Giant doesn't believe her. He has begun an awful habit. He cracks his knuckles, one at a time. From the sound Jody would swear he was breaking his own bones.

She tells herself that if she can just hold on to him for two more days everything will be all right. They will be leaving; as long as she can keep the truth from him he won't change his mind. Except for when he makes her leave the house to phone the hospital, Jody doesn't let the Giant out of her sight.

She wants to say good-bye to her grandmother, but she puts it off, afraid if she leaves him, even for a few hours, he will not recognize her when she returns. She tells him he's nervous because he's never been on a plane before. She tells him they will fly past stars. And, when his back is turned, she takes the batteries out of his radio and runs cold water over them until they are worthless. He will never hear the news, but he knows the truth anyway, and he knows it is his fault.

When the Giant sleeps his dreams are sour, filled with rage and twisted trees. He tries to keep himself from dreaming. He closes his eyes and pretends to be asleep when Jody gets into bed, but he cannot pretend he doesn't want her. He is disgusted by himself, by his clumsy desire. He thinks of the look on the little girl's face and wonders not why Jody doesn't see what a monster he is, but when she will.

He has to be with her one more time, and as Jody is falling asleep, he begins to make love to her. When he moves his hand between her legs, Jody reaches for him, but he slides her hand away. He kisses her and moves his fingers up inside her. He will not let her touch him even after she has an orgasm. He pulls her up so she's sitting on the edge of the bed, then he kneels on the floor. The room is so black it's difficult to tell where the bed ends. His kisses feel hotter as he moves lower. Jody is thankful for the dark. She is the greediest person alive. She would want this to go on forever, if she didn't need time to move more quickly. She can feel his good-bye moving across and through her. When he puts his tongue inside her she has already become something for him to drink.

She is unable to keep herself steady on her arms stretched out behind her. He shifts her on top of him, and when he lurches back on the floor, she follows him down, not daring to let him go. He is inside her, but there is still a terrible distance between them. They are disoriented, used to the confines of a bed instead of this mysterious floor that seems to float in the dark.

Jody moves up and down slowly. She wants them to hurt each other, to cry out loud, to burn away what is wrong between them. The Giant is silent and covered with sweat. He doesn't flinch when she digs her fingernails into his skin. He doesn't make a sound. Jody is not surprised in the least when he doesn't go back to bed with her, but instead spends the rest of the night in a chair by the window. From here he can see the empty chicken coops and the garden that will soon yield lettuce and peppers and a peculiar red cabbage so sweet it makes some people burst into tears when they shred it for cole slaw, and others complain and add shake after shake of salt.

ELIZABETH Renny is furious with herself for having such bad vision. She missed the Giant completely at graduation, and now when she asks if she can meet him Jody says he is much too shy. That doesn't stop Elizabeth Renny from thinking about what may happen when they come home from California. The Giant will change all the light bulbs in fixtures out of her reach now that she is too unsteady to climb up a stepladder. She will invite them to brunch and serve pancakes with sour cream. She will buy them a cat for a homecoming present. When she feels she knows him well enough, she may ask the Giant to cut down the pine tree. One thing is certain, Elizabeth Renny does not plan to die anytime soon. At least not until they're back home and settled in. She wonders if the Giant will prefer her house to his own, although surely her next-door neighbors would not appreciate his keeping chickens here.

Since Jody ran off, something odd has begun to happen to Elizabeth Renny. She is growing younger. One morning she notices the brown spots on her hands have disappeared. The next day her hair is measurably thicker. She rides Jody's bicycle once around the yard and doesn't feel pain in her legs. When Laura or Glenn calls to see if there's any news of Jody, Elizabeth Renny is as snippy as a teenager. Laura tells herself her mother's voice sounds so high because of crossed phone wires. She has no idea that her mother has stopped wearing her old polished flats in favor of a pair of soft black ballet slippers or that her old-woman's insomnia has been replaced by deep, dreamless sleep. She would never believe that Elizabeth Renny can now touch her toes twenty times in a row, as though there has been a shifting in her bone structure.

Once again she feels a young girl's agitation and is reacquainted with both impatience and desire. She knows that Jody plans to go to California, and she can't stop thinking about all the things she herself has never seen. She waits for her granddaughter, she keeps her door unlocked, and when at last Jody appears, on the night before she leaves, Elizabeth Renny grabs on to her hand and will not let go. She pesters her with questions. When Jody tells her the Giant has no shower and she's had to wash her hair in the sink, Elizabeth Renny insists she take a hot shower. She follows her granddaughter up to the bathroom and keeps talking as Jody showers. In the steamy bathroom Elizabeth Renny's skin is flushed; her hair curls around her forehead. Jody steps out of the shower and imagines she sees a young woman handing her a towel. Jody waves her hand, making circles in the steam.

"Don't tell me where in California you'll be staying," Elizabeth Renny tells her. "I might slip and let the cat out of the bag."

"San Francisco," Jody says.

"Don't tell me!" Elizabeth Renny says. She trails after Jody and sits on the bed while Jody towels her hair dry. "Hotel or motel?"

"I don't know," Jody says. "I'll write to you as soon as I get there."

Jody takes a small suitcase from the closet and packs a cotton dress, two white shirts, underwear, a pair of sandals, her tortoiseshell hair combs. Why is it that she can't shake the vision of arriving at the airport in California alone? She is waiting for her suitcase to travel along the silver luggage wheel. Above her, jets fly so low their roar shakes the cement floor.

When they go downstairs, Jody puts her suitcase down by the door; she then takes a diet soda she's left behind out of the refrigerator and pops open the can. She feels about a hundred years old. Sinbad jumps onto the counter and rubs against her arm. She does not regret lying to the Giant after her phone calls to the hospital, but each lie has taken something out of her. She reaches for her soda and spills it.

"I'm a little nervous," she says. "That's all."

Elizabeth Renny reaches into a metal canister meant to hold flour, takes some money and puts it on the table. Jody stares at the money. If something inside her wasn't missing she would burst into tears.

"Take it," Elizabeth Renny says when Jody hesitates.

Jody slips the money into her pocket. When she hugs Elizabeth Renny she's surprised by how small her grandmother seems.

Jody backs away, then gets a dishrag and cleans up the spilled soda. She stares out the window above the sink as she rinses out the dishrag. There are lights turned on next door, in the kitchen and the upstairs bedrooms. Although the sky is still light in the west, darkness has settled over the lawn and Vonny and Andre's house seems small and far away. Jody carelessly bites her lip; she tastes a drop of her own blood. She knows it's time to go.

The telephone rings. Jody and her grandmother stare at each other. The sound is thin and high-pitched and Elizabeth Renny just lets it go on ringing. It can only be Laura, and she'll never believe no one's at home. When she can't stand the ringing anymore, Elizabeth Renny picks up the phone, then quickly hangs it up again. It may only be that Jody is used to her grandmother's hair being pinned up, but from the back, she could swear that her grandmother is no older than eighteen.

"Go on," Elizabeth Renny says to Jody. There's a slight hiss in her voice, as though she were speaking to one of her cats.

Jody picks up her suitcase and goes out the door. She looks back inside and sees that her grandmother has already turned away and is rifling through a cabinet where the cat food is stored. As soon as the phone begins to ring again, Elizabeth Renny slips a Tina Turner tape into the cassette player Jody's left behind. It is amazing how music can drown out any other sound, how it can fill an empty room and seem brand-new even when it's a song that's been played a thousand times before.

JODY finds him out in the yard, wearing old jeans and a white T-shirt.

"Eddie," Jody says, startling them both by saying his name out loud. "We have to leave now."

He goes inside and puts a white-and-blue striped shirt over his T-shirt. He cannot bring himself to touch the hidden strongbox in the chicken coop, but he gets their suitcases and carries them outside. Jody is already waiting up the road. The back door of the taxi she's called has been flung open. The taxi driver swallows air and doesn't move a muscle when the Giant opens the trunk and settles their suitcases inside.

The driver doesn't say a word to them, but every once in a while he looks at the Giant in his rearview mirror. He knows he will faint if the Giant speaks to him, but the Giant and the girl both look out their windows in silence.

The Giant's legs press against the driver's seat; he has cramps in his thighs from folding himself into the car. He remembers the night he first came to the Island, he remembers the wooden bench he sat on during the crossing, and the roll of the ferry in the dark. There was cigar smoke and rain and the scratchy black coat against his neck. At the age of ten he knew enough to go out only at night. It is now almost noon. The trip Jody has planned is a long one. They're avoiding Duke's County Airport, where Jody might be recognized, and flying from Logan Airport in Boston instead. Jody has disguised herself by wearing a scarf tied over her hair and a pair of metal-rimmed sunglasses, not realizing that as long as she's with the Giant no one will give her a second look.

When they pull up to the crowded dock and get out of the taxi, the Giant is stunned by the sunlight. While Jody pays the driver, he gets out and takes their suitcases from the trunk, but his head is reeling. Jody gets their tickets, and as they walk toward the ferry, she checks her pocketbook to make certain she hasn't forgotten anything. There are too many people here. The Giant cannot breathe. Jody doesn't notice that people are staring, but the Giant knows. He keeps his eyes straight ahead. He tries to concentrate on the ferry and the white foam spraying upward as waves hit the bow, but the sun is directly overhead and every step he takes forces him to walk through his own shadow.

"Damn it," the Giant says when they reach the wooden ramp leading to the ferry.

Jody remembers the taste of her own blood. She would not be strong enough to hold him, even if she tried.

"I left my plane ticket in the cab," the Giant tells her.

He drops the suitcases and turns away.

"Wait," Jody says.

She is wearing a sundress and white leather sandals. The hem of her dress moves in the breeze.

"I'll be right back," the Giant says.

As soon as he begins to run, people dodge away and stand to the side. The space created for him fills in with people straining to get a good look once he's safely passed them by. Even though the crowd comes between them, Jody can see him for a very long time. She watches him run past the ticket booth and the taxi stand and the parking lot. Her cotton dress keeps her cool, even in the hot sun, lucky for her since it will be even hotter on the bus to Logan Airport. At last call, Jody gets on the ferry and stands topside, by the railing. She knows that by now he is on the road home, but she keeps on watching the shore anyway, even after the ferry has begun to pull into the harbor. The water is like glass, green and clear, and not even the ferry's churning engines can disrupt the calm surface for long. As they move toward the mainland the path they chop disappears and is replaced by calm water, as though they have never even passed this way.

*   *   *

At the funeral her parents do not look at you. It was a mistake for you to come. You know they can read your thoughts. Their child's death haunts you. You cannot think her name without something inside tearing, and yet a dozen times a day you think, Thank God it wasn't my child. All the way home from the funeral, you rub a quarter between your fingers, but the force field is oddly absent and you have no symptoms. You do not consider pulling over to the side of the road and weeping a symptom.

Every day you tell your child it was not his fault. He is dangerously confused. Someone has told him that when people die they are returned to the earth and now he is waiting for his friend to return. He says he sees her shadow on the lawn, ready for her when she comes back. He begins to disappear each day but you and your husband decide not to worry. He needs some time alone. Then when you are practicing, driving back from the market where you shop for your neighbor, you discover where your child has been going every day. The little girl's house is already listed with several real-estate brokers, but there your son is, waiting for his friend. You pull over and call to him, demanding that he get in the truck. You shift into gear, eager to get away from that empty house. He sits leaning against the door, wearing red shorts and a short-sleeved shirt with three buttons, all undone. You tell him nobody returns. You tell him not to wait. You tell him she will always be alive in his mind. Most people, you assure him, do not die until they're very old, maybe even a hundred, older than turtles, older than the trees.

"You won't ever die," he says to you.

You keep driving.

"If you ever died," he says, "Daddy and I would die too."

You keep both hands on the steering wheel. You do not cry.

"No," you say. "You and Daddy would not die. Every person's death belongs just to that person."

When you pull into your driveway he gets out of the truck without saying a word. You cannot stand the fact that he is suddenly afraid of loud noises. Raised voices or the sound of dogs barking make him burst into tears. He is detached, no longer interested in his pets or in new toys. What you have been waiting for has finally happened. Clothes bought at Christmas no longer fit. Although he is still smaller than most children his age, when you measure him against the counter you begin to cry before you can stop yourself. But your son does not seem to care. He has taken to slouching. Though he is miles beyond any form of bribery, your husband has come up with a plan to get him interested in something. He goes out to the store and returns with a ball and a hoop he attaches to the shed. Even if your son continues to grow at this rapid rate your pediatrician has warned that he will never be above average height. His future in basketball is probably limited. Still, your husband insists he learn the game. You hear thumping as they practice dribbling the ball in the dirt. You watch through the window. At first your son is not interested. He stands with his arms crossed, a parody of adult boredom, as your husband shoots basket after basket.

You cannot help feeling that the accident has proven you right. You wonder if phobics comb the newspapers for crimes and disasters that corroborate their world view. You have suspected there was danger out there, now you know you were right. The sound of the basketball hitting against the shed makes you even more aware of all you can lose. At night you dream you are a child. Your father is in the kitchen, rolling out dough for pies. You recognize the sound of a knife cutting apples and everything seems familiar: the sound of the parkway, the color of the sky. Even though you are asleep, you realize that in your dream your father is younger than you are now. You wake up remembering how he used to sing in the car, and that he once had a beautiful voice. This is what you have realized: your father will not continue to be alive after he has died. You truly have not known this before. You have viewed death as though you were a five-year-old. You have imagined battling with your father after he was dead, trying to convince him you were worthy. You are no longer concerned with being someone's daughter. But at least your struggle with your father has allowed you to know what you are to your own child. You are the person who never dies, you are a parent, not quite human, there only to love him.

You have begun to think about babies, and you want one. You forget that babies mean getting up in the middle of the night, you forget bending low over a crib to check and make certain your baby is breathing. To create life in the face of death is a show of strength. You make love with no birth control fourteen days after your period, and afterward tell yourself the two beers you had made you do something so stupid. When you really consider all the dangers any child brought into the world must face you are immobilized. You stop driving up your road. You ask your husband to pick up your neighbor's groceries. You refuse to go outside. But now you begin to be afraid in your own house. You think of faulty wiring, spontaneous combustion, lightning striking, sudden infant death. When your safe place begins to feel dangerous it can mean your pattern of phobias is breaking down. This can be a sign of recovery. Why is it, then, everything seems difficult? Why are you so certain that unless you start all over again you will be lost? Having broken through the force field, why do you still feel its sharp edges? You think about this for as long as you can stand to and then one morning you go out and drive back and forth in the driveway. By the time you have made your third run down the driveway you have stopped asking yourself why you have to start all over again. You are simply a woman practicing the art of real life.

Simon likes the way the dust rises up when he dribbles the ball. He likes the sound of metal as the ball touches the hoop, then ricochets into and through the basket. His arms begin to feel loose after he plays for a while, heat moves up his limbs to the center of his body. Each time he scores a basket he feels as if he's eating thunder. There's a crash inside his throat. The thunder is what's making him grow taller, it's exploding inside him, taking up all the space beneath his skin.

Nelson lies in the shade and watches, his eyes darting back and forth as Simon runs toward the basket. Simon tries not to look at the dog, because every time he does he thinks about death. In Simon's mind the accident has become a single flash of light. He sees the light behind his eyes as he falls asleep at night and whenever he enters a dark room. He sees it every time he hears a loud noise, like the slamming of a car door. But when he plays basketball everything turns blue. It is not just that he tilts his head up as he aims for the basket. It is more blue than the sky.

No one will ever make him believe the accident wasn't his fault. He still doesn't quite believe that he can't take it all back, like a tape rewinded, then replayed without any mention of the Giant. He will always think of the house down the road as Samantha's, even after it is sold, and he alternates between imagining that Samantha is in New York with her family and believing that she is somewhere in his yard. She seems extremely real to him, realer than last winter when she sent him a postcard from New York.

Simon tries to think only of basketball. Usually, he's easily frustrated. When he can't button a button he sometimes pulls it off his shirt. When he can't lace a shoe, he throws it across his room. But when his father instructs him on how to hold the ball and aim, Simon amazes them both by listening. He knows that if he really tries, this is the one thing he can do. It helps him to forget that he cries at night and sometimes wets his bed. He does not understand why people have to die. What happens to them when their bodies stop working?

Sometimes he thinks Samantha is inside him, and that is why her shadow stays in their yard and hasn't gone back to New York City.

He knows his father has been trying to make him happy. Andre played ice hockey when he was growing up in New Hampshire and he doesn't even like basketball much, and now he cannot have a conversation with Simon that doesn't include Larry Bird and the Celtics. A mechanic he knew in Boston sold him two season passes for the Boston Garden for the coming season. Just the two of them, they'll stay in a hotel near the Charles River, they'll eat junk food till they drop.

But when the Celtics tickets arrive in the mail, Simon locks himself in the bathroom and will not come out.

"This is it," Andre tells Vonny. "This is the fucking limit. Nothing I do makes him happy."

Simon doesn't know how to tell his father that he doesn't deserve to see the Celtics. Since he was the one who knew about the Giant, he was the one who should have been hit. How long, he wonders, will it take before he stops missing her? How long before he no longer sees that flash of light?

In the hallway, his parents argue. Andre vows to take the bathroom door off its hinges, even though this means he will be late for work. Simon hears his mother telling him to unlock the door. He hears her start to count to three. He unlocks the door and walks right past Vonny and Andre, into his room. Vonny follows him and stands in his doorway.

"Don't you ever lock yourself in there again," she tells him. "Do you understand?"

He nods his head. He understands perfectly. He should be sent to his room for disobeying, so when his mother goes downstairs he closes his door, punishing himself. He will not allow himself to play basketball for two days. He will not allow any TV for three. He lies down on his bed and falls asleep with all his clothes on and he dreams that Samantha steps out of the sky. Her dress and shoes are blue, her hair is pulled into a ponytail. All around her is that amazingly bright light, bright enough to fill his eyes with tears. When Simon wakes he is wet all over. He has peed in his pants, his body is coated with sweat. He takes off his clothes and puts on a dry T-shirt and shorts.

Except for the hum of the wheel as his mother works on the porch, the house is quiet when he goes downstairs. Andre is at the garage in Vineyard Haven and should not be home for hours. Simon's rabbit, Dora, is eating from the bowl Vonny has made for her. RABBIT is stenciled in black letters below the rim. Vonny has been setting out her food and water, and Dora no longer follows Simon from room to room. Simon hears the call of a bobwhite. Out on the grass gnats hover. Simon still feels hot. He gets himself a glass of lemonade, and when he sits down at the table he notices that the rabbit has finished her food. He takes a spoon and ladles sugar into the rabbit's bowl, then watches her eat. Every once in a while she stops and is perfectly still, then returns to the bowl. Simon pets the rabbit, who's been so ignored lately she's suspicious. Next to the stove, Nelson is snoring. Simon realizes Samantha will never be any older. She will never learn

to walk the tightrope; she will never be any bigger. Who is
Simon to go on without her? How dare he grow, go to school,
own a pet? He goes to the door and opens it, then leans
against the screen until it sticks open in place. The rabbit sits
and watches. Nelson hears the opening door in his dream and
sits up, bleary-eyed but, as always, ready to go out. Simon
pushes the dog away. He picks up Dora and puts her directly
in front of the open door. The rabbit does not move. There
is sugar stuck to her whiskers. Simon gets the sugar bowl and
starts a thin trail along the kitchen floor, out the door, down
the porch steps. His chest feels tight and his stomach hurts;
sugar sticks to his damp fingers. The rabbit begins to slowly
follow the trail, at last hopping down the steps. Simon slowly
walks past her, into the house. He closes the door and
watches her through the screen mesh. When she finishes all
the sugar she sits there. Her body moves up and down when
she breathes.

"Run," Simon says through the screen.

Dora sits up straight, as though she's heard him.

Planes pass by overhead and Simon can hear the rhythmic
creak of Vonny's wheel out on the sun porch. He leans his
face up against the cool wire mesh of the screen. After a while
he goes outside and picks up Dora. It's a hot day, the first of
many, and even the brown rabbits who come to eat grass at
dusk are hidden in dark places under the bramble bushes.
These rabbits are not so silent as they seem. Sometimes, in
the middle of the night, they begin to scream and no one
knows why. Are they calling to each other? Have they picked

up the scent of an owl? Or does the cry push out of their
throats simply to break the spell of their silence?

Gravel and rocks spin out as Andre's truck pulls up in the
driveway. He leaves the truck idling and slams the door open.
In Simon's arms the rabbit shivers.

"Goddamn it," Andre says.

He's yelling, and Simon's not sure why.

"You're not going to do this to me," Andre says.

Ever since leaving the house, Andre has been thinking
about his father. He's been thinking so hard he no longer
knows if he's furious at his father, his son, or himself. All he
knows is that if he measured himself against his father right
now, they'd be just about equal. That's what's killing him.
Equal amounts of distance and silence. The sum of zero.

As he walks up the driveway he sees that Simon is afraid
of him. He must look like a crazy man. He's been working
on a transmission and his hands are covered with grease. He
doesn't give a damn. He goes up to Simon and grabs him by
the shoulders.

"Talk to me!" Andre says.

Simon holds on to his rabbit and backs away.

"I said, talk to me!"

"I won't!" Simon says.

Andre tears the rabbit out of Simon's hands.

"You're hurting her!" Simon cries.

Andre ignores Simon. He runs up the steps and tosses Dora
inside. Simon charges his father; he has never hated anyone
more. As he slams himself against Andre's legs he can feel the

thunder inside him moving toward his fists as he punches his father, he can feel it come out of his mouth as he makes a terrible noise. Vonny comes running, her arms streaked with clay the color of blood. Andre has reached down and he has one arm around Simon. He turns when Vonny opens the door.

"Stop it right now!" Vonny says. It's not clear who it is she's talking to.

"Don't come between us," Andre warns her. "Don't do that to us."

Simon is crying and his face is streaked with grease. If Vonny takes one more step he'll run to her, he'll wrap both arms around her legs until she bends down and lifts him up. Vonny steps back, takes the handle of the screen door with both hands and pulls it tight. She turns her back to the door so she doesn't have to watch.

Andre kneels down and lets Simon hit him.

"Talk to me," he says. "Simon."

Without the thunder inside him, there is an unbelievable emptiness. Simon leans all his weight against Andre. This time when he opens his mouth no thunder comes out.

"I don't want anyone we know to die," Simon says.

Andre cannot imagine what he would have thought if he had ever seen his father cry, but he doesn't try to stop himself. He puts his hands on Simon's shoulders more gently now, and holds on even after he's pushed his son away.

"We can't hope for that," he tells Simon. "Let's just hope we remember. Then she'll always be with you. Will you remember?"

"Yes," Simon says.

"Yeah," Andre says, "I think you will."

ELIZABETH Renny eats only oatmeal, thinned with milk, flavored with brown sugar. She eats it for lunch and again for dinner. Every spoonful makes her shudder. The oatmeal is too delicious for words. Every now and then she has the urge to drop down on her hands and knees and crawl. She discovered this when she lost a needle while hemming a dress and had to get down to search the floor. It was such a comfortable position she could barely force herself to get up again. She is smaller than she used to be. She knows this from sitting in the overstuffed chair; her feet no longer touch the ground, she sinks into the pillows. She sleeps more than she used to. She falls asleep sitting upright in the chair. Until she was six she shared a room with her sister, and sometimes now at night she thinks she can hear her sister breathing. When one of the cats gets into bed with her, she imagines the creature is a stuffed animal and holds it a little too tight. One morning she loses a tooth, which she wraps in tissue paper and places under her pillow. Vonny comes over with her groceries, but now Elizabeth Renny doesn't remember who she is, although she doesn't let on.

"You're sure you're all right?" Vonny says to her. She has her little boy with her, he's bending down petting the white cat. Elizabeth Renny smiles. She reaches into her pocket and offers the boy a sourball.

"You're not supposed to chew these," Elizabeth Renny says conspiratorially. "That way they last longer."

While Simon is unwrapping the sourball, Vonny goes into the kitchen and looks through Mrs. Renny's phonebook. Mrs. Renny has not been able to go on walks with her for some time, and although Vonny is often concerned, she's respected her neighbor's independence. She does not know where to draw the line. How can she know when it's right to interfere? The garbage hasn't been taken out and the dishes haven't been done. While they're visiting, Simon has to pee, but he comes out of the bathroom after only a moment and insists they go home. Vonny drags him back to the bathroom, but he's right, it smells terrible, and when Vonny switches on the light she sees there's feces on the floor. After they've come home, Vonny gets herself a beer and stares at the phone. Then she calls Mrs. Renny's daughter. She starts out saying, "It's none of my business," but that's not exactly the truth.

"I'm worried about your mother," she tells Laura. "I'm worried enough to suggest you come as soon as you can."

Laura arrives the next day, suddenly, without bothering to phone ahead. As soon as she walks in the door she breaks into tears and Elizabeth Renny does not know why. The house is a disaster. Bowls of crusted oatmeal sit in the sink, dishes of uneaten cat food litter the floor. Laura immediately begins to do the dishes, crying as she washes.

"Mom," she says, after she makes some tea and sits Elizabeth Renny down at the table, "You can't go on living alone."

Elizabeth Renny takes her daughter's hand and looks at her diamond ring. It shines in the light, colors are caught and reflected in the stone. That night Laura tucks her mother into bed. Elizabeth Renny smiles and reaches up her arms to hug her daughter. It is a beautiful summer night, blue and clear and filled with stars. There is a low tide and the air smells like seaweed and salt. Elizabeth Renny recognizes her daughter as Laura is opening windows to let in some air.

"Where are your nice boys?" Elizabeth Renny asks.

"With their disgusting father," Laura jokes. She does not know why tears continue to well up or why her throat feels so tight. She should have seen her mother more. She should not have moved so far away. And yet, the house feels exactly as it did when she lived here. The same furniture, the same heat. It is as though she has never been away. If she had lived closer would she be any more ready for this?

Elizabeth Renny signals to her and Laura leans closer.

"Do they cry when you leave them?" Elizabeth Renny asks.

"No," Laura says. She touches her mother's forehead and then her cheeks. "They don't cry."

"You've got nice boys," Elizabeth Renny says. "You've got a beautiful daughter."

Elizabeth Renny feels happy. She holds Laura's hand. Her hand is so small it is nearly lost inside her daughter's. Elizabeth Renny thinks of a baby sitting on its mother's lap, looking at the sun. She smells crackers and milk, she feels the warmth of someone's body against her own. There is a hand-sewn quilt decorated with bluebirds and letters of the alphabet. Elizabeth Renny curls up and brings her knees to her chest. She loves the way her pillow smells, like fresh soap, like powder.

Laura gets into bed beside her and puts her arms around her.

"Shh," Elizabeth Renny hears her say. "Go to sleep."

Elizabeth Renny smiles in her sleep. All of her dreams are white. She dreams she sees sunlight. She sees the walls of her room at home, she hears her mother in the kitchen, cooking cereal, her father running water in the sink as he shaves. She hears her sister opening the curtains, and the traffic on the street. Laura is still asleep when Elizabeth Renny wakes up. On this morning Elizabeth Renny is so small she could fit inside a high chair. She knows words inside her head, but she can't remember how to talk. She lifts herself up and looks out the window. The sun has just begun to rise. On the lawn she sees a flash of color. She no longer remembers the name for what she sees, but she smiles when the piece of color lands on the porch railing. "Pretty," she thinks to herself. "Pretty red bird."

Your mother always calls you at the wrong time. When you are making love with your husband or sitting down to the sort of dinner that will be dreadful if not eaten hot. This time she calls you on the one morning your son is sleeping past eight and you have the chance to sleep late. You run into the kitchen. You let her talk and pour yourself a cup of coffee. The day is already hot and you think you see two green her-

ons outside flying above the shed. Your mother is complaining about the heat in Florida, not that it bothers her, but next summer perhaps she and her husband will rent a place on the Vineyard. You are reminded of the empty house next door. You remember that as a child when you went to the beach with your mother she always made you wear plastic beach shoes so you wouldn't be bitten by crabs. You cannot recall any death in your childhood, but when you tell your mother this she begins a litany: a cocker spaniel, turtles, your second-grade teacher, your grandfather. You have survived all of these, and you wonder if your son will be so lucky. You see a new sort of caution in him. He knows something he did not know a year or even a few months ago.

"My God, you can't protect him from everything," your mother will say, but that is exactly what you want to do. Your mother will remind you we don't know the half of what goes on in this world. She will tell you that just last week she and her neighbor sighted a UFO.

"Mom," you will say, "you are wrecking your credibility."

The UFO was silver and round, like a ball suspended in the sky. She and her neighbor were having iced tea and Stella D'oro cookies on the neighbor's screened-in porch. They heard a hum they thought was from those huge Florida mosquitoes, but then they looked into the sky. What this has to do with keeping death away from your son you do not know. What this has to do with the look on his face when you sat him down and tried to explain that your next-door neighbor was old and had had a good life you have no idea. You want

to ask your mother why people have to die, but instead you
get yourself more coffee, which you drink black and scalding
hot.

Your mother will try to describe the green light that formed
a halo above the UFO. When she and her neighbor called
NASA to report the sighting they got a recording and had to
leave a message. You wonder why your mother is more real
to you over the phone than she is in person. Every time you
see her face to face you argue, you snap at each other the way
you did when you lived in the same house and were dreaded
adversaries. You think of her out on the porch drinking iced
tea, watching the sky. For years she could not leave her house,
even to drive around the block, and now she tells you she
would go up in a UFO if asked. All of this makes you miss
her.

When you get off the phone everyone will still be asleep.
You will go out to the sun porch. A hundred years ago the
porch was used for sleeping on hot July nights. A whole family dragged their mattresses down here and listened to cicadas.
They whispered and looked at the stars. Red clay sits in a
barrel of water, softening. The surface of the water looks
thick and brownish red. When you reach into the barrel the
clay moves between your fingers like a living thing. You take
what you want and wedge it, kneading the clay until the air
bubbles pop. It is silent outside and the sky is flat with heat.
You sit at the wheel and begin to kick it with your right foot,
you slap down the clay and watch it revolve like a misshapen
planet.

Across the yard, birds gather on the porch railings, on the steps, on the roof. Every day they grow bolder. They are taking over the house, and some of their songs begin to sound familiar. While you are centering the clay, you realize that the force field has begun to shrink. It is now small enough to fit in a matchbox that you keep in your pocket. Sometimes you can feel it pulsing, just to let you know it is still there. You have been to two funerals, and yet summer has never smelled so good or seemed as hot. Now you know what your son meant when he insisted that shadows remain after people die. You see long patches of shadow in unexpected places. You feel as though your neighbor still lived right next door, even though you have been inside the empty house, and your husband is the one to mow the overgrown lawn. A hundred years ago the family on this porch waited for a breeze from the sea to bring some relief from the heat. The lilacs had already been planted, but weren't much more than twigs. On the hottest nights the family kept jugs of water by the door, the mother and daughters wore white nightgowns and braided their hair in the dark before pinning it away from their flushed necks. How clear the planets must have been in the sky, how dark the roads at night. Millions of fireflies must have appeared in the bushes, pale yellow lights blinking on and off all through July. You wish you knew the hour when they all fell asleep, lulled by fireflies and heat. There was a time when people believed the sap of a locust tree was as thick as blood. They believed the soul of a dying child could be caught and kept in a bottle. Who can believe that nothing remains? Who does

*not strain to see the tiny fragments of a life that refuses to be
extinguished?*

*When you press down with your thumbs you can feel the
clay's energy pushing back at you, but it is no match for your
fingers. You open the center of the clay, then begin to raise
the sides with your thumb and forefinger. You keep a steady
pressure on the clay. With your left hand inside, and the fingertips of your right hand following, you begin to pull upward. You think about the dishes in your house when you
were growing up that were never used, white china edged
with a rim of gold and pink. Much too breakable. That is not
at all what you're after.*

*By now you know you will always be afraid. Even when
the sky is flat and clear. Even when your husband and son
are safely asleep in their beds. You know that every time you
drive alone to the store to buy a quart of milk a part of you
will expect the earth to swallow you.*

You will go to the store anyway.

After she leaves, the silence is unbearable. He paces his house,
but there's not enough room to contain him, and one night
he tears out at dark and runs more than five miles, to the
hardware store. He goes around the back, jimmies open a
window, and climbs inside. After his eyes adjust to the dark,
he makes his way past the bags of fertilizer and seed to the
appliance section. He grabs a cassette player from a shelf and
stuffs his pocket with tapes. His hands are shaking, but he
manages to light a match so he can make out the price tags

and leave enough cash to cover what he's taken. He runs all the way home. The sky is black and filled with stars. A few tapes fall out of his pockets and scatter on the road, and when he reaches his house his clothes are drenched with sweat. He sits at his table and examines the cassette player. There are no instructions. He chooses a tape at random, slides it in, and presses Play. He cries when he hears the music.

He is heartsick and each day he grows paler. He is willing himself out of existence. His paintbrushes are untouched, his garden so ignored that weeds have taken over. Customers no longer expect to find anything at the farmstand. No one bothers to stop anymore. Except for the woman who comes to torment him.

The first time the pickup made a U-turn without pausing. He noticed it only because the tires squealed and the sound sent a shiver down his spine. Then the truck began to pull over and idle. It is there every day and the Giant can now distinguish the sound of its motor above all others. One morning the woman gets out of her truck. The Giant, who has stepped out his door to get a better look, recognizes her as the mother of the little boy he kept from seeing the accident. He runs back inside his house and doesn't come out until she drives away. The next morning she is back. The Giant watches from the window. He times her. She stands by the side of the road for exactly five minutes. She comes back each morning. She becomes the only thing in his day. When he hears her truck on the road he stops whatever he's doing and turns off his cassette player. The Giant knows she wants something, she wants it badly. He knows what that's like. He wanted something too.

He cannot know how Vonny's hands sweat whenever she grabs the steering wheel. He cannot know that sometimes, when she gets home, she is sweating so much she goes to the shed, turns on the hose, and runs water over her head. He cannot know that she comes here because it is the spot on earth she is most afraid of. Or that at night her fear turns to desire and she wants her husband so much she scares herself. She has to put her fist in her mouth so she won't make noise when they make love.

It is long past lilac season. All Vonny has to be able to do is stand by the side of the road for fifteen minutes, then buy something and go home.

She gets out of the truck for longer times each day. Seven minutes, then ten. She smokes a cigarette sometimes and always checks her watch. There is a lot of traffic on the road at this time of year and the annoying hum of rented motor scooters and bikes. The Giant's throat hurts when he watches Vonny. He has all but stopped eating. Occasionally he remembers food, then he opens a can, heats it, and wolfs it down, whatever it is, beef stew or vegetable soup.

The Giant does not want to change the sheets on his bed, but at last he does. When he pulls them off he finds one of Jody's hair clips, a thin silver band, forgotten between the mattress and the sheet. He puts the old sheets back on the bed, then he holds the hair clip and studies it. He jumps when he hears a knock on the door. He cannot imagine who would even know he's alive other than the woman, and she's already been and gone. Through the window he can see the police officer, Hammond West. For two days straight the Giant has been listening alternately to Brahms and Johnny Cash and he wonders if his fingerprints have been detected on the dusty shelves of the hardware store. He doesn't bother to hide the cassette player. He opens the door and stands there without inviting Hammond inside.

"Thought I'd see how you were doing," Hammond says.

Hammond is out of uniform. He wears worn khaki slacks and a plaid shirt. The Giant stares at him rudely.

"What does a guy have to do to get a drink around here?" Hammond says.

"Help yourself," the Giant tells him. His voice is hollow, not as deep as anyone would guess.

Hammond walks past him and goes to the refrigerator.

"No beer, huh?" Hammond says. He takes a bottle of apple juice out and looks on the counter for a glass.

"There aren't any," the Giant tells him, so Hammond drinks from the bottle.

"I guess the girl's gone," Hammond says. When the Giant doesn't answer, he adds, "Her parents are still looking for her. They'll find her when she lets herself be found. I didn't think you'd go with her."

"Sure," the Giant says. "You figure I'm a freak."

"No," Hammond says. "I figure this is your home."

"Are you here to arrest me for something?" the Giant says.

"Not unless you've done something I should know about."

"Arrest me or get off my back," the Giant says.

"Seems like I'm bothering you," Hammond says.

"I don't have to talk to you," the Giant tells him. "I don't have to explain anything."

Hammond's done his job. He caps the apple juice and puts it back in the refrigerator. There's nothing much inside: a package of cheddar cheese, some wilted lettuce, two sticks of butter. Hammond closes the refrigerator, then sees that the Giant is crying. Hammond quickly turns away and looks out the back window, into the yard. It's empty out there.

"I worked here for your grandfather one summer when I was a kid," Hammond says. "He just about drove me nuts. He had me cut wood till I thought I'd drop, but that wasn't the worst part. He talked all the time and I wasn't used to it. My parents were deaf and we all used sign. I got dizzy from all his talking, it shook me up. He had a rooster named Primo and when your grandfather wasn't talking to me he was talking to Primo."

"I knew Primo," the Giant says. He sounds like a kid; his voice is soft and flat from crying. "Or maybe it was his great-grandson."

"Bastard of a rooster," Hammond says. "Wouldn't you know he'd live for fifty years."

All this time the Giant has been holding the silver hair clip. He puts it down on the table and can't take his eyes off it.

"Let's go get them," Hammond says.

The Giant turns to him, puzzled.

"You must have taken your chickens somewhere. Now let's get them back."

The Giant looks at Hammond and when he sees this isn't a joke, he gets an empty seed bag from under the sink.

"I'm going to be breaking the law," he says to Hammond.

"No, you won't," Hammond tells him. "I'll see to that."

They take the patrol car and drive down the road to the neighboring farm, then park and wait for dusk. When it's dark enough they get out, run over to the slatted fence meant to keep cows from straying, then crouch down low, on their bellies.

"Go on," Hammond West urges. "I'll be right behind you with the flashlight."

The Giant crawls forward, under the wooden slats. A car goes by, illuminating the road, and the Giant pushes his face into the earth.

"We're okay now," Hammond says when the headlights disappear.

There's a tall wire fence around the poultry yard. The Giant's been here once before. He hands West the burlap bag.

"I'll catch them," he says. "You just keep them in there."

The Giant scales the fence easily, then gets down on his haunches, waiting for Hammond, who gets stuck on top of the fence and rips his shirt coming down.

"You okay?" the Giant asks, and Hammond nods impatiently. They go into the first henhouse. The Giant recognizes some of his chickens from the tone of their clucking. He quickly grabs two hens and elbows Hammond to open the bag so he can get them in before they start squawking and alarm the others. It's too dark to find all of his stock, but they manage to get twelve before Hammond says, "Time's up."

They go back the way they came. The Giant lets Hammond go first, then he climbs the fence while holding the bag of chickens in one hand. They run to the patrol car, and when they get in, the Giant lifts the bag of chickens into the backseat, then he lets out a whoop. "All right!" the Giant says, and he pounds Hammond on the back a little too hard.

"I hope we got the best of them," Hammond says, "because I'm not going back there."

"I thought I might have to leave you up there on the fence." The Giant grins.

"Very funny," Hammond says. "I'd like to see you try it when you're my age."

They're still running on adrenaline; every now and then they laugh for no reason at all. The bag on the backseat cackles and moves and sets them off all over again. When Hammond pulls up alongside the farmstand, the Giant grabs the bag, lifts it over the seat, and sets it on his lap.

"Listen," he says. "Thanks."

The Giant gets out of the car and Hammond gets out too. Hammond steps up so he can lean on the roof of the patrol car. "I'll tell you one thing, Eddie," he says. "If I have to see a chiropractor and get my back realigned, I'm sending you the bill."

"You do that." The Giant laughs.

Crickets are calling, their song quickened by the heat.

"It's going to be even hotter tomorrow," Hammond says.

"Yeah," the Giant agrees. "That's July for you."

"Yeah," Hammond says, and they laugh.

It doesn't matter that the hollow is pitch black as the Giant walks down it; he knows this path by heart. He walks behind the house and over to the coops. He kneels down and takes the chickens out slowly, one at a time, holding each hen on the ground until her wings stop flapping. Then he opens his hands wide and lets go.

The Giant goes inside and makes himself the first good meal he's had in weeks—a cheese sandwich and a salad. He's too excited to sleep much and he wakes before dawn and goes outside. Hammond is right, the day is hotter. Already. The chickens are scratching in the dust and the Giant throws them some feed. He knows that if he ignores his garden any longer the heat will scorch the flowers on the melon vines, the sunflowers will become brittle and their stalks will snap in half. The Giant gets out the hose and waters. Then he begins to weed, just a little because the earth is so easy to work now that it's drenched, and before he knows it he's cleared a line of lettuce.

He makes himself some coffee and sits down on a wooden crate outside to drink it. The sky is growing light and, beyond the trees, there is a brilliant streak of crimson in the east. The Giant goes back to work; he weeds until he's covered with sweat, then he takes off his shirt. He fills the crate with heads of lettuce, with the season's first tomatoes and green beans, then carries the crate up to the farmstand.

Blisters have formed in the palms of his hands, but he's still working when Vonny's truck pulls up. The Giant walks around to the side of the house so he can get a better look.

Vonny's out early this morning; she leans against the truck and watches cars go by. There are times when it's hard for her to leave this place. She sees now there is at last something to buy and she goes over to the farmstand. Carefully she chooses lettuce and beans. She folds two dollar bills through the slit in the coffee can, then decides to take the bunch of cosmos the Giant has found growing wild underneath a tangle of brambles and searches her pockets for change.

Vonny sees him just as she is about to get back into the truck. Instantly she sees how young he is. He is staring right at her and for this one moment Vonny feels as though he belongs to her. If she leaves now she can still go to the beach with Simon and Andre. They've promised to wait. Vonny juggles the flowers and vegetables into the crook of one arm so she can wave. The Giant lifts one hand in the air, then watches her get back into the truck. His back and arms are strained after working so hard, but he returns to his garden and sets out bowls of salt to keep the snails away. Soon, he knows, Vonny will no longer stop here. She'll drive a little farther each day until the farmstand is just a small reference point rather than a destination. But the Giant will have other customers, some of whom will swear his vegetables are better for them than medicine.

Tonight the Giant will sleep on clean sheets, and above him there will be uncountable, unknown planets. He wants to stay awake forever, he wants to always remember the way he feels right now. But his arms ache and he realizes just how tired he is. He lies down in the grass and, stretching himself out to his full height, looks upward, through the green leaves.